DO NOT RESUSCITATE

HOSPITAL EVIL: WHERE NO ONE CAN HEAR YOU SCREAM

SCOTT EVELOFF, MD

Black Rose Writing | Texas

This is a work of fiction. Names, characters, businesses, places, events, and incidents are either the products of the author's imagination or used in a fictitious manner. Any resemblance to actual persons, living or dead, or actual events is purely coincidental.

ISBN: 978-1-68513-663-5
LIBRARY OF CONGRESS CONTROL NUMBER: 2025936203
PUBLISHED BY BLACK ROSE WRITING
www.blackrosewriting.com

Printed in the United States of America
Suggested Retail Price (SRP) $21.95

Do Not Resuscitate is printed in Minion Pro

*As a planet-friendly publisher, Black Rose Writing does its best to eliminate unnecessary waste to reduce paper usage and energy costs, while never compromising the reading experience. As a result, the final word count vs. page count may not meet common expectations.

Praise for
Do Not Resuscitate

"*Do Not Resuscitate* - An inventive combination of high-stakes hospital drama mixed with supernatural horror, fueled by a terrifying villain from beyond the grave who turns a medical intern's life upside down with his nefarious plan to get revenge for his own death. The author's background as a physician lends authenticity to his main character's difficulties as he comes under fire from hospital higher ups for a series of "code blue" medical crises and dying patients that he gets blamed for. With no one else able to understand or willing to believe the real evil behind it all, he's the only one who might be able to stop it. A fun scary ride!"
–Erik Bork, author, screenwriter on HBO's *Band of Brothers* and *From the Earth to the Moon*

"*Do Not Resuscitate* is an impressive debut novel from Scott Eveloff. Still grieving from the loss of a child, Dr. Harry Lindmark tries to lose himself in his internship. When a series of tragic events strike the patients in his care, Harry wonders if there's a killer lurking among the hospital's staff or if he's cracking under pressure. As he gets closer to the truth, he finds himself in an otherworldly battle that threatens Harry and everyone he cares about. Part ghost story and part medical drama, *Do Not Resuscitate* brims with medical detail, superb characters, and surprising twists you won't see coming."
–Travis Tougaw, author of *Death Grip*

"An unsettling medical mystery combined with spine-tingling horror that fans of both genres will enjoy. *Do Not Resuscitate* is a chilling blend of medical thriller and horror that keeps readers on the edge of their seats. Set in a hospital where unexpected deaths are happening with alarming frequency, the story follows a dedicated medical resident, Dr. Harry Lindmark, as he delves into the mystery unfolding within the hospital's corridors. With each unsettling clue he uncovers, Dr. Lindmark begins to suspect that something far darker than negligence and human error are at play but maybe, he's just losing his mind.

Masterfully weaving together medical realism with supernatural elements, Scott Eveloff builds tension with every page and keeps readers guessing right to the very end."
–James Foley, author of *Treasure Coast*

"Eveloff's supernatural novel takes the reader on a realistic journey through unexplained medical mysteries, leaving you desperate for answers and positive outcomes. Dr. Lindmark's gift feels more like a curse as he attempts to save his patients from a malicious spirit while working to keep his paranoia and psychosis from ruining his career. The first person experience facilitates empathy and gives the reader a somatic stress response as they go through a rollercoaster of emotions in the race to save lives. It is a realistic account of what it is to work in healthcare and the immensity of the responsibility that comes with it. This page turning novel was a gripping read, an artistic rendition of justice and the complexity of death in healthcare."

–Megan Jamieson, author of *The Ties That Bind Us*

"*Do Not Resuscitate* is a gripping medical thriller that plunges readers into the shadowy corridors of a hospital where the line between life and death blurs into something far more sinister. Author Scott Eveloff, MD masterfully blends the stark realities of critical care medicine with an unsettling supernatural undercurrent, leaving readers questioning what is real and what lurks beyond the veil of science. Through the eyes of Dr. Harry Lindmark, a young intern navigating an ICU plagued by unexplained deaths, Eveloff delves into themes of medical ethics, paranoia, and the unseen forces that may guide—or manipulate—fate itself. Is the hospital merely a setting for human error and malpractice, or is something far more malevolent at work? With razor-sharp tension, chilling horror, and a plot that spirals ever deeper into darkness, *Do Not Resuscitate* keeps readers on edge until its final, shocking revelation. This is a novel that doesn't just ask who is responsible for the deaths—it dares you to question what is pulling the strings."

–Julia Shraybman, author of *Lucky Number 6*

"Being a resident in internal medicine is hard. No one knows this more than Dr. Harry Lindmark. Not only does his senior resident have it in for him, but his previously recovering patients keep taking unexpected turns for the worst, and the blame keeps falling on Harry. Even worse, he is seeing things – things that are unpleasant, scary, and downright evil – that seem intended for his eyes only. Questioning his sanity, Harry dives into the history of Narragansett General Hospital and learns there is a malevolent presence lurking in its halls. With time running short, he realizes the only way to protect his patients and loved ones is to make the ultimate sacrifice. Weaving elements of paranormal horror into a fast-paced medical thriller, *Do Not Resuscitate* is the gripping story of a young doctor's encounter with dark forces beyond medicine and just how far he is willing to go to fight them. I highly recommend this book."

–Laura Cody, co-author of *Call Game*

DO NOT RESUSCITATE

CHAPTER 1

A gnarled hand shot out from under the starched sheets and clutched my arm in a death grip. The old man in Bed 22 pulled himself up with his claw tightened on me. "If something happens–just let me go," he rasped. "I want to be a No Code. You understand what that means, right? Right, Doctor. . ." His other hand skittered around the front of my white coat until it gripped my name badge. "Right, Doctor Lindmark? You hear me?" His watery eyes darted back and forth, then widened as he fastened on something behind me. "Listen to me, goddam it—" Violent coughing interrupted his words. He fell back, wracked by hacking spasms.

I turned to see what had scared him, but only the beeping cluttered machinery of the Intensive Care Unit stared back at me. *What had the old man seen*? I'd read about sleep-deprived ICU hallucinations in medical school. Or had his aging brain given way to some medication-induced side effects? I scowled down at the unkempt patient, resisting the urge to jerk free of his clammy grasp. Instead, I pried each finger loose as gently as possible until the withered claw fell away.

The hair on my neck stood on end as cold knifed against my skin. I spun around again, greeted only with the smirk on my supervising resident's face. I backed away from the bed, trying to shake off the unease worming through me.

"Doc Travis bothering you, Lindmark?"

Dr. Martin Bethany was a short squat man whose red beard covered pudgy cheeks and jowls that flashed from pink to crimson, depending on his mood. His fiery visage matched his combustible disposition, creating an intimidating presence both inside and out to those of us interns under his tutelage.

"No sir, Dr. Bethany. I was just discussing, uh, advance directives with the patient. He does not want any life-support measures in case—"

"What the hell are *you* discussing code status for, Lindmark?" Bethany snapped. "You're just an intern in the goddam Intensive Care Unit, where we try to make sure patients won't ever *need* a code status. Understand?"

Chastised, I rubbed at the red marks left by the patient's grip, imagining some lethal ICU infection eating its way through my skin.

"Now let me tell you about Doctor Travis," Bethany continued as we walked away from the bed. "The good doctor was one of the few staff physicians at this hospital for a long time. Pretty well-respected, I'm told. Of course, that was back when leeches and blood-letting were cutting-edge medicine. Whatever happened to him, now he's just an old demented guy who keeps babbling about dying and dead people. This time he came in kicking and screaming from the nursing home with chest pain."

"Hey, Lindmark."

I turned back towards Travis. The old man had raised himself off the bed with both skeletal arms and was glaring. "Get over here. I'm not finished talking to you."

Bethany shrugged. "Go deal with him, but hurry. The family of the new chest trauma in Bed 28 wants to ask his doctor some questions. I've nominated *you* to be 'his doctor.'"

I set my jaw and returned to the bedside, careful to stay out of arm's reach.

"You got to listen to me," Travis said. His breath wafted in fetid testament to the remnants of the chicken stew on the tray in front of him. I couldn't imagine this disheveled old man had once been a doctor in charge of people's lives.

"I want my chart to read *Do Not Resuscitate*. And no IV medications. Hell, just take the damn IV out. You got it? I don't want any intravenous medication at all. That's how they do it, you know." I could only nod. He had sounded so rational, but it had lasted all of one sentence. "They don't want me yet though, Lindmark," Travis continued, his voice lowered in a conspiratorial mutter. "Not with the younger patients you got in here. They kill the young ones first. The young ones. Remember that, Dr. Bismarck."

"Lindmark. I'm Dr. Harry Lindmark, And I really—"

"They got their sights set on me, though. I know it. Because I know too much." His bloodshot eyes ricocheted back and forth. "They're gonna keep killing. Watch the young ones, hear me?"

I nodded, deciding that any response would be like giving food to a hungry dog. The old man's words triggered a rush of dark memories. I instinctively rubbed the scar on my neck but couldn't relieve the squeeze of anxiety gripping me. The beeping from the old man's monitor quickened as if it were reading my own pounding heartbeat.

Travis's voice dropped to a whisper. "They're getting better at killing, you know. I've been around here a long time, and I've seen it happen, Lindmark. That's why I want my chart to read Do Not Resuscitate. Then I want out of this place. They *never leave*. They watch and they learn. Learn how to kill."

CHAPTER 2

The young accident victim occupying Intensive Care Unit Bed 28 had either been a team captain in college or had shared an attractive gene pool with many sisters, because I had to elbow my way through several shapely young women surrounding his bed. Lying swathed in gauze and bandages, he resembled more a mummy than a patient. Wires and traction devices stretched taut, conjuring in my mind the image of an ancient medieval torture rack. IV lines, multiple catheters, and ventilator tubing sprouted from every orifice and limb like tendrils of a strange parasitic organism.

Someone squeezed my arm, breaking my trance. "How is my son, Doctor?" a poised well-dressed woman asked. "Anthony. Anthony Richman. I'm his mother Janice."

I rifled through the papers on my clipboard. "He's holding his own, Mrs. Richman," I said, trying to paint the concussion, punctured lungs, and multiple fractures in as positive a light as possible. "He's responding to commands, and the bleeding into his lung has slowed. Still critical, but no reason not to expect a full recovery as young as he is."

Richman's mother and every member of his blonde fan club stared as one at me, seeking comfort and reassurance. Was the mummified trauma victim's prognosis really that good? Only a few months out of medical school, I cleared my throat. "I guess what I meant is—"

A nurse wedged herself through the crowd. "Dr. Lindmark, Dr. Bethany wants you at Bed 5 right now."

"I'll be right there." I offered Mrs. Richman as confident a smile as I could muster. "I really think your son will be okay. We'll obviously be watching him closely. . ."

"Thank you so much, Doctor," she replied, as if I had really done something.

I glanced once more at her son. Pumps pumped, the ventilator breathed, the monitor. . . monitored. All steady, all working in concert to keep Bed 28 alive. Nothing out of place. Something I'd heard earlier nagged at me, but I shrugged it off, squeezed Mrs. Richman's hand, and hurried off to Dr. Bethany and Bed 5.

I opened my eyes as cold wrapped around me. A pale face glared at me from across the room. A dainty goatee framed a thin-lipped slash of a mouth. His eye sockets were empty, just two bottomless pits. He glided away without even a whisper of rustling clothing breaking the silence of the room. The cold left with him. I shook my head, wondering when the dream would end. A faint light flickered from another corner. I squeezed my eyes shut like a terrified child in a room full of shadows. When I risked opening them, a teenage boy stood in the corner. His head swiveled in my direction, only blank white existed where his eyes should have been. He blinked once, twice, then dark pupils appeared, staring hollow and piercing at the same time. Not like that other vision. He approached me, not really walking but just. . .gliding. Pale twisted arms reached out. His hands touched my neck. A scream stuck in my throat. The hands tightened, shaking me, strangling me.

"Doctor Lindmark! Hey Doc! *Harry*!"

I bolted upright, clawing at my throat.

"Dr. Lindmark, it's me, it's Eva!" The ICU nurse stopped shaking me. "Wake *up*, Harry. Sorry to wake you but—"

"It's okay, Eva, it's okay," I mumbled. On call in the ICU and all I could do was fall asleep and dream nightmares? I rubbed where Eva had shaken me awake.

"No, it's *not* okay, Dr. Lindmark." Her tone was urgent. "Dr. Bethany needs you in the ICU. Richman's coding."

I leapt out of bed and threw my lab coat over my scrubs. Richman? Who the hell was that? What bed? The little demented lady with heart failure? The diabetic with pneumonia and kidney failure? A roll call of bed numbers and diagnoses blended together as I bolted out of the on-call room. Thank God Bethany was already there. Of *course* he was there. I was only an intern on my first rotation out of medical school in the damn Intensive Care Unit no less. I rounded the corner and the blur of thoughts screeched to a stop.

A crowd of nurses spilled out of a far room. A red light, the emergency light, flickered above the doorway of Bed 28, whose mother I had comforted and reassured.

I elbowed my way into the room. Bethany stood at the foot of the bed, barking orders to nurses, therapists, pharmacists. A heavy-set nurse pumped on the boy's chest with grim determination. "What happened, Dr. Bethany?" I asked, shaken by the surrounding turmoil.

"You tell me, Lindmark, he's your patient."

"I, he. . .was okay when I went to bed," I stammered.

Bethany's words spewed in a torrent as his eyes darted from monitor to patient. "I'm impressed you feel multiple long bone fractures, internal bleeding, two punctured lungs, and blunt head trauma is 'okay,' Dr. Lindmark. I guess you'll stay awake when things get really serious, huh?" He looked up from the monitor to the nurses milling about the bed. "Where are those stat labs? Make sure the fluids are running wide open. Still getting breath sounds on both sides?"

A nurse pushed a sheet of paper at him. "Better look at this, Doctor."

"Hold compressions, check for pulses," Bethany barked while scanning the paper.

"No pulses, Doctor," another nurse declared after several agonizing seconds. She kept pressing on the large artery in the boy's groin, searching in vain for any throb of life. I swiped away the sweat erupting on my forehead. He *had* been doing okay. He *had* been stable, all things considered. . .

Bethany scratched his scalp with both hands as if trying to put out the fire of his red hair. "Damn. Resume CPR," he commanded. "Lindmark. What's the normal range for blood sugar?"

"It's 80 to 120."

"Give him an amp of D50, *now*! No, make it two amps. He needs as much sugar into him as possible." Bethany said without turning away from the bed. "Then why the hell is his blood sugar *ten*, Lindmark?"

Ten? TEN? "I don't know, sir. It wasn't—"

"Should I shut off the insulin drip then?" a nurse asked, her hands running up and down the jungle of intertwining IV tubing surrounding the bed.

Bethany glared at me as he answered. "*Insulin drip*?" His words changed from rapid-fire staccato to an icy growl. His face reddened until it became impossible to see where his beard stopped and the crimson of his face began. One hand resumed the odd scratching and rubbing on his head. "*An insulin infusion*? Of *course* shut off the damn insulin drip, unless you'd like to try for a new world record of most severe brain damage caused by a wrong medication." He exhaled a long, exaggerated breath and said, "Then start a D10 drip." He glared at the nurses. "Hold compressions."

A long silence. Then, "No femoral pulse."

"No carotid pulse."

"Goddam it," Bethany muttered. His voice raised to a strident pitch as he spat staccato orders like bullets. "Resume compressions. Give him an amp of epinephrine. Keep fluids wide open. Make sure that insulin drip is off. Give him another amp of D50."

I stood rooted in place, a petrified spectator of the turmoil swarming around me. I wanted to run away from all the orders, away from the steady thumping of the boy's body against the bed as nurses continued their chest compressions like they were trying to beat the life back into him. His mother was probably resting peacefully at this very moment, because I had told her everything would be okay. I dared a glance at the boy on the bed. My patient. His eyes were wide open, the whites swollen and engorged with blood. His skin was blue. A thin trickle of clear fluid ran from the corner of his mouth.

"All right, everyone, we're gonna do this one more time." Bethany's declaration was terse, emotionless, and jolted me as if he had screamed the words. "Check for pulses."

No one answered. Several nurses silently shook their heads.

"I got no rhythm here," Bethany said. "*Anybody feel a pulse?*" Head shaking from everyone in answer.

"Goddam it." Bethany scanned the room. "All right, unless anyone has any objections, I'm calling it."

The rhythmic hiss from the oxygen bag pierced the silence as a respiratory therapist squeezed air into the boy's lungs.

"That's it. I'm calling it. Time of death is. . ." He looked up at the digital clock on the wall. "3:17 a.m." He snapped off his latex gloves and threw them on the floor.

That was it? A young man, *my patient*, declared dead with as much emotion as morning roll call?

Others in the room shut off pumps, snuffed out hissing oxygen valves, turned off beeping monitors, and retreated. I turned to leave, but a low moaning wail made the hair stand up on the back of my neck. I twisted around. The boy's white corpse lay motionless, open dead fish eyes staring. The wail rose to a keening torment that assaulted me from every direction. I covered my ears but others in the room seemed oblivious. They continued to perform their mundane ritual of cleaning up after death, ignoring that awful sound and the dead person at the center of it all.

Anthony Richman suddenly twitched, arched his back in a violent spasm, then collapsed back onto the bed. The shrieking rose to an unbearable pitch as the corpse's eyes *exploded*. Red gelatinous matter spewed into the air and splattered onto the floor. Fingers of cold air brushed across my face. The terrible screeching stopped. I scanned the room, afraid I'd be the only one to have seen what had happened. But everyone else had stopped what they were doing and were staring at the awful thing once again motionless on the bed.

"Now there's something you don't see every day," Bethany's dry voice broke the silence. "Better call housekeeping. . ."

CHAPTER 3

"It's the truth, Connie," I insisted, but my wife kept moving around the kitchen, putting clean dishes away and wiping down counters as if I weren't there. "First my patient coded out of the blue. Heart beat and breathing stopped, unresponsive, the whole thing. Someone screamed, but no one else heard it but me." I stopped as the words "my patient" struck me like a slap. The excitement of recounting the bizarre happenings around that Code Blue sickened into a roiling in my stomach. Had I been responsible? Maybe I should have—

Connie stopped her cleaning and looked at me. "Harry, I'm sure it's all very exciting, being a doctor and all, dealing with all sorts of exploding-eye disorders, but I'm just having another bad day."

Regret piled on regret. "I'm sorry, Connie," I said as I put my arms around her. "Of course you're having a bad day. A bad year. *We're* having a bad year. And I get to leave it and go to work."

"It's so lonely here, Harry. You're gone during the day, and you're gone every third night on call. And I can't stop thinking about. . .him." Tears overflowed her eyes. "When you *are* here, you're reading articles and studying."

"Connie, we both knew internship would be tough. I do have to keep reading. I get grilled every day about what's normal, what's not. That code last night happened on my watch." I didn't add, *I need to find out what I did wrong.* "My first month as an intern, I'm in over my head."

"I'm in over my head too," Connie said, her voice sinking to a whisper. "Here in this apartment all alone, Harry. I knew it'd be tough when you got accepted. You did warn me the first year of your residency, being an intern, was just one step up from slave labor. And then two more years of being a resident physician after internship. I just didn't know it would be *this* lonely. I wouldn't feel like this even if we'd wound up on the moon if I had a baby, *our* baby, to care for. You know?"

I tightened my arms around her. "We can try again. And I'll knock off the reading early. Maybe, in the meantime, another visit with the therapist? It could help, you know?"

"Maybe Harry." She didn't bother to say what we both knew. No doctor could tell us if future children might suffer the same genetic fate. No therapist or antidepressant would lessen the fear of such uncertainty.

Connie eased out of my grasp and returned to the sink. "I know you're tired. You were up all night." She offered a wan smile without trace of humor as tears ran down her cheeks. "With you hearing and seeing things no one else does, maybe I'm not the only one who should see a therapist."

I trudged up the stairs to my bedroom, the bed offering a refuge from guilt and worry and sleeplessness until Richman and all the other terribly ill patients pushed into my thoughts. All those *infected* patients, with all those germs. Opening my mouth at the mirror, I inspected carefully. No weird spots or strange blisters showed up in the mirror. I stripped off my scrubs and searched my body up and down for rashes or ulcers, sure I had picked up something. The unreasonable conviction I had stuck myself with a needle itched at my brain. Scrubbing my arms and hands furiously did nothing except make my skin burn, then brushed my teeth an extra three minutes trying to sterilize myself against all the horrors I'd been exposed to.

The anxiety I'd battled throughout medical school certainly hadn't improved, even after forcing the several deep breaths my previous therapist had taught me. Resisting the urgency to check my entire body for ominous rashes, I instead checked the prescription bottle in my drawer once more, reassured that I was still weeks away from a refill.

Exhausted, I threw myself onto the bed, the warmth of the covers finally offering refuge against what I'd left behind at the hospital.

CHAPTER 4

The Intensive Care Unit was business as usual, as if losing a boy with his entire life ahead of him had never happened. I walked past the rows of glassed-in cubicles housing wasted patients. The same tangle of machinery and tubing snaked into each patient like tentacles. Same vacant-eyed, sallow family members sat in their endless vigil beside each bed.

I shook off the grimness around me and hurried to find Bethany. What happened the night before was not my fault. . . was it? What the hell had happened? Had I overlooked something? If not, then what had happened? That insulin drip had killed Richman.

"Lindmark. Glad you're here early." So absorbed, I'd almost bumped into Bethany.

"Dr. Bethany, could I talk to you about Richman? I need—"

He peered at me, squinting eyes almost buried by pink fleshy cheeks. "You don't look so good, Lindmark." He hung an arm around my shoulders. With anyone else it might have been comforting, an expression of reassurance, of shared empathy. With Martin Bethany, I expected his paw to curl around my neck in a chokehold as punishment for whatever medical error I might have committed. "Listen," he said, his voice low, his tone jocular instead of biting. "All that with Richman? Brutal. But do you know what the most violent place in most cities is?"

I'd been an intern long enough to know that when Bethany went educational on his underlings, any answer was probably going to be wrong at best, ridiculed at worst. "The inner city?" I ventured. He shook his head. "Municipal jail?" Another headshake, exaggerating despair as he gazed up towards the heavens.

"Jesus, this was supposed to be easy. The Intensive Care Unit. Needles stuck in patients at least three or four times a day, without sedation or anesthetic. In painful places like necks or groins. Arms and legs restrained. Plastic tubes jammed down airways, leaving patients gagging and unable to speak. Then we have at least one Code Blue daily on these horrendously sick patients, where we pound on their chests, stick in more large needles, jam tubes into chests or genitalia, and don't forget the electric shock paddles. But violent, Lindmark. All one big painful torture chamber. Get used to it."

It was a strange if not novel perspective I'd not heard before. Dr. Bethany was, if nothing else, a very strange if not novel human being. "You're saying Richman's code was just a terrible but expected critical care—"

He bit off my words. "I didn't say 'expected.' You have a lot to learn. You didn't have to explain to a mother why she was told her son was doing well one minute, and then she was getting told he had died the next. You really told her that her multi-trauma comatose son was doing well?"

"No, I didn't say he was doing well, exactly. But she needed hope. And with his age and previous health, he could have recovered. There was nothing terminal there. I did give her hope, and I didn't lie to her. I *did* think he would recover."

Bethany glared at me. I waited for the flush of crimson predicting an imminent Bethany eruption that would reduce me to a pathetic dunce. But nothing. I jumped like a drowning man clutching at a life preserver. "And something else, sir. I never ordered that insulin. Someone else did. That's what killed him, right? Not the broken bones or punctured lungs. There was an autopsy, right?"

Bethany nodded. "Cardiac arrest, Lindmark. Big shock, huh? Thing is, a post-mortem won't show a fatally low blood sugar after all the glucose he got during the code. Nor the insulin drip that caused it, either." His voice hardened with each word. "It's just going to show the damage caused by such an incredibly stupid mistake."

"What if. . . what if it wasn't a mistake?"

"Keep your voice down, dammit." Bethany lowered his head toward me. "I went over the chart after the code. Fact is, *nobody* ordered it. There was no order for any insulin anywhere in the chart. But Pharmacy received an order through the hospital's computerized system, and they filled it. I saw the order myself. But it didn't come from the chart or from any of us." He shook his head, defeat replacing his bravado. "Maybe intended for some other patient. All I know is it caused a young kid to die, on my watch."

"But who?" I asked. "Pharmacy wouldn't have filled an order without the doctor's name."

Bethany drew closer. "Travis. Dr. Leland Travis. But that's not to go any further."

"The old guy in Bed 22? *That* weird babbling doctor?" Bethany nodded. Then it struck me. Travis had warned me about the young ones. That's what had nagged at me earlier. Richman should have recovered, *as young as he was.* Had Travis been faking his craziness to cover up his hatred of anyone healthier or younger? He could have—

"Someone used his name," Bethany interrupted as if reading my mind. "Old Doc Travis may be a walking warning against outliving your brain, but he was in his ICU bed the entire day. I've alerted the Chief of Staff. Not a word to anyone about this, Lindmark. We may have one of those 'Angel of Mercy' nurse killers running around." His face had regained its color. He glanced at the bustle building around us. "Meantime, let's try not to let anyone else die before they're good and ready to die, right? Meet me in front of Bed 5." He gripped my arm. "And Lindmark, *never give* a patient or a family member a prognosis unless you're sure. Give someone hope without giving them *false* hope. That kid's mother told me she never would have left his bedside if you hadn't assured her he would be okay. She didn't get a chance to tell him goodbye. Remember that, Lindmark."

I'd remember those words for a very long time.

"Lindmark, define cardiogenic shock and tell us what the best treatment is."

We had stopped in front of my most complicated patient, Aaron Shirkey. Mr. Shirkey was a fifty-year-old man with an eighty-year-old body. An exceptionally large body. He suffered from high blood pressure, swollen feet, heart disease, diabetes, sleep apnea, and kidney disease. A man, Bethany had explained, who was living one pizza slice away from total system collapse. He'd developed chest pain while stirring "Marinara by Aaron-ara," his own homemade sauce, and had come in for a simple heart catheterization.

Mr. Shirkey apparently also suffered from bad luck. The catheterization had damaged his kidneys and thrown him into congestive heart failure. That led to a heart attack that the catheterization had been designed to prevent. He was on a ventilator hovering on the verge of dialysis. Nothing nefarious, just a perfect storm of bad luck inflicted on bad health. I had already reviewed each intravenous drip he was on but at the cost of time spent with Connie, again.

"Cardiogenic shock is a condition where blood pressure is reduced because the heart has simply lost too much pump function," I said, confident in my answer. "In this patient's case, his heart attack destroyed a significant amount of heart muscle." I glanced at the patient. Aaron Shirkey's eyes were bulging out of his swollen face, darting from white coat to white coat. It occurred to me, too late, that he was not comatose like most of our other patients and was taking in every word.

"So far so good, Dr. Lindmark. What's the treatment?"

A rattle above the bed caught my attention. The tubing twisted by itself: long transparent worms unwinding slowly and straightening out down their length then snapping back. A swirl of freezing air brushed against me.

No code. He's a No Code. I startled. Who had whispered that to me? The other intern several feet away peered at me expectantly as did the rest of the team.

"Someone call the nurse to fix those pumps," Bethany demanded. "Lindmark, finish up. We've got other patients to round on."

The rattling stopped. The IV lines hung limply over the bed. I looked from side to side, unable to quiet a sudden foreboding. An alarm went off above Shirkey's bed. Shirkey's heart rhythm stuttered and skipped as frequent premature beats interrupted the tracing. Apprehension exploded into panic, squeezing the breath from me.

"Dr. McCormick, please nudge, slap, or do something to your fellow intern to wake him up. Remind him we're on morning rounds." Bethany's words blurred as if he were speaking from a distance.

"Dr. Bethany," I forced out. "Shirkey's going to die, like Richman. They must've done something to *his* drips as well." I began inspecting each hanging bag of fluid, running my hands down each length of tubing. Whatever Angel of Death was lurking around would not get another of my patients.

"Everyone go on to the next patient. Dr. Lindmark and I will sort this out," Bethany said before hissing in my ear. "I thought we agreed not to say anything about what happened. What the hell's going on?"

"Something's wrong with his medications," I said, eyeing the bags that had to be dripping death into my patient. "I saw them. . . moving."

"Uh, huh," Bethany said. He flipped each bag around, eyeing each label. "It all looks okay to me. I think maybe Richman got to you more than we thought, huh?"

Make him a Do Not Resuscitate. I whirled to my left, but saw no one. "He's not to be coded," I mumbled, confused.

Bethany's head jerked up. "When was that decided?"

Sweat poured down my face. "This morning, I think." The irregular beeping faded into a reassuring regular cadence. The vise of panic released its grip. Shirkey rested peacefully as the ventilator exhaled its steady breaths of life.

Bethany took me by the arm and led me away from Shirkey's bedside. "Harry, let's think about this." His tone had lost its abrasiveness. "We have a man whose barely fifty with a family and a long life ahead of him. He's young, he's aware, and could easily survive. Does that sound like someone we should let die if he codes?"

It did make sense. Bethany continued, "And besides, it's a little late. He's on a ventilator. He's on blood thinners. He's on a gazillion correct intravenous medications. Is there any part of him that's *not* already being artificially kept alive?" His voice hardened. "Let's catch up with the rest before your fellow interns really do kill someone. Shirkey will be okay, if you just pay attention."

I wasn't reassured. Bethany hadn't heard that whisper. A whisper from nowhere. I scratched out the start of the No Code order, peered once more around the room, and followed Bethany to where the rest of the team stood waiting.

"Hey Doc, anyone gonna peek in on me today?" Too late, I'd walked in full view of Dr. Travis.

"Morning, Dr. Travis," I said. "You're looking better today." In fact, he was looking better. Someone had shaved him and washed his hair. His eyes were brighter, his skin less sallow.

"Better, but still a lot like a dried-up turd. Isn't that what you meant to say?" he said, his sneer and thrust jaw daring a response. Something along those lines was exactly what I was thinking. "Yeah well, I'm ready to go. I'm pain free, no heart attack, and I survived the night. Which is more than I can say for some people in here. Did you write that Do Not Resuscitate order in my chart?"

"Well yes, but—"

"I don't trust that protecting me. I don't trust you protecting me. The nurse told me what happened to that boy in 28. I warned you, didn't I? I want out of this place." Fear crossed his expression. "Transfer me. Take out my IVs, let me go. I am a No Code, after all. Right?"

"What happened has nothing to do with your case at all. You must know that, being a doctor yourself. I can't just—"

"No, I don't know that, dammit. You don't know what they can do. What they've done. Check on it, if you don't believe me. Check into Myron Frazier and the rest of them. Daryl McCalmon. Todd Blazer. I know all of them. I know what happened. Sylvester Morrow. . . especially that one. You'll see. Morrow is getting smarter. And better."

This was not good. Dr. Travis needed to be transferred out, to a psychiatric hospital. Or at least, sent back to his nursing home. I'd speak to Bethany. I backed out of the cubicle and hurried off to catch up with rounds.

Whispered voices, demented warnings faded from my mind. I focused instead on the onslaught of numbers, diseases, and medications I had to recount or learn as we made our way through patients I could see, not imagine. Patients that I, at the ripe old age of twenty-six, had become personally responsible for as the intern of record.

The day finally ended, despite the best efforts of my patients to succumb to the diseases ravaging them. Efforts I would never blame them for, but that still translated to a burgeoning intern to-do list. I hurried out of the Intensive Care Unit, reminded of an early cold front that had snuck in from Canada making the leaf-peeping autumn temperature of Rhode Island much colder than usual. Just great, I thought, a frigid end to an already uncomfortable day. The underground tunnel between buildings had to be better than trudging across the frozen tundra of the parking lot. Several flights of stairs down, I arrived at the door to the tunnel system under the hospital. A long hallway lit by a string of naked bulbs, lined with exposed twisted pipes running like veins along the walls, loomed as a creepy remnant of the hospital's origins.

The ominous gloom reminded me of a motto I jokingly carried with me as an avid consumer of true crime and crime drama television– nothing good ever happens in parking garages. But a tunnel? I smiled at the ridiculous Hollywood truism and shrugged. I'd take "warm" over creepy and archaic.

A scuffing noise broke the silence behind me. So what? I couldn't be the only one who took this shortcut to stay out of the cold, but I stopped and listened.

Silence.

Anxious to get home and hopefully clear my mind for a while, I hurried forward until slow, thudding footsteps echoed off the walls from somewhere back in the gloom. My pace quickened. Every so often those footsteps were interrupted by a scraping sound as if something were being dragged across the rough concrete floor. A light flickered over my shoulder from the depths of the tunnel behind me. The morgue was on this level, housing dead patients destined for the funeral home or waiting for autopsy.

Unease stole into me and pushed me faster into the tunnel. Footsteps behind me shuffled faster, too. The naked bulbs overhead flickered and the walls seemed to tighten around me. Something moved in the distance ahead. I peered into the murky tunnel depths. It was a. . . kid. Maybe a young teenager? Had someone's son gotten lost down here? Something was wrong about him. He wasn't walking, he was gliding, legs hanging limply. His head swiveled back and forth on an impossibly small neck until he locked his eyes onto mine and stretched out his arms as if to stop me.

His eyes. . . something wrong with those eyes. I'd seen them before. I froze. It was the same frail kid that I'd seen in the call room, right before Richman's death. So it hadn't been a dream? Or was I hallucinating the same strange images? Neither explanation comforted me. I shivered as a chill settled over the tunnel. Something scraped along the concrete behind me, loudly, like a body being dragged. Or dragging itself along the tunnel floor? I squinted into the gloom and saw that strange flickering light bouncing off the walls.

I spun back around, feeling cornered. The tunnel's gloom had deepened almost into blackness. Several bulbs had broken or blown out. The strange boy vanished. I was alone with something or someone sneaking up on me. Icy wafts of air cut through the tunnel as an unnerving cacophony of scraping, creaking, rattling, and plodding footsteps drew closer. That light bounced crazily off the walls. A surge of panic pushed my heart into a rapid stuttering rhythm. I had to protect myself from whatever was down here, and protect that lost disabled teenager wandering down here. I clutched hold of the handiest weapon I could find–my stethoscope, and turned to face the unknown.

"Doc, what the hell you doing down here?" A stooped black man stared at me. He held a flashlight in one hand and the handle of a dented metal cart with a locked wheel in the other. Dragging instead of rolling. I collapsed against the brick wall of the tunnel. The old man's eyebrows wrinkled together in concern. "You okay?"

I slipped the stethoscope back into my pocket, and swiped a sleeve across my forehead. "Sure, yeah, I'm fine," I said. "Just wasn't expecting to find anyone else down here. Who are you, by the way?"

"Charlie, Doc. Charlie Washington." He must have noticed my blank look. "One of the orderlies. You're Doc Lindmark, right? Leland told me you were his intern."

"Right." My voice sounded raspy as if sandpaper were lodged in my throat. An orderly? He looked too old to be a viable patient, much less a hospital employee.

Charlie must have read my thoughts. He said, "I'm getting too old for this. They got me bringing surgical equipment over to the surgery suites in the next building. Didn't even give me a cart that works. I guess it don't matter how long it takes to get the equipment over there. Ain't no surgeries until tomorrow anyway."

The cart looked as decrepit as this venerable aging Narragansett General Hospital itself. Charlie had to be a volunteer from a charitable work program the hospital offered to the community's elderly. It didn't matter. I suppressed an urge to reach over and hug the old man as the thudding in my chest quieted.

Then I remembered. "Charlie, there's a lost child down here. Shine your light down the tunnel, will you?"

His eyes widened. "What did you say, Doc?"

"There's a boy down here in the tunnels. He must be lost and, I'm not sure but there's something wrong with him. I lost sight of him and he was gone."

Charlie peered over my shoulder. "Ain't no kid down here, Doc. Never was. Maybe just some shadows from these damn broken lights, but it was not anyone's kid." He aimed his light into the gloom, his hand trembling. The beam danced along the dank tunnel walls.

"Charlie, I *did* see a boy. More like a teenager, but small and frail. We at least got to tell security."

He grabbed my arm and started pulling me in the direction from which I had come. "Shadows, Doc. Ain't no child down here. Never was, no matter what. We can tell security if you want, but let's go."

"Charlie, what about your cart?"

"I'll get it later. Nothing on it so valuable." His eyes flitted back and forth as he kept hold of my arm. "Don't argue. We got to go."

I had become too tired to argue. I scanned the tunnel once more. Naked bulbs swayed back and forth in the distance. The gloom seemed to shift under them. "Charlie—"

But Charlie was already shuffling back down the tunnel. I yielded to a flash of panic at being left alone and followed him. We chatted about the hospital, how old and rundown the tunnel, the equipment, and he himself had become, how things used to be.

He repeated, "Forget about any child."

I stayed close to my ancient white-haired guardian and his reassuring flashlight and did not look back.

CHAPTER 5

My house wrapped its warmth around me as I walked in from the frosty outdoors. Memories of the ICU and of that tunnel had wormed inside my mind during the drive home and still would not let go of my thoughts. I hurried into the hall bathroom and held my hands out in front of me but saw no tremor or weakness, not even an unexplained rash. I opened my mouth at the mirror. No thrush, no lesions leaped out at me. I breathed a sigh of relief. Whatever had caused my hallucinations didn't appear to be a tumor or an ominous neurologic disorder. None of my medical school classmates had ever confided that they felt symptoms of every disease they had read about, and I had never divulged the certainty of my own countless disorders to them.

I smiled at myself in the mirror, having apparently managed to outlive the hundreds of illnesses afflicting me during those four years. Once again my anxiety had turned against me, stirring up hallucinations instead of physical symptoms. I shook my head at how the person in the mirror had graduated medical school mentally intact. A chronic anxiety disorder wasn't exactly a *mental illness*, right? I glanced down at the prescription bottle in my drawer and wondered if I should double the dose of the anxiety medication. In the next second, I remembered that a possible side effect could be hallucinations. I shrugged and closed the drawer, resolving to live with a little anxiety.

Like everything else in this Providence neighborhood, our apartment was ancient. We'd moved from the Providence suburban cookie-cutter beige to urban Providence to be closer to my medical school and to its teaching hospital, Narragansett General. Our new neighborhood reflected the New England reputation–so proud of its history that even ancient buildings and colonial infrastructure remained used and only modestly renovated.

"Just a necessary stepping-stone on my way to a high-paying practice after the year of internship and two more years of residency," I'd reassured a skeptical Connie. Besides allowing a shorter travel to and from the hospital, I didn't add that maybe leaving the house we had been in when we lost our baby would ease the grief. But this house offered Connie only depressing dilapidation and did nothing to cure her loneliness and sadness of a baby come and gone. I resolved yet again to replace the ache and regret with a promise of love and better things to come. It was the best I could do at the moment.

The warped hardwood creaked under my weight as I trudged into the kitchen. A woman I didn't recognize sat at the table next to Connie.

"Harry, I invited a new friend over. Denise Schlager, this is my husband, Harry."

The woman exposed celebrity-white teeth in an engaging smile. "Hi, Dr. Harry." She was a tall, dark-haired bejeweled contrast to my wife, whose unblemished features and slim figure belied her age without excessive makeup or top-line clothes. Denise sported stylish high-heeled boots, snug fitting jeans, and a fancy embroidered sweater. Gold bracelets jangled as she stretched out her hand to shake mine. My mind raced through the possible credit card charges this new friendship could generate.

Clicking and humming sounds came from the living room, then a small figure in a motorized wheelchair rolled around the corner. A skinny pale girl greeted me with the same toothy grin as Denise. Her wide-open green eyes and the smile almost diverted attention from the rest of her body.

Almost. Her head was pulled down and to the right by taut, ropy neck muscles frozen and contracted. One hand curled tightly around the joystick of the wheelchair. The fingers and the entire arm on that side were pitifully thin and shriveled. Both legs protruded shrunken and twisted from under her dress. Her feet dangled downward unnaturally. Something about them seemed strangely familiar.

Denise's smile widened as she turned toward the wheelchair. "And this is my daughter Audrey. Audrey, this is Dr. Lindmark."

The girl looked up at me up at me with wide expressive eyes, her head remaining immobile on a twisted neck. "Are you really a doctor?" she asked. Her speech was hesitant and slightly slurred, reminding me of how I sounded when drunk.

I couldn't help a rueful grimace. "These days I don't always feel like it, but yes, they tell me I'm really a doctor." The nightmare of Bed 28 forced its way into my thoughts.

"Most of my doctors are assholes, Dr. Lindmark," she said in that slurred warbling voice.

"Audrey!" Denise said, her smile gone. "Do *not* say those words. Now apologize."

"Okay, I'm sorry they're assholes. They don't joke, they don't even talk to *me*."

"Uh, Audrey, what grade are you in?" I interrupted, anxious to avoid any response from her mother.

"I'm not in school. I sit at home all day and cruise inappropriate websites."

"You. . . uh. . . "

"Very funny Audrey," Denise said. Then a subdued smile lightened her pokerfaced expression. "Dr. Lindmark asked you a polite question and expects a polite answer. Your thoughts?" Her tone was gentle, not angry.

Audrey spun around in her wheelchair to face her mother. "I think he deserves the truth, Mom." She turned back to look at me. "She's right, Dr. Lindmark. I really do go to school. I don't cruise the websites until I get back home."

Denise's jewelry jangled a response as she buried her head in her hands in mock disgust. I couldn't hold back a laugh. Denise looked up at me with deadpan eyes over a pouty smile. "She doesn't get that from me, Harry. I promise."

The combination of exhaustion and lingering unease from the hospital distracted me from further socializing, and from my promise to Connie to be more present. The need to find out more about Leland Travis, and pursue who had killed my patient, preyed on me. "I need to take care of a few things before dinner," I said in as lighthearted a tone as I could muster. "It was nice meeting the two of you." I spoke directly to Audrey, remembering her words about doctors. "If you're good, Audrey, maybe the next time you're over we can spend all afternoon on my favorite educational websites. Think of all the fun facts you could learn."

She shook her head as much as her contracted muscles would allow, her message of derision still coming through loud and clear. I couldn't resist chuckling. I'd almost forgotten how to do it. My laughter felt good. That girl released something that had laid dormant and forgotten over the last year.

Hoping Connie's new adorned friend would be the answer to my wife's loneliness I took my leave and headed for the stairs. Connie had shrunk from most social contact over the last year after our newborn's death, her withdrawal broken up only by part-time swim therapy work. She'd hated meeting other couples after our move, with their newborns and toddlers. Denise and Audrey, though, were different. Maybe they would show to Connie how enjoyable life could be despite hardship, instead of covering up or denying life's blemishes in the name of appearance.

Guilt over leaving Connie and her first real break from isolation followed me up the stairs. I sighed and sat down at my computer, logging into the hospital website. Bethany may be smart, but that insulin drip couldn't have been just a mistake. Not with Leland Travis as the ordering doctor. Travis didn't strike me as the second coming of Bill Gates. How the hell had he hacked into the system? Did someone know he was too crazy to defend himself if they used his name? No one else seemed bothered enough to investigate. Was everyone that scared of a lawsuit? Or were they scared of something else?

All I knew was it hadn't been me. I just needed to convince everyone else of that. I focused on the screen and entered my password, before sleep overwhelmed me.

CHAPTER 6

The hulking edifice of Narragansett General Hospital loomed against a sky barely touched by dawn as I pulled into the parking lot. The building reminded me more of Dracula's castle than a modern place of healing.

The Intensive Care Unit was quiet when I walked in for morning rounds. I still hadn't become used to such a place. Nowhere else in any civilized world were there so many people so close to death, so many fighting for their very life every moment of every day, with so little fanfare or even disruption of routine. Sometimes I felt like I was walking into a prison housing miserable inmates trying to survive torture instead of miserable patients and families trying to survive severe illness. I shook my head in resignation

"Something bothering you, Dr. Lindmark?"

I broke out of my reverie at Bethany's bark. "No, I was just thinking about, well, I was just thinking."

"What a banner moment for you, Dr. Lindmark. I always knew you interns would eventually get around to thinking. Hopefully, your fellow interns will follow your outstanding example and master brain function just as well as you have. Meantime, tell me about how this patient's kidneys are responding to the treatment for his heart failure. Do you happen to have his labs for this morning?"

Rounds mercifully finished just before lunch without further embarrassment or catastrophe. As we had admitted no new patients to the ICU so far, Bethany told our team to go on to Grand Rounds for the lunchtime lecture. Of course, I was called out of the lecture only minutes after I'd collapsed into a chair at the back of the auditorium. I took my half-eaten sandwich with me on the off-chance I would find a few spare minutes to finish it. The odds of ever tasting that chicken salad again were not good.

"We got a possible admission," Bethany greeted me when I walked into the ICU. "Not a lot of teaching value, though."

I hoped that if I ever became seriously ill, I would also have very little teaching value. The Great Cases I heard described by other interns or residents were always the victims of some rare or fascinating disease. Not just rare, but usually a disease that led to progressive infirmity, unbearable pain, or inevitable death. No patient attracted more admiration or attention during bedside rounds than one with an odd heart murmur, a hugely enlarged liver, a possible exotic infection, or a classic stroke finding. In other words, A Great Case for doctors in training, not so great for the afflicted patient.

Timmy, as his parents called him, was a nineteen-year-old mentally impaired boy with a delicate seizure disorder. He did well at home, but over the last week had developed a stomach flu. He had vomited most of his seizure medications and had suffered several major seizures over the last twelve hours. His parents had brought him into the emergency room only when his lips and fingers started turning blue.

Dr. Bethany spoke to me without breaking stride or even looking at me. "I'm told this kid seizes at least once a week when he's doing well. He's starting to wake up now that he's gotten some meds in him here in the Emergency Room, so he probably doesn't need the ICU but we've been called down just in case." He lowered his voice and leaned into me. "Might be a good idea to find out if his parents have ever made any decisions about Timmy's code status. Sounds like this may keep happening and one of these times he may need life support. We need to find that out. Are you up to it?"

Talk to parents about whether we should try to save their son's life or allow him to die peacefully? I wiped my hands on my coat and swallowed against a mouth gone dry. Bethany was staring at me intently. "Of course, Dr. Bethany, I can do that."

"Yeah." He stared at me. "My own view, Lindmark?" For a brief second, I thought his eyes flitted back and forth in a face contorted with fury. I blinked several times and saw only his features hardening from a smirk to flinty-eyed intensity. "I would try to dissuade them from making their son a 'No Code.' Mental impairment or not, he could have a long life, and seizures are treatable as long as his guardians act responsibly and give him his medications, right?" He didn't wait for any agreement. It seemed a strange command out of the blue, but he was the Great and Powerful Dr. Martin Bethany. "But be careful, Lindmark. Mrs. Richman is probably still recovering from your last heart-to-heart." I hadn't been all that confident even before he flung those last words at me.

Bethany stopped in front of a middle-aged couple sitting in front of a curtained-off room. "Mr. and Mrs., um. . . " he glanced down at a sheet of paper. "Strickland?"

The man nodded. His face was hardened and coarse, his hands were ingrained with dirt. Threadbare khaki pants rode up his calves, exposing weathered cowboy boots. He was holding a Teddy Bear. His wife's flowered blouse stretched over a large stomach and was tucked into faded jeans tattered at the bottoms. Creases puckered her mouth, betraying the countless packs of cigarettes inhaled for too many years.

"I'm Dr. Bethany. This is Dr. Lindmark. We're doctors in the ICU here. We—"

"Can we go in and see our Timmy?" Mrs. Strickland asked. "He gets scared when we're not there."

Bethany shrugged and pulled the curtains aside. Another resident was just stuffing his stethoscope into a pocket. "He's all yours, Martin," he said and walked out past Timmy's parents without another word. Timmy looked older than I was expecting. Thick black hair sprouting disheveled cowlicks framed a long face with disfiguring bony ridges. Large buck teeth and swollen gums pushed out through drooling lips.

He glanced back and forth in obvious fear, until his mother stroked his head and laid the stuffed bear in his hands.

"Will he be okay?" his mother asked. "We can't stand it when he gets sick."

Bethany and I looked at each other. The Stricklands looked as if they'd be much more successful caring for Bessie the ailing milk cow than monitoring doses of complicated seizure medications.

"Mrs. Strickland, does Timmy talk? How, um, how functional is he?"

"Of course he talks, Doctor," his mother answered. Timmy mumbled and showed a crooked toothy smile. "See?"

I nodded. "Your son had some severe fits. You understand that, right?" I approached carefully, using more simple terms. She nodded. "I hope it won't happen again, but we should probably clarify what you would want to happen if he had a very severe episode here in the hospital. Or at home."

"What do you mean?" she asked, still stroking Timmy's head. Timmy smiled up at her and clutched the bear more tightly.

"Well, should he become very sick after a seizure, or should anything very serious happen, would you want him resuscitated? You know, I mean, would you want us to save his life? Put him on a ventilator, on machines to keep him alive?" Even as I was saying the words they sounded brutal and selfish, as if I were punishing both parents for having the gall to burden the hospital with their disabled son. I wanted to comfort Timmy's mother, not slap her in the face with the brutality of her son's future. Why the hell did Bethany make me do this?

Tears welled up in Mrs. Strickland's eyes. Oh God, they hadn't discussed it before. Could it be they'd never even considered this issue?

She turned to her husband. "Norm, did we bring any of Timmy's other special animals?" She turned to me. "Dr. Lindmark, you asked if Timmy was 'functional,' if he could talk. Is that so important? Every day Timmy talks to us. Right now he's telling me he loves me, and he knows we'll protect him." I looked at Timmy. He was looking up at his mother with wide unblinking eyes, smiling that misshapen grin.

Mr. Strickland rose from his chair and clumped over to us. "Can I see you boys outside for a second?"

We gathered outside the curtains. "Timmy means everything to us," he said without hesitation. "I don't know how this happened. Norma and I always measure out the exact right amount of Tegretol and Topamax. The last levels were therapeutic just a week ago." His expression turned thoughtful. "He had a little virus a week ago. You might want to check his liver enzymes. Some illnesses can affect the liver, which could change drug levels." His tone hardened. "Let me tell you boys about my son's code status. Timmy is not ready to die, and we're not ready to let him. We're all the three of us have. We want everything done. Full resuscitation, intubation, mechanical ventilation if he aspirates or has another bad seizure. Is that understood?"

I nodded. My talk had been completely unnecessary. Timmy had always been a Full Code, out of love. Even Bethany looked a little dazed, but probably more from the unexpected sophistication flowing from the American Gothic figure than from the actual decision. I'd focused on two people named Norm and Norma finding each other and had married, until taken aback by the man's erudite instructions.

"Don't look so surprised, doctors," he responded to our unspoken thoughts. "Do you really think I've lived through hospitalizations, doctor visits, ER visits, so many seizures, without learning a few things? You think all those medical websites are open only for college graduates who wear suits instead of shoveling cow shit for a living?" A sad smile creased his wrinkled unshaven cheeks. "I'm sure you boys learn a lot in medical school when your grades depend on it. I guarantee you one thing. You learn a lot more when your boy's life depends on it." He looked at us suspiciously, then reached out a paw to shake our hands. "I better get back with the wife. Timmy likes it when we're both with him. He hates hospitals. So do we."

Neither of us said anything for a while as Bethany and I retreated from the Stricklands' cubicle. "Lindmark, tell the floor team to come down and admit him to a regular floor. There's no evidence of aspiration, and he shouldn't seize again. Let me know where he's admitted to. I may want to check up on him, just in case. When you're done, we can change some intravenous lines on your patients." He glanced back at the Stricklands. When he turned back to me, his brows were knit over a scowl. "Can't argue with what Doctor Farmer-In-The-Dell said, even though I would have gotten to those liver enzymes myself." I dared not smile at Bethany's injured ego.

I glanced at my intern's clipboard and sighed. The to-do list had now grown long enough to become a bucket list. I sighed again as I called one of my fellow interns about Timmy. She would not like getting another admission. At least I could blame it on Bethany.

CHAPTER 7

My last day in the ICU had finally come and gone. I'd weathered Bethany's daily barrage of questions and had even brought up points the Great One hadn't considered. Hadn't considered *yet*, he'd made sure to qualify. More importantly, no one else had exploded, bled out, or died unexpectedly. Some patients had even improved. Aaron Shirkey had weaned off the ventilator and all his infusions. As he was being wheeled out to a stepdown floor, he'd promised to bring us all some pasta from The Marinara Man when he was back at work.

Anthony Richman's death still nagged at me. Apparently, I was the only one who still thought about it. Life and death had gone on in the ICU as usual. The ICU pharmacist had told me he couldn't answer any of my questions, because the case was under litigation. At least that meant someone was looking into it, that *someone* cared about how that damn insulin order had made its deadly way into the boy's veins. It had kept me awake the night before. I'd awakened today, my first Saturday off, still uneasy. Because 'under litigation' meant that the 'someone who cared' was a collection of lawyers and paid consultants who cared about lost money, not lost life.

Which is why, on my first proper day off, I was headed back to the hospital. I'd told Connie I was catching up on errands because even my wife would question the sanity of virtually heading back to prison after just getting paroled. At the hospital, I put on my identification badge in case I met one of the elderly security guards. They were the running joke around my intern class. *Patients who lived to be discharged back to a nursing home never made it. They just got recycled back to the hospital in uniform. . .*

I was about to walk through the front door when it occurred to me how ridiculous I'd look as an overworked intern going back to the hospital voluntarily instead of enjoying a weekend of freedom. For the same reason I'd lied to Connie I looked for an unseen entrance, which meant the tunnel. It was at worst an old decrepit passageway in an old decrepit Narragansett General where reputation and medical education held sway over infrastructure. So why did that tunnel scare me so much? What about that lost kid? Had he ever been found? I'd heard nothing about it since I'd reported it to Charlie. Something else I'd have to look into. But first, I *had* to find out the truth behind Richman's death. I owed it to him, if for nothing else because I'd offered such careless reassurance to his mother. We *all* owed it to that poor kid, because he'd died under our watch.

I gritted my teeth, gripped the handle of the dingy side entrance at one end of the parking lot and opened the door. Maintenance had mercifully replaced the broken bulbs. The long passage in front of me loomed gloomy instead of black. Although it was still warmer than the outside, I closed my collar around me and hurried towards the hospital entrance. Naked pipes still coursed along the walls. Condensate dripped loudly, as if the walls were sweating. I passed a red Hazardous Material container, stained coffee cups and plates, and old newspapers. Charlie was right–there probably were druggies and homeless that used this tunnel as refuge from the cold. Maybe that child was one of their kids, homeless and lost?

The gloom shrouded everything and dampened the echoes of my footsteps. A rustling seemed to emerge from the walls and surround me. Water running through those old pipes? Rats swarming behind the walls? Imagination stoked my already heightened anxiety, provoking visions of even scarier denizens of this crypt of a tunnel. Sweat dampened my shirt despite the chill. Why had I come down here again? The rustling sank to a whisper, but in the next moment grew louder and more insistent. The entire tunnel seemed to be breathing in and out. Without warning silence descended as the tunnel held its breath. I looked from one side to another, unease churning in my stomach. The sudden stillness was broken by a thud and breaking glass from somewhere behind me.

I couldn't help jogging down the tunnel instead of walking, obeying the burst of fear that had erupted. Just as the door to the main hospital finally appeared, I heard a low sighing noise from behind me. It was a sound of wind moaning through trees with an odd tinkling mixed in. A woman's shrill scream seemed to twist in and out of the moaning. I spun around as the noise grew louder. Dots of shadow sped along the walls towards me. Shards of broken glass, syringes, needles, and bloody strips of gauze exploded from around a corner. Bloody instruments scraped against the wall as they whirled and twisted down the tunnel.

I ran.

Metal and glass clinked, frigid air moaned and wrapped around me. I flailed at anything, at nothing, and kept running. A break in the wall appeared ahead of me, where several pipes branched off into a metal cabinet. I threw myself into the small crevice, pressing against the wall. Slivers of glass and crusted hypodermic needles flew past into the wall beyond me seconds later. I felt a sharp pain in my chest and knew one of those shards had pierced me.

I pushed myself back out of the hollow in the wall and looked down. A fresh surge of fear gripped me when I saw the spot of red on my shirt. Something from that medical waste container had hit me. What if it had come from an AIDS patient, or a hepatitis patient? I reached down to see how deep the wound was and brushed against a sticky, wet outcropping of brick. My heart beat slowed to a gallop as I realized I'd scraped against the wall, instead of suffering a puncture by flying death.

What the hell had happened? I looked up and down the tunnel, seeing nothing but shadow, hearing nothing but my own heavy breathing. I wiped clammy palms on my pants, then clambered up the stairs to the safety of the exit door. Only a few last steps from refuge, the door squealed open.

"Hey, Doc," Charlie Washington greeted me. "What the hell—"

I was never so happy to see another person in my life. I reached out and hugged the old man. He gave off a pungent scent of aftershave mixed with the rich aroma of pipe smoke. "Doc, you don't look so good. You coming here as a patient or as a doctor?"

I held a trembling hand in front of me and looked down at the tear in my shirt with a red stain around it. I *did* look as bad as I felt. It was all I could do to keep from ripping off my shirt and hurling myself down to the Emergency Department for a thorough inspection and decontamination. I needed to scrub myself raw right then and there. "Charlie," I finally said. "Have you worked here long?"

"Only as long as penicillin has been around," he answered. "I think the equipment they give me has been around for that long, too."

"Have you ever noticed anything. . . strange around this place?"

His soft dry chuckle sounded like rocks shaking around in his throat. "Doc, not a day goes by there isn't something strange going on in this place." His rheumy eyes widened as he peered more closely at me. "You're scared, ain't you?" I shrugged. "What happened in that tunnel? Something happen? Someone hiding down there? We've had people from the streets come in looking for drugs, you know. Or just a warm place to sit."

"Yeah, maybe one of those people was down there. I, uh, got a bunch of needles and contaminated waste thrown at me. Can you believe that?"

He squinted at my shirt. "One of those things hit you, Doc?"

"I must have scraped against the wall ducking out of the way, I guess. And whoever it was tried to scare me even more by howling and screeching. Some asshole, huh? A woman, now that I think about it. Whoever she was, she was angry." I shivered at the memory of that unearthly scream. "Have you heard anyone else get caught like that down here, Charlie?" I touched the wound on my chest, my fingers coming back reddened.

The old man's expression turned worried. He rubbed a hand against his curly white hair. "A woman you say?" I nodded. "You stay away from the tunnels, Doc. I'll send security down to look it over, but maybe using the front entrance like most people might be better."

"It's cold outside, Charlie."

"It can get pretty cold inside too, Doc. You do what I say, okay? Stay out of the tunnels." We had by this time entered one of the main hospital corridors. The bright lights were a welcome relief from the shadows behind us. Groups of hospital personnel scurried about their routines as if nothing had happened. Of course, none of them had been witness to the near-death experience I had just survived. Surrounded by well-lit normal hustle and bustle, I felt foolish over my previous panic.

"Charlie, let's just keep what I said about all that in the tunnel between us, okay? Homeless people and junkies, right?" Charlie's affable shrug prompted more cautious sharing. "But as long as we're keeping things between us, do you, uh, do you ever see other things around here? That maybe aren't, you know, explained?"

"Doc, I never ignore nothing around here. Just don't go shooting your mouth off to anyone else about that. That's how people get gone around here."

"Yeah, but Charlie, you're only a—" I stopped and avoided the old man's stare. "I didn't mean that—"

Charlie grasped my arm with a surprisingly strong grip. "Only an orderly? Maybe I am, Doc, but no one else is gonna believe you. So we're stuck with each other. Now—weren't you on your way somewhere?"

I ducked into the intern call room and sat in front of the computer. I couldn't deny that I felt more secure around Charlie. Anthony Richman's dead corpse and bleeding eyes invaded my thoughts and pushed Charlie Washington out of them. I hoped the hospital computer would surrender more information than my remote connection from home did. A flood of lab values immediately crowded the screen when I punched in Richman's name. Blood sugar levels, acid levels, electrolytes. All immediately visible, all horrendously abnormal, all too little and too late since they came from the Code Blue. I scrolled to the orders and breathed a sigh of relief when all my signed orders seemed to be what I had remembered. No order for insulin or for anything else that could possibly have led to the boy's death. I clicked the central pharmacy link, looking for that insulin order from "Dr. Leland Travis."

PASSWORD: ______________.

Password? None of us had needed a password to review pharmacy orders. We needed that access to manage minute-to-minute changes in patient medications. I tried again, with the same objection. Bethany had gotten in. How else had he known about that order?

I shook my head in annoyance. Must've been the lawyers. I thought of Travis's words. Maybe he *did* know more about this. According to Bethany, someone had thought enough of him to use his name. What had the old man said? Someone Frazier. Sylvester Morrow. I focused on the names Travis had babbled and entered 'Frazier, Myron' into the database. The screen spat out its tale. Myron Frazier admitted two years previous with chest pain. I scanned through the records. Cardiac arrest, successfully resuscitated. 'Successfully' was debatable, as he survived with major neurologic and personality injury. Discharged to nursing home, 'full care.' Something caught my eye, at the bottom of the code blue record. Martin Bethany MD, Code Blue supervising resident.

I punched in Sylvester Morrow. Nothing.

I scrolled to another name Travis had thrown out, admitted three years ago with diabetes and an infected foot. Cardiopulmonary arrest. Insulin reaction suspected. Did not survive resuscitation. The record included the other medical personnel who had assisted in the resuscitation. A name leaped out at me.

Martin Bethany MD, intern.

Bethany had assisted in the Code Blue resuscitation efforts of both people Travis had mentioned. Something else I had skimmed over hit me as I reflected on that coincidence. I scrolled up and fastened on words that suddenly had taken on meaning: *Insulin reaction suspected.* My hands went cold, an embarrassing symptom of my exploding anxiety. Could that really be just one more coincidence in a hospital where medical errors are bound to happen?

I sank into the chair and tried to slow the racing thoughts with deep breathing. Not so unusual in a teaching hospital, right? That's what interns and residents were for–to handle things that happened in the hospital when their private physicians weren't there. After my own year of internship, I would hopefully graduate to become a more experienced resident physician. We were expected to manage emergencies and hopefully save those patients. But these were patients Leland Travis had warned me about. The same Leland Travis whose name had been used to kill one of my patients. Anthony Richman had been yet *another* patient under Martin Bethany's care. These dots weren't connecting. I shook my head. Or they were connecting in a very bad way? No way. I'd probably find the same thing by looking at records of other residents.

But the same doctor involved in patient deaths where egregious medical errors could have been responsible? Including my patient, goddam it. Medical errors happened. Bethany was one of the most highly regarded residents. Hell, I'd seen him in action. But could he be like the arsonist who set fires, only to put them out as the hero? I needed proof, if even there was such proof. I needed to watch my back, never mind watching my resident. And I needed. . . maybe a higher dose of my anxiety medication?

I glanced at my watch and realized I'd been at the hospital far longer than the errands I had explained to Connie would allow. Not only had I lied to my wife, I'd left her at the mercy of her thoughts and memories without the distractions that for better or worse buffered my own sadness. I resolved to be better, somehow, and logged off the computer's medical records. The hospital had become even busier than when I'd first entered the on-call room, especially for a Saturday. I threw on my coat and headed for the main entrance. It was going to be an uncomfortable walk, but "uncomfortable" didn't begin to cover what a walk through the tunnels would probably be.

CHAPTER 8

A van blocked my entrance into the garage. A blue handicap parking sticker hung from the rearview mirror. I breathed a sigh of relief. Connie hadn't spent the afternoon alone, no thanks to me.

"We're in here," Connie greeted me as I walked in the door. Denise was sitting on the couch with Connie. Her daughter sat inches away from the television. "Harry, you remember Denise and Audrey?"

"Audrey, how about saying 'hi' to Dr. Lindmark?"

Her mother seemed to take Audrey's disapproving frown in stride. "Mom, I was going to say it without you telling me." She looked at me. "Hey, Dr. Lindmark. Don't mind my mom. She doesn't get out much."

I couldn't help smiling. "Sorry I'm late, Connie. I had a few more errands than I thought."

Connie's eyes widened. "Harry, your shirt. What on earth happened? Is that blood on your shirt?"

"Dr. Lindmark, did you get shot?" Audrey sounded excited.

"No, no, everyone, it's all okay. I just tripped. Stupid." I rubbed my hand over the tear in my shirt as those bloody scalpels flew into my memory.

"Oh." I could swear Audrey sounded disappointed, then her tone picked up. "Well, you got here just in time for the party."

"Party, Audrey?" For the first time, I noticed Denise's eyes were red and swollen. "Is everything okay?"

"Today is Audrey's birthday." Denise sounded solemn, not happy.

"So, what are you doing for the party?"

Connie and Denise looked at each other, then Connie took my hand and guided me into the kitchen. "This *is* her party." Her lips quivered. Her eyes were also swollen. "Denise invited Audrey's classmates to a movie today. She sent out invitations, bought a huge cake, reserved a room at the movie theater. She hadn't received any replies, but she thought kids just showed up without bothering to RSVP." She squeezed my hand. "Audrey and Denise took the only two girls who did show up into the movie. They said they had to leave right after the movie ended, so there really was no one there for the actual party. Denise was going to light the candles anyway, just her and Audrey, but Audrey said she wanted to eat the cake with all her friends. You and me, Harry. All her friends." Her eyes no longer contained the tears that spilled over. "So the end to a very long answer to your question, Harry, is that we're going to have a nice quiet party right here. Twelve candles and enough cake to feed the neighborhood."

I walked back into the living room and looked at Audrey. The bow in her hair must have been a special purchase for her birthday celebration. Her dress covered the scrawny twig that was one arm, while her legs dangled almost hidden by the extra-long lacy fabric. "Hey Audrey."

She spun the wheelchair around to look at me.

"I've heard about the parties you throw," I said, unable to suppress my grin. "I'll do the cake and candles thing, but if the neighbors call the police, you're on your own."

I was gratified by her smile. We followed her into the kitchen and sang off-key over the twelve candles with one to grow on. The immense slab of cake emphasized the loneliness of our small gathering.

"You guys eat as much as you want," Audrey slurred. "My mom needs to watch her girlish figure." I looked again at the cake, then glanced at Connie. Her smile was strained and stiff. Denise's eyes were glistening. For one brief moment, I hoped they were tears of joy, an emotional expression of pride in a daughter's special milestone.

But I knew better.

"Hey Audrey," I smiled down at her. "I wouldn't do this if it weren't such a special occasion, but it so happens we do have Netflix here. I'm gonna let you select a movie to watch. Any movie."

"*Any* movie?"

"Any movie. Mrs. Lindmark doesn't even let *me* do that." Her giggle broke the somber mood. I joined her in laughing.

The noise of the television drowned out the voices from the other room. I wondered who was comforting who. Our own sorrow was never far from Connie's mind. It even drowned out the voices in my head, the ones that had been nagging at me since I'd left the hospital. The voices that would not let go of what I'd seen in those medical files, the voices that warned me never to turn my back on a certain medical resident. The antics of Kyle, Cartman, and the rest of the South Park gang managed to quiet those thoughts, until Audrey spun around and looked at me. "I'm really okay, Dr. Lindmark. My mom, she makes too big a deal about things. It's a great birthday. I had cake, I get to watch a show that my mom never lets me watch, and I got to be another year older. This is great."

That wasn't how the usual twelve-year-old girl should describe a birthday. She sounded as if living yet another year was an unexpected gift.

"And now I get to watch South Park with someone, instead of listening to my mom go on about how those other kids don't matter, how she'll speak to their mothers, blah, blah, blah. You do like South Park, right?"

I actually did like South Park. But I would have said so anyway, even if I'd never heard of the show.

CHAPTER 9

Morning rounds continued on to Timmy Strickland's room. "All right, hit it, Dr. Lindmark," Dr. Helen Northrup commanded as we stood outside the doorway.

"He's doing pretty well," I replied.

She heaved an exaggerated sigh. "Thank you for that scintillating summary, Dr. Lindmark. Of course, I could have received the same information from the housekeeping attendant who cleans the room every day. Now–can we get a few more details befitting a recent medical school graduate?"

My new resident, Dr. Northrup, was the Major Houlihan to Bethany's Hawkeye Pierce. A tall thin black woman, she was always immaculately made up, her hair restrained in a bun wound as tight as she was. She walked, or actually *marched*, with determined poised strides no matter the occasion. She ran rounds as a warden would run morning roll call, and had no patience for hesitation.

"Tim Strickland. His oxygen level is improving daily. He's been on IV antibiotics for seven days. It's probably time to change him to oral antibiotics, especially since he keeps picking at the IV. He's had no more seizures, back on all his medications."

"Take a breath, Dr. Lindmark. Sounds reasonable." She entered the room as gracefully as any beauty contestant. I followed, my medical student behind me. Frank Bannister, the other intern on the team, brought up the rear. Frank looked the human equivalent of Big Bird in white instead of yellow, with a similar easygoing personality. He was wearing a bowtie with medical symbols on it that barely contained a jutting Adam's apple. I couldn't resist a chuckle as I stared at that tie. Frank might as well have been wearing a sign proclaiming I AM A NERD.

Northrup shot me a warning glance, cutting off any more quiet laughter. She turned back to the three people in the room. "Good morning, Mr. and Mrs. Strickland," she intoned. She favored the boy in the bed with a tight smile. "Hello Tim," she said, as if addressing a colleague. Her tone had all the warmth of a fast-food attendant speaking through the loudspeaker at a drive-through.

Timmy looked up at her and smiled widely. His mouth could barely contain swollen gums and crooked teeth. He mumbled an unintelligible greeting as he grabbed tightly onto a stuffed giraffe in his lap.

"He's looking a lot brighter today," I remarked to his parents.

Norma Strickland beamed at my words. "Oh, he's a lot better, Dr. Lindmark. We've almost got our boy all the way back, thanks to you doctors."

I laid my stethoscope on Timmy's back. His lungs sounded clearer. In one of his few mistakes, Bethany had been proven wrong. Timmy *had* aspirated during the seizure that had brought him in, requiring a longer hospitalization than expected. "He's made so much progress we can take the IV out and start him on oral antibiotics." I suddenly remembered. "I mean, through his feeding tube. If he remains stable, probably home in a day or so."

My smile froze as a gust of icy air wrapped around me. I looked around for an open vent but saw none. No one else had reacted. Northrup spun around with military precision and walked out without a backwards glance. I looked at Timmy and could swear I saw goosebumps pucker his arms. His eyes opened wide and darted back and forth around the room.

His father walked over and put an arm around Timmy. "Did you hear that, son? Home soon. Back to your room. You're doing great, boy." Under his father's reassuring hug, Timmy burbled something and stopped looking around. The chill left as quickly as it had come.

I looked around the room one more time, then offered my most reassuring smile to the Stricklands. "You guys have quite a son there. I definitely think home soon." I left them in a group hug and followed the team to the next patient.

Aaron Shirkey had followed me from the ICU, recovering enough to make it onto a regular medical floor. "Mister Shirkey, you have come an amazing way," I started off as we walked into his room.

He grinned back through lips still swollen and cracked from the breathing tube. "You bet, Doc," he rasped, his voice box also rubbed raw from the tube. "What you want from Aaron-ara the Marinara Man for all your hard work?"

It was getting scary to consider what he had been like before his hospitalization. "Well, I could start with—"

"I'm sure this is all very important, Dr. Lindmark," Dr. Northrup interrupted. "But if we could focus on all those annoying little medical details, like Mr. Shirkey's elevated blood sugars, and those pesky abnormal liver function tests? Any idea if they're correcting?" Apparently the brief moment I took to look up the lab values was too long. "Never mind." She looked at me as if I were a bug she had barely avoided stepping on. "Make sure you check all the labs before noon conference and review them with me later."

We raced through the remainder of the patients. Northrup gathered us and gave Bannister and me a concise list of duties, then ordered us all to the noon conference. I stopped by the floor's computer terminal and printed off the updated labs on my patients. One number caught my attention. Timmy Strickland's sodium level was 154? It was only. . . I scrolled back through previous labs. Yeah, it had been normal at 143 only two days earlier. He'd looked so normal, or at least normal for Timmy. I knew one thing–Timmy was not going to become another Anthony Richman. I made some quick calculations, then called the floor and instructed Timmy's nurse to start a free water IV drip at my precisely calculated rate. It would mean Timmy's discharge would be delayed and Timmy would need to keep his IV in place, but such a high sodium level could cause another seizure among other disasters.

I shouldered my way through the crowded lunchtime hallways, already late for the conference, until I saw the squat fiery-haired figure of my previous resident striding in the same direction ahead. I hung back, all thoughts of the conference gone, my new mission made suddenly clear. Would he veer into the hospital pharmacy? Were those bulges in his pockets really reference manuals, or were they syringes? He did stop at the main pharmacy doorway. My eyes narrowed as I watched him hand a piece of paper to the pharmacy tech that answered his ring. I needed to see that paper.

As Bethany merged back into the hallway crowd, I decided to stop into the pharmacy instead of following him, walking up to the pharmacy with absolutely no idea of what I'd do next. I reached out to ring the bell, turning stories and explanations around in my mind.

"Harry!"

I jumped at the voice in my ear. I spun around, heart pounding, prepared for another vision that no one else seemed to see.

"Whoa, Harry, take it easy." Terri McCormick stood smiling at me. Another of my fellow interns, she and I hadn't crossed paths much since starting internship. "I've been meaning to give you a message from one of your special patients, but haven't had the chance until spotting you just now. Do you need to finish something?"

I glanced at the open pharmacy window, shrugged and shook my head. I could be taking care of about a billion other things as an intern instead of playing Hardy boys in the hallway. Would Dr. Bethany really hand over some incriminating message to a pharmacist in the middle of a busy hallway? Besides, I couldn't ignore a message from a 'special patient.' I had to hear this. "No, just on my way to conference, Terri," I said. "What's up?"

She smiled. "I was on service when your favorite patient was finally discharged. He wanted me to give you in particular a message. It was a while ago, and I almost forgot about it until I saw you." I shook my head in puzzlement. "The one and only Doctor Leland Travis finally left us."

"He didn't—"

"No, he just got better and better, and louder and louder, until we couldn't take it anymore and sent him back to the Morrow."

"The Morrow?"

"Where have you been, Harry? The Sylvester Morrow Convalescent Center? Most of the residents there need to purchase round-trip tickets to and from this place, because we just seem to recycle them after each infected bedsore or infection. Anyway, he wanted me to tell you, and I quote: 'that other intern. . . Bismarck or whatever his name was, he can take his phony bedside manner, his fat-ass resident, and try to be a real doctor the next time by listening to his patients. And if I ever get admitted again, just stamp "No Code" on my forehead and throw me in a corner somewhere.' His exact words, Harry. I think he really liked you." Her smile widened.

I looked at her carefully. "He really said all that?"

"You think I'd make it up? Don't take it to heart. He's a miserable old man who hates everyone. He couldn't stop fixating on getting out before 'they came for him, when there were no more young ones or healthy ones to take.' Whoever *they* are." She shrugged.

"Did he say anything else?"

Before she could answer, my phone shrilled from Dr. Northrup, calling with another admission. She told me she'd go over everything after I saw the patient and wrote what I thought were appropriate orders. She ended the call abruptly after leaving me a helpful '*Now, please.*' I shook my head and wondered how it would feel to have an intern of my own someday to order around, once I'd graduated to a second-year resident status.

CHAPTER 10

Timmy, my least complicated patient, was becoming way too complicated in a sea of complicated patients. After his initial improvement, he'd become sleepier and more lethargic over the last several days. "This is not my boy, Doctor," his father warned us daily. Northrup and I suspected the seizure medications were blunting him. I was privately frustrated over his damn sodium level, which had remained elevated despite the intravenous water drip I'd been giving him. That kind of electrolyte imbalance could easily cause his symptoms, and I resolved to solve it on my own. I knew I was missing some hormonal process somewhere, and I would not give Northrup a chance to make me look stupid if I revealed it to her.

"How you doing today, Timmy?" I asked as I walked in ahead of my team. His mother was sitting vigil at his bedside, smelling even more strongly of cigarettes than on previous mornings.

"Still sleepy today, Dr. Lindmark," she replied in her son's stead. Timmy opened his eyes at the sound of our voices, but barely looked in my direction before his eyelids fluttered closed. Saliva leaked out from between crooked teeth, which his mother kept mopping away with a towel. "Timmy, can't you wake up for the doctor?" she prodded, her actions and tone as unperturbed as if she were wiping a spill off a coffee table instead of dabbing at her nineteen-year-old son's drool. Timmy stirred but didn't open his eyes. A wisp of cold grazed the back of my neck. I whirled around and saw only my resident standing in the doorway, one plucked eyebrow raised suspiciously.

"Expecting someone else, Dr. Lindmark?" she asked.

I shook my head and turned back to Timmy. His eyes had opened wide, staring at me, before he sank back into his stupor. The cold vanished as quickly as it had snaked around me.

"Why, doctors? Why is Timmy so sleepy? Medications? Have you checked his levels? Sometimes changes in diet can affect metabolism, right?"

I glanced at Northrup, knowing we were thinking the same thing. When had Timmy's parents graduated from a field of corn to a field of medicine?

"Maybe he's just a little sleep-deprived?" I offered. His mother shook her head vigorously.

Northrup said, "We'll look into it, Mrs. Strickland." Resident-speak for *my intern will look into it and we have to get moving to more important patients.* "Dr. Lindmark, we should keep moving."

I cast Mrs. Strickland a reassuring smile and resolved to get that sodium level down as fast as I could before Timmy seized again. I scribbled an order in Timmy's chart to increase the free water drip again, then hurried after the team. My night on call hadn't even started and already I was falling behind.

Get up. GET UP!

The whisper in my ear jolted me awake. I looked around the darkened call room, but saw neither nurse nor apparition. I'd finally managed to fall asleep after my fifth page of the night, the last one from a nurse calling at 2:00 a.m. for a laxative order. A knife of cold sliced down my back. I bolted upright, alert. Nothing in the call room moved. I checked my phone. Nothing. No call had come in with that message. I ran to the door and threw it open onto a hallway deathly quiet and as empty as a mausoleum, but it was still a hospital even at 3:00 a.m.. Where the hell was everyone? *Anyone*?

Frigid air wrapped itself around me, *pulling me* down the empty hall. A figure walked out of a room in the distance. As I approached, it became more recognizable as a small, stooped adult. No, it was the boy, the lost child I'd seen wandering around the tunnels. His head swiveled with eerie slowness until he pierced me with an unnerving staring gaze. He moved towards me, not walking but *gliding*? *Floating*? I could not turn away despite a stab of dread that iced its way into my gut. He came closer on thin dangling legs that didn't move and raised stick-thin arms at me. I felt like the hospital was holding its breath, so heavy was the quiet. I didn't want to get any nearer to this strange boy, still lost and wandering. Was he a patient, or maybe a little lost boy needing help, looking for his parents?

The code horn shrieked overhead, shattering the silence. I started running down the hall towards the room that boy must belong in, not knowing why. Two nurses panted into the hallway from a stairwell. "Dr. Lindmark, there's a code!" one called out as they pounded past me.

"Who? Where is it?" I blurted out. "Is it Shirkey?" It had to be Shirkey. He'd been doing just too well. "Wait, the lung cancer guy, right? Did anyone look at the monitors?" My words were lost in the code horn's blaring. The nurses were joined by respiratory therapists, one carrying an orange resuscitation bag. I joined the growing crowd and looked down the hallway again. The boy was gone, but a red light flashed over the doorway of the room out of which he had emerged. That odd spooky teenager *had* been wanting help.

I skidded into the room along with the rest and felt the cold immediately. There was something happening on the bed. My throat tightened as I elbowed my way through and looked down. Timmy was violently seizing. His fists were clenched, arms and legs jerking without control or purpose. His eyes were wide open but unseeing. A thin stream of vomit spurted out between misshapen teeth with each fresh muscle spasm. Charlie was backing away from the bed, his eyes wide open. He looked at the crush of people pushing through the door.

"Doc! Thank God you're here. I was just walking by when I heard something in here. He was. . . he was. . . "

Someone pushed by me. Martin Bethany bulldozed into the room and leaned over Timmy. "Charlie, out of the way. Denise, push five milligrams of Valium *now*. I need a suction catheter *now*. Hook him up to the monitor, and get him on oxygen. Put him on 100%, but get the intubation tube ready. He had to have aspirated." Bethany was doing that frenzied head-scratching thing, as if trying to awaken more brain cells just waiting under that red curly mop to be called upon.

I almost collapsed with relief. The residents alternated call among themselves, and I'd known he would be with me tonight although my supervising resident was Northrup. I would have taken my third-grade teacher at that moment, as long as she knew how to manage this emergency.

I looked down with horrible déjà vu at another unexpected Code Blue in a young patient with Martin Bethany arriving so immediately at the scene. Timmy finally stopped moving as the Valium kicked in. My heart rate slowed until Bethany straightened up and glared at me. "Lindmark. Get over here. He needs to be intubated. He aspirated, and now he's not breathing. *Now*, Lindmark."

Bethany's growl replaced my relief at Timmy's response with an unease that twisted like a knife in my chest. "Dr. Bethany, wouldn't there be a better time for a teachable moment than this?" I hated how my words came out in a squeak.

"Yeah, I know. You've never done it. But you're here to learn. Don't worry, I'll walk you through it." He turned to one of the respiratory therapists. "Start bagging him, Stuart. And lubricate the number seven tube for Dr. Lindmark."

I shivered with cold, nerves, and *fear*, as the threat of Bethany's menace battled with panic over actually putting a breathing tube in a living patient. "This is not a drill" echoed in my head. I shouldered my way to the head of the bed where people were manipulating Timmy's head. Someone else was noisily suctioning up vomit from Timmy's mouth. Stuart slapped a breathing tube in my right hand while Bethany placed a special light in my other hand. "Put the scope in his mouth, Lindmark, and sweep the tongue to one side. See that upside down 'V'? Those are the vocal cords. Suction away the vomit and slip the tube through that 'V.'"

He sounded so calm, so reassuring. Timmy's slack jaw offered no resistance as I propped it open further with thumb and forefinger, then levered the scope into his mouth. The pounding in my chest eased slightly as whitish vocal cords came into view. Timmy lay motionless, not reacting at all to maneuvers that would have made any conscious person gag and strangle. I pushed the tube towards that target. Intense cold sharpened and bit at my face. My eyes started to water, blurring my vision of those welcoming vocal cords. I had to look away and blink.

Something moved beyond the doorway, capturing my attention. A white-coated doctor was walking towards the room. *Gliding* towards me. I couldn't tear my gaze from that man. He entered the room and raised his head to stare directly at me. His eyes, vacant and empty, bore into mine. I felt fury pouring from them, fury so palpable I felt a searing heat on my skin despite the cold. A gray goatee framed the slash of a mouth. His lips parted and formed a single word. "No." It screeched into my head. Then, "Not yet."

Bethany's head whirled in the direction of my gaze. He paused for several seconds, then spun back around and glared at me. "Lindmark. Harry, dammit! What the hell's wrong?" Bethany's words reached me from a great distance. I couldn't answer. I couldn't even swallow past the sudden dryness in my mouth. The doctor's mouth widened, revealing blackness. I couldn't move.

"*. . . too. . . far gone. . .* " rustled in my ears.

I shook my head, trying to get rid of that noise and shake off the terror that engulfed me.

"Lindmark, goddam it!" Bethany's shout wiped away any other voice. I looked down at Timmy. His mouth gaped open before me. His body lay motionless, so still he could have been—

The monitor alarm went off. A rumbled *NOW* whispered in one ear. I glanced at the monitor screen and saw a flat line broken by feeble occasional beats.

Bethany pushed me aside, muttering, "Jesus, he's not breathing. And when that's not treated, Lindmark, a patient can DIE." He snatched the tube and light out of my hand. "AND CAN'T BE BROUGHT BACK. Bag him! Check for pulses. One amp of atropine now." Bethany waited only seconds, then pushed away the respiratory therapist and peered into Timmy's throat with the light. Seconds later, an interminable lifetime to me, he pushed the tube forward. "I'm in. Inflate the balloon. Listen for breath sounds."

"Breath sounds equal, Dr. Bethany," one of the respiratory therapists replied, his stethoscope going back and forth over Timmy's chest.

"Suction through the tube. Saw a lot of vomit down there. Then bag him vigorously." Bethany's forehead dripped with sweat. His staccato commands kept up with his eyes as they flitted back and forth across the room.

I regained my footing and looked towards the door. Nothing was there. I looked around the room. Bethany and I were the only people wearing white coats. I swung my arm around and swept through warm air. My skin had stopped burning. I passed a shaking hand across my forehead. It came away dripping.

"No pulses, Dr. Bethany," a nurse called out. How many times was I going to hear those damn words?

"Could be fine ventricular fibrillation, not absent rhythm," I heard Bethany mutter. Jesus, Timmy *was* going to die. 'V fib' was the most lethal heart rhythm known. Something caught my attention above me. The IV tubing running into Timmy's arm shook and swirled as if it were caught up in a current. I saw Charlie stumble over through the melee and grab the tubing.

"Clear!" Bethany barked out. Timmy's body arched into the air as the jolt of electricity penetrated through his heart. Nurses immediately swarmed back to the bedside as Timmy collapsed back onto the bed. Gloved hands prodded his body, searching for signs of life.

"All right, he's back in sinus rhythm," Bethany called out as he stood over the monitor. "Pulses?"

"I got a femoral pulse."

"I think. . . yeah, I'm getting a carotid pulse."

"Um, Dr. Bethany?" a young nurse piped up. 'Carol' stood out on her name tag. "Do you still want this free water drip continued?"

"Free water drip? What's that for?" Bethany snapped back. The nurse shrugged. "Lindmark! He's your patient, or was. What's the IV drip for?"

"I was treating his elevated sodium levels, Dr. Bethany. It's been difficult to bring down, but I didn't want another seizure because of abnormal electrolytes."

"Keep checking for pulses. Someone check a blood pressure. And go ahead and shut off that drip until we make sure. I want electrolytes, stat. God knows what's been going on here." Bethany was snapping out his orders to the whole room, but that last sentence landed like a punch. I slunk away from the crowd around the bed and collapsed in a chair against the wall.

"Dr. Bethany, he's opening his eyes to my voice," the same young nurse Carol called out.

"And I have a good strong pulse now," another nurse announced.

The beeping on the monitor picked up speed as Bethany strode to the bed and leaned over Timmy. He whipped out his stethoscope out and began listening intently over Timmy's chest.

"Doc, you okay?" I felt an arm drape across my shoulders. I turned and saw Charlie bending over me.

"Not really, Charlie," I managed.

"You don't look okay, Doc. In fact, you look like crap." He looked back at the commotion still surrounding Timmy's bed, then glanced around the room. I could swear he looked more scared than concerned. Something nagged at me, something about Charlie, but that vague feeling was pushed aside by the terror of what I'd witnessed. I had to tell someone.

"Charlie, I really don't care if you laugh, or tell the Chief Resident about me. I don't care, because none of this is right. If you really want to know, well, I've been seeing. . . *someone*."

The old man stopped looking around the room and stared at me. "Doc, I ain't here to judge. If you want to play doctor with someone besides your wife, that's none of my business. And this ain't the time or place." He looked over his shoulder. "We got more important things to worry about."

I stared back until it hit me. "No, Charlie," I muttered. "Not like that. *Seeing* someone, or *something*. I swear. He looked at me. No, he looked *through* me, then he stopped me from intubating Timmy. I almost killed him because of that man, that doctor. Then I swear he just disappeared."

Charlie's eyes darted over to the bed where Bethany and the nurses were still adjusting drips, listening with stethoscopes, and talking among themselves. His eyes widened. "You are right. Doc. There's a hell of a lot around here that ain't right. Especially—"

"I saw the IV tubing move. . . by itself. You must've seen it too. I saw you. I think I screwed up, Charlie."

"You're fine, Doc. But tell me what this doctor looked like." He wasn't smiling. His expression tightened with suspicion.

"He was old, with a goatee. Lips so thin I could barely see them. Then when he opened his mouth, it looked like blackness that never ended. And I felt *hate*, Charlie, hate that smothered me like a blanket. He wore an old doctor's white coat. And his eyes—"

His grip on my arm stopped me in mid-sentence. "Don't say nothing else," he muttered. "Doc, I'm warning you. After you get off later, meet me at the Sylvester Morrow Nursing Home." His death-grip around my arm belonged to someone years younger.

"I'll be getting off call, Charlie. A night of call like *this*. And you want me to go to a nursing home?"

"I do," he answered. "We need to talk. And whatever you do, don't say anything to anyone about it. They listen, you know." He gripped both arms with that surprising strength. "Don't go through the tunnel. Take the long way out of the hospital. You hear me?"

I nodded. His tone had hardened as much as his grip, reminding me of what had bothered me before all hell had broken loose. "Charlie, what were you doing here? You were here before any of the rest of us were here. Right by Timmy's bed. How'd you know?"

He released my arms, fixed me with one last glare, then straightened up and hobbled from the room. I stood on shaky legs and walked over to Timmy's bed. The remaining nurses whispered to each other as I walked by. The respiratory therapists stopped talking as I approached Timmy's bedside. Timmy himself was awake and calm. The breathing tube protruded from his mouth, he'd sprouted two more IVs, and his chest was branded by two large pink squares where the electricity had burned his skin. Bethany's weird soliloquy about 'the most violent place in any city' suddenly didn't seem so weird. I shivered.

"Why don't you go back to bed, Lindmark?" Bethany murmured in my ear. "I'll get Dr. Bannister to help move Timmy to the ICU and get him plugged in."

"He's my patient, Dr. Bethany," I protested. "He's on my service. I can bring him to the ICU. Just so you know, I've been managing his electrolytes, so I don't want to let him go now. As for that tube, it just, I saw—" Charlie's words stopped me from spewing about what I'd seen. "I guess I just panicked."

Bethany guided me over to a vacant corner. "Timmy is not your patient. He is no longer on your service. As for your *management. . .* " He handed me a sheet of paper. "We got these stat labs during the code."

My face grew hot as I focused on one value that seemed to leap out at me: Sodium – 115. *One hundred fifteen*? Any suspicion of Bethany vanished as I stared at those numbers. How could it be so low? It had still been elevated in the 150s only yesterday.

"One hundred fifteen, Lindmark. And you were actually trying to lower his sodium even more with that free water drip. No wonder he seized. No wonder he coded," Bethany said quietly. "Harry–were you trying to kill him?"

"I—"

"A mercy killing, Harry? Was that it? The road to hell, you know? Did you decide on your own that someone so mentally disabled shouldn't be getting hospitalized so much?" His complexion had darkened from middle-of-the-night sallow into an alarming blotchy crimson. "Didn't Northrup oversee all this?"

"She didn't know. I wanted to take care of this on my own." My words sounded more like a confession than an explanation. In the movies, the next words would have been 'Do I need a lawyer?'

Bethany took the paper from my hand. "Harry, go to bed. Bannister and I can finish up. Really." His eyes bore into me and said more than any verbal explosion could have.

I grabbed his harm. "Dr. Bethany. There were. . . " I remembered the whispered word I'd heard. "You'd said he was too far gone, I think. Remember? At least I think it you. Maybe I heard—"

Bethany's eyes narrowed. "What did you say, Lindmark? You're blaming this shitshow on me? What the hell—"

"Coming through!" a therapist called as Timmy was wheeled by. The respiratory therapist was squeezing oxygen through the breathing tube as he walked beside the bed. Bethany turned away and lumbered after the crowd, barking out instructions. I fisted my hands and slunk out of the room, heart dragging on the floor.

Once back in the call room I considered the end of life as I had known it. I dropped my head in my hands and tried not to contemplate what I would face the next morning, or the next thousand mornings. I'd screwed up, horribly, almost killing *Timmy*, for God's sake, the most innocent of the innocent. I *had* killed him, or would have if it hadn't been for Bethany. No matter what the mistake, no matter what the catastrophe, Martin Bethany seemed to know exactly what to do.

I looked up, fixing on the computer glowing silently on the desk. *Bethany always knew what to do.* Always. Nothing seemed to faze him. No matter what the outcome, he came off looking like the Albert Schweitzer of the hospital. I reflected on Timmy's near death. Bethany had burst in almost before the code horns had stopped blaring. Why had he been so close? Everyone knew he was aiming to be Chief Resident next year. What better way to polish his credentials than to be known as the doctor who could bring patients back from the brink of death? Like a firefighter committing arson, so he could be the first one in and put it out. What better way. . .

I couldn't shut down the thoughts ricocheting in my brain. Maybe I had imagined that strange doctor at the code, but maybe not. Maybe he *had* been real, someone Bethany had worked with in the past, someone who revered Bethany as much as we all did. My head pounded. I *hadn't* imagined that it had been Bethany who had looked into that insulin order on Richman. But I'd just taken his word for it. I'd been framed then, and now with Timmy. I couldn't fathom what deranged purpose was governing Martin Bethany, I just needed to prove it.

I *hadn't* imagined those high sodium levels. Bethany could be hacking into the system with false values. Someone who knew their way around the hospital and the computer system, *like Bethany,* must have ordered Richman's insulin. He could have easily originated the order with someone who could take the blame, like an old demented Leland Travis. I hadn't imagined that voice either, telling me Timmy was already too far gone. So was it *all* really my fault?

I almost bounded over to the computer. Bethany had been present at the only other code I'd been involved in. Hell, he'd already been there by the time I'd arrived at Richman's code. How many more medical catastrophes had my genius of a resident supervised? I searched for 'Martin Bethany–Patients.' The list was huge, of course, as Bethany had been here for the last three years as an intern and the as a resident. I filtered the list into "Cardiopulmonary Arrest–Martin Bethany MD." The terminal grinded for several long moments until a list emblazoned the screen. Three per month? Seemed like a lot, even for a resident serving at a trauma center like Narragansett General. I sat back and thought. We were on call every third night. Any resident could be involved in emergencies, because they were in the trenches along with very sick patients on the brink of catastrophe every day. I typed in "Cardiopulmonary Arrest, last three years" in the PATIENTS window and waited. Patient names and details populated across the screen. I re-typed the search again, my hands shaking. The same list appeared and seemed to be yelling out its message. I scrolled up and down the list.

I stared at the screen, the thrill of vindication overwhelmed in the next instant by a stab of dread. Who would believe me, even with this proof? Was this even proof at all? Who could I even talk to about it?

CHAPTER 11

"Connie, I have to go," I pleaded. "It has to do with work. I need to follow up on patients who were discharged."

"A nursing home, Harry? You've been at the hospital for over a day, I've been alone, and now you're going to a *nursing home*?" It wasn't anger. I heard the desperation through the phone as clearly as if I were at my wife's side. "I haven't seen you at all, Harry. It's hard enough being alone when you can't help it, like when you're on call. But now? When you could be home?"

"Connie, you may not believe this, because I can hardly believe it myself, but those patients dying in the hospital I tell you about? It's not my fault."

"I never said it was, Harry. But what does that—"

"Everyone else thinks it is my fault, Connie. I'm in trouble. So I need to go and, well, I need to get help."

The phone stayed silent. I thought she'd hung up when she said, "Harry, I know internship is stressful. I can't imagine, really. Just don't forget there're other stresses for both of us. Here at home." She laughed, a light, breezy whisper in my ear. "At least I know you're not having an affair. Even an idiot would come up with a better excuse than meeting someone at a nursing home. And it must be important, because nothing else would make an intern coming off call want to see someone at a nursing home instead of collapsing in bed. I love you, Harry. I'm doing my best here. Please come home soon."

My wife deserved something special. I sighed, because I couldn't give her the only thing she'd consider special. We'd had that special thing once, for a few short incredible minutes, but had been unable to get pregnant since. "I'll be home as soon as I can."

The Sylvester Morrow Nursing and Convalescent Center looked every bit like a dilapidated warehouse for human beings past their expiration date. Charlie limped down the crumbling concrete steps as I pulled up. "Let's go, Doc. I want to be here about as much as you do." I followed him as he shuffled back up the stairs so slowly I could almost hear him creak.

"Charlie, I left my wife alone for this. Hopefully, I'll still have a marriage, not to mention a medical license, when I get home. I just want to curl up in a fetal position on my bed. Can you tell what the hell can be so important at some nursing home?"

He kept trudging up the steps, "Can't really tell you, Doc. It'd take too long, and you'd think I was as crazy as some of the people at the hospital are beginning to think *you* are." He turned and looked at me. "Hell, I know you're not. I know what happened in that boy's room last night, and I know it's not your fault. Now be quiet and just follow me, okay?"

"You know it wasn't my fault? *How* do you know?" I was talking to his stooped back. "I think I know whose fault it is. You're not going to believe it. I can barely believe it, but I am *not*—"

Charlie had reached the top of the steps when he turned at the door of the nursing home. "Dr. Lindmark, you are starting to make me regret the only part of my body still working well is my hearing. When I said we need to talk, I meant *I* need to talk and you need to listen."

We walked through the imposing wooden doors of the entrance. As soon as the doors closed behind us murkiness descended. The walls were made of institutional green bricks, chipped and scratched by years of wheelchair and gurney collisions. Huge ornate lights hung at regular intervals along the hallways, but their glow made few inroads against the gloom. I felt I had walked into a distant past decade where wood and brick were considered up-to-date materials for healthcare facilities. Yet another homage Rhode Islanders paid to preserving buildings past their prime, then using them to preserve other Rhode Islanders who were past *their* prime.

The only sound was the hollow clicking of our shoes. As we passed a tarnished plaque on the wall, I stopped to read the inscription: "Dedicated to the Memory of Dr. Sylvester Morrow – Friend, Caring Physician, and Benefactor. September13, 1989." The burnished portrait on the plaque showed an unsmiling older man wearing a lab coat. With a small dainty goatee. I stood frozen in front of that plaque as the man's graven image resurrected Timmy's frantic resuscitation in my mind. The doctor, that horrible vision who had stopped me from intubating Timmy, was a doctor who had died in 1989? The face on the plaque kept staring at me, like it had in Timmy's room. "Charlie," I croaked.

"Hurry up," Charlie urged. I shook out of my paralysis and followed the old man as we turned a corner and came upon a nursing station. Several nurses sat behind a huge mahogany wooden desk, which would have been a fashion statement in a hospital from the 1950s. One nurse was writing in a patient's chart, but the others were reading newspapers, knitting, and finishing up something spread out on a Taco Bell sack.

"Well hey, Sugar, it's been a long time," one of them exclaimed as Charlie walked up. "Kind of late for visiting, isn't it?"

Charlie's face crinkled into a small grin. "Getting in the way of your beauty sleep, Charlotte?" His grin faded. "Think he's up for visitors?"

Charlotte wiped grease from her mouth. "Is he ever?" she replied, then glanced at me and smirked. "Does your friend know what he's in for?"

"He's met him. Think we'll take a chance. See you girls around." I followed Charlie past a large television around which six or seven elderly patients sat propped in wheelchairs. They all stared as one at Dr. Phil, whose lecturing drawl boomed out at them. We passed other residents until Charlie stopped in front of one of them, a wizened man whose skin was mottled and scaly. Oxygen prongs ran from under his nose to a tank on the back of his wheelchair. He glared at Charlie with eyes that were angry and empty at the same time. They gave off a fury I'd seen somewhere before.

"Go away, Washington," he croaked, then coughed weakly.

"I'm not here to see you, Myron," Charlie said. I thought a cringe of fear crossed his wrinkled features.

"Not Myron, Washington. You know that. Turley. You can at least give me that. Now go away," the man rasped again. His glare burned into me.

"It's okay, Doc. He can't hurt you, or anyone. That's Myron Frazier. At least he used to be Myron Frazier. Worked in the hospital a long time ago." Charlie's voice thickened. "He was a good man. He was a good doctor. I liked working for him."

Frazier? I'd heard that name somewhere. I stared at him as his words hit me. *Used to be* Myron Frazier? Charlie had always sounded so intact. But he was old. Maybe he shared more with these demented relics than just age. I suddenly felt very unsure about why I had followed him here.

Charlie shuffled on past spare unadorned rooms all looking the same, whether or not a huddled form lay on the bed. The pungent odor of urine-soaked clothing assaulted me. We stopped at a room that was more brightly lit than the rest. An old man sat on the edge of the bed, a tray of food in front of him. The congealed film floating on the soup revealed the length of time it had been sitting there.

"About time, Washington," Leland Travis said. "Oh, I see you brought an esteemed physician with you. Long time no see, Dr. Lindmark."

The old man appeared far better than he'd looked in the hospital, but not by much. He still wore the same scruffy stubble, but his face had filled out and had lost its sallow, unhealthy pallor. "I didn't know you and Dr. Travis were friends," I remarked to Charlie.

"Why would I want to brag about something like that?" he replied.

Travis interrupted with a loud phlegmy huff. "So Washington, I'm sure you didn't bring Dr. Schweitzer out here so I could get a free house call. What's happened?"

Charlie leaned forward and relayed in muted tones what I'd told him, and everything he had personally seen. Every now and then, he broke off and peered around.

Travis turned to face me. "Know what I think, Bismark?"

I winced.

"I believe it all. Because I've been there too." Around us the shadows seemed to grow, pushing in and smothering the lights in Travis's room. From somewhere down the hall, a moan floated up at us. Squeals of rusting wheelchairs echoed from unseen places. "Listen up, Landmark. Know why I stopped working?"

I shook my head. Speculation about premature dementia and inappropriate behavior crossed my mind. "It's Lindmark, Dr. Travis." It was a waste of a perfectly reasonable sentence, but I couldn't think of anything else to say.

"I tried telling anyone who'd listen. Doctors, administrators, whoever, that my patients weren't just dying. They were being murdered." Silence hung over the room and stifled any attempt at response. Even Dr. Phil had gone silent. The distant wailing had also succumbed to the oppressive quiet.

"So you stopped working because of the stress? Or fear?"

"No, I had my privileges revoked. I was relieved of my duties."

"Because you thought your patients were being killed by someone?" I couldn't keep the disbelief out of my voice, especially given what that computer in the on-call room had revealed. Had they even had computers when Travis was practicing?

Travis pursed his lips and worked his jaws before answering. "No, because I tried to warn them that my patients were being killed by some*thing,* not some*one.* I told them they were being murdered by ghosts." He thrust his jaw out and glared at me, as if daring me to smirk or laugh.

"Come on, Dr. Travis. I mean, well, what do you mean, ghosts?" I ventured.

"Let me ask you something, Lindmark. That doctor you saw in the doorway, during that code. The one that stopped you from intubating the patient. Was it an old man? With a stupid little goatee?"

My mouth dropped open. Either I wasn't going crazy, or *many* of us were going crazy and sharing the same hallucination. Maybe it was toxic fumes in that hospital. Yeah, it was old and there had to be—

Travis must have read my thoughts because he held up his hand at me, cleared his throat, then spat noisily into a cup. "That man was a staff physician named Sylvester Morrow." I thought of the plaque on the wall. "Yes, *that* Sylvester Morrow. Friend, caring physician, and don't forget–benefactor." His voice took on a biting edge. "Dr. Morrow has been dead for decades."

I looked over at Charlie, expecting to see a toothy grin as he played along with the hazing he and Travis must have been planning. Charlie's features were grim. His expression was impassive, as if he were listening for the fifth time to Travis recounting a favorite anatomy lecture. Then he nodded.

Travis continued, "I worked with Sylvester Morrow at that damn hospital. I was honored when he offered to be my son's doctor." His jaws clenched and unclenched. "Honored. . . " He mumbled the word at the floor as his head sank. After a long silence, he recovered and fixed me with the intense stare of someone years younger. "Morrow died a few years after that, at the peak of his career. President of the medical staff, largest practice at the hospital, rich and respected. No, revered." Travis was spitting the words out, as if they were burning his mouth with an acid taste. "If only everyone really knew."

What did that mean? I looked at Charlie, who shook his head.

Travis wouldn't stop. "The esteemed Dr. Morrow died because of a horrible unforgivable mistake. The most important doctor in the hospital had come in because of abdominal pain. All we found were gallstones. Old Sylvester even directed his own evaluation. The morning of what should have been routine gall bladder surgery, he was wheeled to the pre-op room and given the usual pre-op medications. Except we found out afterward the orders for the medications to be given *during* surgery had been accidentally placed where the *pre-op* orders usually were. The pharmacist, of course, followed his routine duties and filled both sets of orders. All the syringes were laid out as usual with the best of care, and everything was administered with the best of care by the pre-op nurse. While she went to check on another patient scheduled for surgery, those medications took effect. But instead of the mild sedative intended to relax Morrow *prior* to surgery, he was given the drugs to be used *during* surgery. Pavulon."

"He was given a paralyzing drug?" I whispered.

"And given with no sedative at all, since he would have been completely anesthetized before Pavulon *had it been given in the operating room, when it was supposed to be given.*"

"Oh my God," I said.

"There he was, unable to move a muscle or breathe, completely paralyzed, but awake and aware. Couldn't cry out while he slowly suffocated. The nurse later reported that when she went to check on him, he was 'resting comfortable'. Sure, he looked comfortable. Anyone completely paralyzed would look comfortable, all the while suffering unimaginable torture under that calm exterior." Travis shook his head. "They worked on him for an hour, but never got him back. So the great Dr. Morrow dies, and the hospital was thrown into turmoil. Everyone blamed everyone else. The hospital donated a wing of this building and named the whole place after him. But of course all that didn't stop the lawsuits. I kept working as an attending physician on the staff. About a year later, one of the resident doctors called me in to the hospital one night for an emergency." He stopped talking and slumped down. His eyes darted back and forth, then settled on a spot on the wall behind me.

"Leland, you okay?" Charlie laid a hand on the old man's shoulder. "You need a drink or anything?"

"I sure as hell do. Did you bring something?"

"I meant water, Leland. You want a drink of *water*?"

"Hell, Washington, I got that on my tray. Thought you'd bring me something I could use, instead of bringing me Dr. Kildare over there."

"What happened that call night, Dr. Travis?" I prompted.

He glared at me, then squinted at the doorway of his room. He turned back to me, eyes now dulled and no longer angry. "I thought I saw a light flicker in the hallway. I kept looking and saw Sylvester Morrow staring at me. Just. . . walking, in the dark. He'd been goddam dead for a year. No one else around that time of night." He wiped a shaking hand across his mouth and swallowed noisily. "Patients started dying. *My* patients. Young ones, old ones, and all when *I* was on call. We'd expected some of the older patients to die. Back then there wasn't as much to do for them. But the young ones, in for tonsillectomies or bad stomach flu? Damn. Goddam it."

He slurped water from a glass on the tray. "By then I'd become pretty good at CPR and advanced resuscitation. I managed to save two or three of them, but then wished I hadn't. They survived with severe brain damage. One of 'em, another staff doctor, lived but developed such severe lung damage from aspiration during the code he couldn't even talk without getting short of breath. His whole personality changed. Nicest guy in the world before it happened. Now he's a hateful old wreck."

Charlie interrupted. "You saw him when we walked in, Doc. That was the 'Dr. Frazier' we ran into. I knew him back before it happened. He'd been a nice guy and a good doctor. It's like that code damaged his lungs *and* burned his brain and his personality, right Leland?"

"He didn't seem so nice out there, Charlie," I said. As if the hate that shone from his eyes had consumed his body and his soul. Something else struck me. "He said to call him 'Turley,' Charlie. Remember? What the hell did he mean by that?" I wanted that question back as soon as I had said it. Of *course,* low oxygen during the code would have damaged his brain, injuring his memory and cognition as well as his personality. Just more unfortunate results of someone to whom resuscitation had given back life but had stolen vital brain function. I should have recognized—

"Eh? What was that, Linkmart?" Travis had sat upright and leaned forward, rheumy eyes staring with sudden intensity. "Said he was 'Turley?'" I nodded, wondering if that was some sort of octogenarian code word. Travis looked at Charlie, his expression grim.

"Never mind about that, Doc." Charlie met Travis's gaze with his own stern, unblinking stare, even though his words were directed at me.

"Yeah, whatever, Charlie," Travis said gruffly. "Anyway, if you're still interested, everyone said all my patients had died from mistakes. Wrong medications, mixed up lab results, wrong interpretations of labs. Said they were *my* mistakes."

I stumbled backwards, landing on one of the rickety folding chairs in the room. The man's experiences could have been mine.

Travis went on as if I weren't there. "Hell, I was the one who resuscitated them. They would have died if I hadn't acted. The chief of staff, the state examiners, they were gonna chalk it all up to stress. But I knew better. Guess I didn't help myself. All those suits were going to let me go on with supervision, until I told them Morrow had to be responsible." He dropped his head into his hands. "The great Dr. Morrow took all that hate, all that agony while he slowly died, into death with him. Releasing it all on me and my patients from the other side. I tried telling them that." He shook his head back and forth, his face still buried in his shaking hands. "I actually blamed it on ghosts. Jesus. After that, things got worse. They thought I might have even killed Dr. Morrow for what he did to my son. They suspected *me*. Then they said I was a danger to patients and staff. They insisted I undergo therapy before letting me back." He looked up at me. "Never got the therapy. Obviously, never went back. But I'll never take back what I said."

Charlie walked over and sat beside Leland on the bed. "After Leland left—"

"After I was kicked out and humiliated," Travis said through clenched teeth.

"After Leland was kicked out, the death rate settled back to what would be expected in a hospital." He draped an arm around Travis. "But I believed Leland. I still believe him. It's just like he said. I've seen too many things I can't explain. Patients who died that shouldn't have, patients that died in strange ways. Can't blame any of that on Leland anymore. *You* looked pretty scared that other day in the tunnel yourself, Dr. Lindmark. You've seen things too, right?"

Was crazy contagious? Two elderly men with visions, one of them a disgraced decrepit physician who may have actually killed his patients, blaming his medical errors on a dead doctor? And now me, a young apparently sane intern, believing that same dead doctor had prevented *me* from saving one of my patients? Both Travis and I seeing lab tests that had never existed? Charlie meant well, I knew it. But just maybe he had fallen in with a bad crowd of one, who must have sucked gullible Charlie in with his Tales From The Crypt. I looked closely at Travis. Maybe Bethany had just perfected what Travis had tried years before, both of them going after glory or better experience by resuscitating patients they had injured in the first place?

My patients were dead or dying in flesh-and-blood reality. But a small voice refused to surrender to rational thought. I couldn't completely ignore a nagging possibility that ghosts and haunting after death, just maybe, weren't confined to movies and books. So I had to ask, "What do these. . . things want? Why are they doing this?"

Travis cleared his throat, unable to clear the gravel in his voice. "Where the hell else are they going to go, these souls released after death? Gonna get transferred to the nearest haunted nursing home, like they do with us living people?" Spittle collected around the corners of his mouth. "What do they want? They want revenge. They want to make sure the living will never get to enjoy what they had taken away. Or they're pissed off at the people who just couldn't perform well enough to keep them from dying. People like me." He uttered something between a sob and a choke, bony shoulders jerking. "Hell, *I* should be asking for revenge on Morrow after what he did." He glared at me, as if I shouldered some of the blame for his misery. "For what he did, when he was still in the flesh."

"You didn't always fail, Leland," Charlie broke in softly.

"Like old Frazier? Just look at him. He's not exactly grateful for what I did, is he?"

"There're others, Leland," Charlie said. "You know what—"

Leland kept talking *at* me. "I tried to tell you all this, Lindork, but you and that wise-ass tubby resident just laughed at me like I was a demented old nobody."

"It's Lindmark, and no, we—"

"I knew they'd kill me sooner or later. They do it through the IVs. And all you could do is tie my hands down so I couldn't pull that IV out." His lips twitched into a cold smile. "Just what the late Dr. Morrow ordered. I don't know how he kept doing it back when I was practicing. All I know is my patients died, overdosed on medicines or solutions that I'd never ordered. Sound familiar?"

It did. "Okay, Dr. Travis, okay. So what do we do?"

"Do?" he spat. "If I were you, I'd make sure everyone I cared about was never hospitalized in that place. Or any other hospital, because medical errors and unnecessary deaths occur everywhere. Then I'd find a new job before you get blamed."

One of the nurses walked in. "Sure do hate to break up a party, but visiting hours have been up for a while. I let you both stay because I like having Charlie Washington around." She winked at him.

"Watch out for yourselves," Travis called out behind us. "Remember they're dead. *Dead.* You listen to me this time."

The nurse waved back and laughed. "They'll listen to you, Leland honey. In fact, we'll all watch out for those mean old dead people."

Our footsteps echoed down the empty hallways. Once outside, I gulped in large breaths of night air as if I'd been drowning, then turned to Charlie. "You really believe him, don't you?"

"Doc, you need to believe *me*, because I do believe *him*. I got more trust in Leland than you'll ever know. I was a—" He stopped, then quickly resumed. "I was nothing more than a black assistant. Yes sir, an assistant when that man was the smartest doctor in these parts. Even Dr. Morrow thought Leland was the best resident he'd trained. Took him under his wing." His tone softened. "Leland wrote only Morrow's pre-op orders that morning. He didn't write the orders for Pavulon. I read the orders myself."

Doubts about Charlie cropped again in my mind. Why would a lowly assistant have read such orders, much less know what they meant? And why would that unshaven, defrocked physician command such worship? Doubts turned to suspicions. Bethany commanded that kind of respect, too.

"He had nothing to do with that mix-up," Charlie continued. "And he came close to resuscitating Morrow. People still blamed him. All after that thing with his son. And through it all, he still did his best for his patients." He paused for a second. "So yeah, Doc, I believe him."

"What about Leland's son, Charlie?" I looked at Charlie's face in the dimming light. The roadmap of wrinkles and blemishes spelled out only concern without guile or pretense. "Is that something you couldn't talk about in front of Dr. Travis?"

"Don't want to talk about it now either," Charlie said. "That has nothing to do with this. Just pay attention to what he said, okay? What you should be asking is, why is it happening all over again? And why have they picked you?"

"No, Charlie," I said. "You brought me here, you defend that old man, you want me to understand what he's gone through. Well, I need to know everything. Especially something as important as what happened to his son. Because I think that started it all, didn't it?"

Charlie squinted at me, wrinkles crevassing wrinkles, then chuckled. "You watch how you speak to your elders, son. And I am definitely an elder. But you're right. Leland never spoke one word about it after it happened. I guess I've just gotten into the same habit after all these years."

"Never spoke one word about what, Charlie?"

Charlie swallowed noisily and leaned against the car. "No one ever knew what Kevin's problem really was. He'd been born limp and almost died in the nursery. Some sort of muscle disease, the specialists said. You have to remember, we didn't have the machines and tests they have now to look into these diseases. All they knew was he'd never make it out of childhood. That's what they told Leland. All those doctors also told him to put Kevin in an institution, where at least he'd be watched over until he died."

"What did Travis say?" I asked in a hushed tone.

Charlie flashed that blinding grin again. "What the hell do you think he said? He told them he'd find neurologists who knew what they were talking about. Then he marched into the nursery, picked up his son, and took him home to an empty house. His wife took off shortly after learning her darling son was 'a defective.' Somehow he managed to become the best resident this program ever had, impress the hell out of Dr. Morrow, and still dedicate himself to giving Kevin a childhood. He told me once he knew Kevin would die young, and if he couldn't give him a longer life, he'd make sure Kevin would have a happy one. And somehow he did it. Least, that's the way it always looked to me."

"Yeah, but—"

"He got the best doctor to look after Kevin's medical condition. That 'best doctor' was Sylvester Morrow. He did about everything he could to find out answers. Called specialists all over the country. Those days, though, no one did much for kids who couldn't even move an inch on their own. Usually just warehoused them or made them comfortable." I nodded solemnly. "That was usually all that could be done. I think Morrow finally realized there just wasn't anything medical science had to offer for Kevin. Didn't stop caring for him, but I know that's why he did. . . what he did."

Charlie was gazing down at the ground, frail shoulders slumped. He sighed, then looked back up at me. "But damn if Kevin did better than anyone thought. He outlived childhood. He was on his way to being a teenager." He shook his head as if overwhelmed by his own story. "Kevin just goddam kept on going despite what all the best minds predicted. Then he came in with pneumonia. Morrow came in special to look after him. Antibiotics, heated mist treatments, but his cough got weaker and weaker, and his fever climbed higher and higher. I was here that night. Leland was actually on call in the hospital and managed to drop by every so often to check on him. Next day, Leland took it upon himself to bring up putting Kevin on a ventilator. Would never do it himself, to his own son, but he got the process started. It should have been done sooner, except Morrow wouldn't hear of it. Even I knew Kevin was going downhill, and I was just, well, cleaning the ICU."

He glanced around him, but everything was quiet except for cars and the occasional ambulance driving in and out of the nursing home's lot. "I overheard when Leland took Morrow aside that morning. Told him *never* to give up on his son. Morrow told him he just hadn't considered such a drastic step like life support at the time. Leland told him again that the pneumonia was getting the best of his son, and he needed to be put on a ventilator. Then he insisted Kevin was *not* going to die just because of a little cold." Charlie's smile was a sudden beacon of humor flashing white against the dark of the evening and the dark of his story. "Leland told Morrow apple-picking season was starting the next week, and that Dr. Sylvester Morrow was the only doctor who could be trusted to pull his son through in time. Morrow puffed up at that and told Leland to get some sleep. Everything went fine after that, Doc. For about an hour. I'd stayed with Kevin while Leland was sleeping in the call room. Kevin told me to get his dad, that he was feeling more short of breath. I could hear the stuff gurgling way deep in his throat. I got terrified as hell, Doc. I was. . . well, I was only a. . . "

Why was he hesitating?

"Anyway, I panicked," he continued. "I just wanted to give Leland a break, and I didn't feel like he should be father and doctor all at the same time. Besides, there were a few other good doctors in the hospital at the time." He darted a quick glance back at the nursing home and shook his head. Silence lingered for a long several seconds, then he looked back at me. "Lot of good doctors around this place then, Dr. Lindmark. Chuck Turley was one of them. But I avoided him because of his bedside manner, and got Morrow instead. He was Kevin's real doctor, but he just stood there shaking his head as Kevin got more short of breath. He should have put Kevin on life support right then. Coulda saved his life, Doc." His voice sank to a whisper. "He told Kevin he'd make him feel better. He said he was not going to let him suffer any more. Then he called for a nurse, and he told me to run and get some new supplies for the room. I was so damn relieved, I ran off and didn't wake Leland." He breathed a deep sigh. "That was the last time I saw Kevin. Morrow did make Kevin more comfortable. He gave him some morphine, and then just turned up the oxygen."

The brutality of his words hit me like a physical blow. I actually staggered several steps back.

Charlie kept talking. "He tried telling Leland, later, that he did it because he felt sorry for the both of them. Why put his son through all that, when he wasn't expected to live that much longer, anyway? That's what he said when Leland arrived. Had he really wanted his son to suffer needlessly? *He asked Leland that, Doc.* I heard it all. He said he'd done what he was expected to do as a doctor. Kevin died dignified and comfortable. Except it wasn't Morrow's decision to make. Leland Travis was never the same. I think if he hadn't blamed himself for sleeping, he would have strangled Morrow right then and there. Everyone knew how he felt. That's why it was easy for people to think Morrow's death wasn't so accidental, and suspect Leland wasn't so innocent. Bunch of bullshit, Doc. Leland had nothing to do with it. He hated himself even more than he hated Morrow. Living with that kind of guilt over his son did something to him. And then when all his patients started dying, well, everything went to hell after that."

Silence settled between us. Charlie led me away from the building, looking over his shoulder several times. "I been around here a long time, Doc. I've watched, I've listened. Leland Travis is not crazy. Morrow is still here. So are others, their souls ripped from their bodies when they weren't supposed to. Unfinished death, that's what it is. Leaving their souls to just suffer in that purgatory of a hospital, instead of moving on to a deserved peace. And now they got it in for you, like they had it in for Leland. They drove him crazy. Morrow wanted revenge then and he still wants revenge now."

"Why me, Charlie? Why the hell *me*?"

"I don't know, Doc. But I can tell you, I think Morrow wants more than just revenge. I know it, Doc. Because I seen what happened to Frazier and the rest. You know what happens when we die, Dr. Lindmark?"

I wasn't sure if he wanted the scientific explanation, the metaphysical explanation, or the religious explanation. I went for what I knew best–science. "Um, heart stops, Charlie, brain wave stops, decomposition—"

"Not that. The soul leaves, right? Everything that makes a person, deserts the body after death. The soul leaves an empty shell, you know? Ripe for the taking." He tapped his head. "Got it all right here, Doc. I've learned about them, just as they've learned how to do it better."

"Ripe for the. . . Charlie, what the hell—"

A group of nurses burst from the front door, their voices and laughter carrying across the parking lot. Charlie glanced at them, an expression of unmistakable fear deepening his leathery wrinkles. He shook his head then hurried away towards his car, his shuffle reminding me of the hesitant jerking gait of a toy robot whose battery was running low.

"What do I do now, Charlie?" I called after him. "You brought me to hear him out. So now I've heard him out. I heard *you*. So how do I protect my patients? How do I protect *me*?"

He stopped and turned slowly. Even from a distance I saw his smile shining out against the evening gloom. "Just think of being at work like driving through a bad neighborhood, like where I live. If you drive with the windows up and doors locked, and don't stop for nothing, you'll make it through. They won't bother you when you're with people, working or walking around. Understand?"

Frazier's twisted features flashed through my mind. I recalled the bloodstained needles and broken syringes flying at me in the tunnel. I *had* been alone then. But I'd been with a whole damn group of frenzied people during Timmy's code, and I still saw that. . . Dr. Morrow. No, I didn't understand. I felt scared as shit. "Thanks Charlie. I have the weekend off. I'll see you on Monday."

I collapsed into my car, feeling even less reassured about everything than I'd been before this nursing home pilgrimage. I drove home on autopilot, never noticing or remembering the route I must have been following. Questions broke through thoughts of life and death, of life *after* death, of spirits and souls and goddam ghosts. Why was it all starting again? And why *me*?

CHAPTER 12

I awakened the next morning to a strange light I hadn't seen since starting internship–the sun. I'd slept long past sunrise. I almost jumped out of bed, the mundane errands I'd put off and the time I should have been spending with Connie all pushing me to get up. Just as quickly, my burst of enthusiasm was quashed by the recollection of Timmy's code, by the accusing looks, by that sodium level that had been thrust at me. I finally rose from the bed, this time with all the energy of an eighty-year-old.

"Coffee, Harry?" The aroma was soothing. Connie's smile helped even more. "I thought maybe we could spend some time together. I know things have been tough at work. I guess that's why you had that important meeting with all the specialists at the nursing home last night."

"No, wait, Connie, I—"

She smiled. "Don't worry, Harry, I understand. Well, I really don't understand, but I can't imagine what having patients die must be like. But you do have a wife. So I'll let you make it up to me. Denise and Audrey invited us to a picnic in the park. That means you and me, Harry. It's sunny, too."

"I thought you wanted some time with *me*, Connie. Some alone time, you know?"

Her features darkened under brows knit together.

I regrouped. "You know, a day at the park sounds like just the thing, Connie. What a great idea." Maybe it would be enough to take my mind off Timmy. Being with a kid I didn't know, trying to find common ground with her rich elegant mother. . . more than enough annoyance to go around. In the same instant, I realized why Connie sounded so eager. Maybe Audrey would take up some of her empty space instead of reminding her about what we'd lost. I was sure that's why she had kept up her aquatic therapy classes, with so many happy kids. Kids that still weren't hers. I smiled back at her. "Really a great idea," I repeated. "From a very understanding wife."

The playground at the park was swarming with families, but it wasn't hard to pick out Audrey and Denise. Audrey's wheelchair stood out like a tank on the deserted baseball field. I watched with amazement as Denise pulled out a plastic baseball bat from a backpack. She wrapped her daughter's hands around it, then stepped several feet away. The ball she tossed in Audrey's direction hit Audrey squarely on the side of her face. I expected the worst when no one moved. Then the two of them burst out laughing.

Connie and I started high-stepping down a hill towards the two of them. Audrey saw us coming and headed towards us at ramming speed. "Hi Connie. Hey, Dr. Lindmark! It's about time. We had to start playing without you."

"You guys looked like a real team out there," I said. "Not sure what kind of a team, but still a team." She actually dragged a smile out of me. Timmy and Travis and dying patients stopped their unseen nagging.

"If my mom knew how to throw a ball, I coulda hit it, I know it. She's kinda lame with sports, you know? I bet you play baseball pretty well, don't you?"

I had a tough time keeping up with her words, even as slurred as they were. "Well. . . "

She circled around me before I could offer any better answer. I felt a gentle nudge on the back of my legs. "Is this the nice ass section?" I heard her squeak from behind me. I whirled around and bumped into her wheelchair.

"What did you say?" I asked, sure I'd mistaken the slurred words.

"Is this the nice—"

Denise clamped a hand over Audrey's mouth, bracelets jangling loudly. "She's quoting from Eddie Murphy in 'The Nutty Professor.' I thought it would be fine for my daughter to watch. It had to be a step up from South Park, I thought. Apparently not, huh Audrey?"

Connie tried to hide a smile. I chuckled out loud. "I thought that's what I heard. If it's so inappropriate, why do you let her watch those movies?"

Denise shrugged and smiled at her daughter. "I can't help it. She knows how all those streaming channels work better than I do."

I jumped at a sharp pinch from behind. I whipped around and saw Connie smiling at me slyly. "I guess this *is* the nice ass section," she whispered in my ear. It boded well for our time after the park. The rest of the day was pleasantly distracting, even relaxing. Audrey roamed the playground at high speed, leaving in her wake gape-mouthed children and adults alike. Denise had brought along an assortment of deli meats, cheeses, rolls, mustard, fruit cups, and wine disguised in sparkling water bottles. Between the feast and her unashamed performance on the field with her daughter, Denise Schlager was rapidly rising above my initial impression.

"So, am I ever going to meet 'Mister Denise'?" I asked as I sank into a chair, exhausted. It was a satisfying welcome exhaustion, so different from when I'd collapsed in the same chair with the life sucked out of me following days at the hospital.

"You mean Denise's husband? *Mister Schlagle?*"

"Yeah, the man behind the carats," I said.

"Denise's husband left her and Audrey about a year after Audrey was born. It was just too much, or too depressing, or too whatever for him," she said. "Not a mean man, according to Denise. He just couldn't fit Audrey's condition into what he'd expected out of life."

"He left her pretty well off," I remarked. "What does he do?"

"Just a middle management job. Before he passed away from cancer, anyway. But they won a pretty large malpractice suit, which still wasn't enough to keep Denise's husband around. Apparently Denise's uterus was slowly rupturing even as the Ob-Gyn kept telling her the pain was normal and to stay home. Audrey was born on the *inside*, and suffered severe low oxygen damage. It's amazing she's alive, never mind as smart as she is. I think Denise deserved to direct a little of the settlement to buying some carats, don't you?"

My phone cut off any response. "Harry? It's me, Terri. Terri McCormick."

Terri? I was suddenly confused. Why was an intern calling me at home? Confusion erupted into panic. Did I really have the weekend off? Had I failed to show up for a weekend shift? And after what I'd done to Timmy? Oh shit, oh damn.

"Harry? Are you there?"

"Yeah sure, Terri. Is everything okay?"

"No, Harry, everything's not okay. Everything is shit, Harry."

Goddam it, I knew it. I'd missed a shift. "Say no more, Terri. I don't know why it happened, but I'll be right in."

"You already knew, Harry? How'd you hear about Charlie already?"

"Charlie? What are you talking about, Terri?"

"Charlie almost died last night, Harry," she whispered.

My brain froze. "Charlie?"

"Charlie Washington. The orderly. We all knew him. He's in the ICU on a ventilator."

Charlie? I'd been with Charlie the day before. "What happened?"

"A new admission last night. Young guy, maybe in his 40s, way too young to come in with a stroke. I think he was a smoker. Whatever. One of the other interns was on last night. Thank God it wasn't me."

"Terri, *what happened to Charlie*?"

"Sorry Harry, it's just that I'm scared," she said. "So anyway, the new admission with the stroke, he coded sometime in the middle of the night. According to Gene—"

"Gene?"

"Gene Austinaur. Another intern in our group. Do you live under a rock? Anyway, according to Gene, a nurse found this guy unresponsive in bed. Eyes wide open and staring. The nurse told Gene his mouth was pulled back in something like a 'screaming smile.' That's exactly what he said, a screaming smile, like his mouth had been pulled in opposite directions."

That vision assaulted my imagination.

"Charlie showed up to the code like he always does. The patient needed to be shocked. Ventricular tachycardia. What no one knew was that one of the IV bags had somehow started leaking its solution onto the bed rail, then down onto the floor. It ran all the way to where Charlie was standing. Gene said Bethany had called for everyone to clear before delivering the shock. But Charlie was standing in that puddle of IV solution, which apparently conducts electricity very well given its salt load." A shuddering breath interrupted the rush of words, followed by a long silence. "Did you know Charlie has a metal plate in his skull from some past accident?"

I shook my head, oblivious that she couldn't see me. "The CT scan showed it. The electric current from the paddles passed from the bed through the trail of water to his feet up to his head. Gene said it was as if Charlie had been in an electric chair. He was—"

"Executed," I whispered.

"Yeah, Harry. Electrocuted. It was horrible."

"No, Terri, he was executed. Charlie was being punished. Or shut up." He'd talked me into listening to Travis's ramblings, which suddenly didn't sound so much like ramblings. Charlie believed everything Travis said, which meant he believed everything I'd experienced.

"What? No. It's horrible, but a horrible *accident*. He must have been standing where the floor was warped and sloped, for that fluid to flow towards him. That whole hospital is so old, you know? Anyway, Bethany had to leave Charlie's resuscitation to a whole other team since he was trying to resuscitate the patient on the bed. The patient died, but they were able to shock Charlie again into a normal rhythm."

"Has he woken up yet?" I mumbled, trying to gather myself.

"No. He's in the ICU on a ventilator."

"They killed him, Terri. They killed Charlie." I had trouble catching my breath. "Wait, you said Dr. Bethany was there?"

"That's what Gene said. Bethany must have changed with Gene's resident for the night. I hope when I'm on call—" The wail of a code horn erupted from the phone. "Harry, I've gotta go." Background commotion muffled any further words before the phone went silent.

I couldn't breathe, unable to erase the images swirling in my head. A screaming smile. Charlie in an electric chair. Words broke into the pictures, skittered around in my thoughts. Travis always so insistent with '*my patients being murdered, they want the young ones.*' Then those words of Terri's. *Young guy,* maybe in his 40s. . .

"Harry? What's happening? Who was that?"

I jumped at Connie's voice and glanced around as if coming out of sleep. All thoughts of Denise and Audrey were long gone. I stared at the phone, holding it out as if I were warding off some evil with its magical power. "It was Terri, another intern. There was another patient death at the hospital. I had nothing to do with it, this time. One of my friends, he's on a ventilator. They're all dying, Connie."

I felt an arm around my shoulders. "Harry, I have no idea what you're talking about." Her voice was calm, soothing. "But this job is really getting to you. Those people are in the hospital for a reason. They're sick. Some are going to die, because they're sick. That's all. Maybe you need to be somewhere that isn't so stressful, that isn't so intense?"

"I know you're trying to make me feel better, but you don't understand. I thought it was Bethany. You know, murdering patients but making it look like innocent but horrible medical errors. Him, or someone else with enough medical knowledge to know how to kill medically, making it look like an error or an accident. So it has to be a doctor. A good one, like Martin Bethany."

"You're scaring me, Harry. Are you really saying there's a serial killer loose in your hospital? Some deranged doctor? That's just. . . that doesn't happen in real life—"

I shook my head. "Something else is happening at that hospital. I mean, it may be Bethany. He's there every goddam time, but there's something else. Something dead, just like Travis was saying. Just like he was saying, Connie." I couldn't slow my thoughts as they tumbled out in a babbling torrent.

She gently lowered my arm and took the phone from my hand. "Harry, I think you need to go lie down." She looked directly at me with glistening eyes. "We're going to get through this. Do you think our baby is finally catching up with you? Maybe it's not unexpected patient deaths, maybe it's our baby's unexpected death that you never really dealt with, that's affecting you now? Do you think, Harry?"

I tried shutting my brain off, but peace wouldn't come. Connie's insight seemed possible. Her words mixed in with Travis's words, with Terri's tale, with Charlie's warning. I tossed and turned almost in rhythm to the bubbling stew of thoughts as they churned against my skull.

I greeted the dawn under the weight of a hangover from the night. The hospital still pulled at me like an invisible snake that refused to release its stranglehold. Connie had to be wrong. She and I may have held our baby as he passed away. But I *had* dealt with it. I'd gotten out of bed every damn day since then and carried on with life, finished medical school, started internship. *That* was dealing with it. My hand involuntarily rubbed the puckered scar on my neck. I'd dealt with that, too. My newborn baby's death, *and* that awful experience of my own before that. I'd faced life with enough courage and fortitude, to quote an old friend, to last a lifetime. It sure didn't mean I was imagining what was happening now.

I crept down the stairs for a cup of coffee, and knew what I needed to do. I owed it to Connie, and to Richman and Richman's mother and to Timmy and Charlie and the other victims of something unspeakable. I would not become an old, bitter, defeated victim of the dead.

CHAPTER 13

"I'm Dr. Lindmark," I declared to the single nurse at the nursing station. Coming in on a Sunday left only a skeleton crew to face at the nursing station, and thus left fewer people to wonder why I seemed to have no life outside the hospital. I was buoyed after finding out Timmy had quickly recovered, weaned off the ventilator, and had been transferred out of the ICU to a step-down floor. "Just stopping in to see Timmy Strickland in Room 122. Is he up to seeing people?"

"Did you say 'Dr. Lindmark?'" the nurse asked.

"Harrison Lindmark. Yes. One of the interns." I flashed my name badge for proof. "But this is more of a social call than professional. He's not my patient, but I was taking care of him. Just wanted to see how he's getting along." *And to prove to myself that I really hadn't killed him.* "I'll just go on down and see him," I said and started walking down the hall.

"Um, Dr. Lindmark, could you wait a second?" she called after me.

"It's really okay," I said over my shoulder. "Timmy was on my service. His parents know me." I heard a boy's voice through the open door of the room as I approached.

"So, when am I getting out of here?" The voice was thick, as if the person were talking with Kleenex stuffed in his mouth.

"Timmy?" I walked into the room. Timmy was pacing around the floor. Someone had combed his curly hair, and he no longer looked disheveled. His lips still barely covered his swollen red gums.

"Who are you?" he answered in the same muffled voice I'd heard outside the room.

"It's me, Timmy. Dr. Lindmark," I answered, then looked over at his parents. "Hi, Mr. and Mrs. Strickland. I can't tell you how good it is to see how Timmy has recovered. And I wanted to tell you all how sorry I am that he had to go through all that."

Norm Strickland walked over with his hand held out. I reached forward to shake it, but he ignored my hand and gripped my arm. His jaw muscles were working under his skin. "I left instructions at the desk that you weren't to come in here," he said in a low, emotionless voice. "Why did you ignore them?"

"I didn't hear from anyone that—"

"My son has done very well since you left his case. Do you know you almost killed him? It wasn't all your fault. The supervision you received was atrocious. In a damn teaching hospital, no less. And you coming in every day telling us it was all okay. You people have a lot to learn about. . . learning, and teaching. But *you* especially have a lot to learn about taking care of people." He released my arm only when his wife came up behind his and laid a hand on his shoulder.

"Mr. Strickland, sir. We all tried our best for your son. He, well, the labs—"

He froze me with his gaze. "Dr. Lindmark, you'd better go. We don't want you here. We certainly don't want you anywhere near Timmy. As soon as he's well enough, we want to be discharged and never sent back to you or to this place. Now get out before—"

"Tim."

I looked to where that single word had been spoken. "What did you say, Timmy?"

"Tim," he repeated. "My name is Tim. And if this guy's a doctor, don't get mad at him. Let him discharge me." The words were fluent but muffled and strained, as if forced through vocal cords rusted with years of disuse. He was better. No, Timmy Strickland was better than better. Could that near-death catastrophe with the low sodium and the low oxygen and the heart standstill have re-wired all those short circuits in Timmy's diseased brain? Rational thought and years of medical education told me that just didn't happen.

"Just go. *Now*," Strickland commanded as if his son hadn't spoken.

Timmy stared fixedly at me. "If you can help me get out of here, please do it. Otherwise, I think you're bothering my parents. So do like he asked." He didn't look angry. He looked blank. Without a smile showing them off in an endearing light, his swollen misshapen gums took on a gnashing ugliness. Timmy was blank and cold. . .and fluent?

I slunk out of the room without another word, their anger almost palpable. I wanted to just keep on going, to leave that hospital and never come back, but I still had one more person to see. I hoped no one would recognize me as I trudged toward the ICU.

Once through the sealed doors, I felt as though I'd never rotated out. The same smells, beeps, and buzzes buffeted me. Several nurses returned my wave, but others smiled uncomfortably and looked away as if I were a leper invading the healthy. I wasn't surprised. Word traveled fast when a doctor was accused of a life-threatening mistake. It became viral if such a mistake was mixed in with the whisper of notorious intent. Laurie, unmistakable with her over-bleached hair, multi-hued nails, and inflammatory lipstick, pointed out Charlie's cubicle. I'd managed to stay on her good side during my ICU rotation. I hoped that would keep her from joining in my shunning.

She rested a hand on my arm. "It's nice of you to come, Dr. Lindmark," she murmured. "Nobody else has been by. Charlie's been a fixture in this hospital longer than most of the floor tiles, and you're the first." I shrugged. "It's just as well you came by now."

"What do you mean?" I asked.

"That shock really scrambled old Charlie's eggs, you know? The brain wave test today," she said. "It looked pretty bad. Every single lead, every place on his brain, showed the same thing. Low voltage. Not quite flat line, but not a whole lot of anything going on. I heard the docs say it was about as bad as it could get without declaring him brain-dead.

They'll probably remove the ventilator and let him pass peacefully if nothing changes."

I forced myself to look at Charlie. A large, white breathing tube sprouted from his mouth. The same gnarled hands that had both lifted heavy supplies and offered gentle comfort lay still without twitching. The frizzy white hair on one side of his head had turned black and matted where the electricity had exited. Swollen IV bags drooped over his bed.

"Charlie?" My greeting came out as a croak. I cleared my throat. "Charlie, can you hear me?" I said more clearly. "It's me, 'Doc.'"

No movement came from the wizened old man on the bed except for the rhythmic up-and-down of his chest in obedient rhythm to the ventilator. I shook his shoulder, then tried a furtive pinch of the skin on his chest. Nothing. The IV bags resembled bloated cauldrons about to spill poison. The air around me became frigid, as if I had stepped into a frosty cave never exposed to sunlight. *They kill through the IVs* pierced my memory, followed by the words I had whispered to Terri when first hearing about Charlie. '*He was executed.*'

Making sure Laurie was on the other side of the closed curtain, I fumbled on a pair of latex gloves then ripped both IV catheters from Charlie's arms. Clear liquid from the IV mixed with oozing blood spattered a slippery crimson pattern on the floor. I tried pressing on both wounds to stem the bleeding, but could only cover one without letting go of the dangling catheters. Irregular heartbeats interrupted the rhythm scrolling across the monitor above the bed, igniting a shrill beeping.

"What's going on here? What are you doing?" Laurie had pulled aside the curtain, her mouth gaping open almost comically.

I dropped the catheters and clamped my hands around both bleeding sites, too panicked to answer.

Laurie walked towards me, her eyes widening as she looked from the blood running down Charlie's arms to the IV catheters dangling in front of me, now infusing fluid onto the floor. "Why did you pull his

IV's out?" she asked, her voice reduced to a trembling whisper. "He is not dead *yet*, Dr. Lindmark."

"That's why I pulled them out, Laurie. I was protecting Charlie. They were going to kill him, with the IV fluid."

"*Who* was going to kill him?" she asked, her eyes narrowed.

I looked around the room. The IV tubing hung impotently. Charlie remained disturbingly undisturbed. I knew what I had stopped from almost happening. "Laurie, just keep an eye on Charlie, okay? There have been mistakes with medications. I thought another one may have been happening with Charlie." God, I sounded weak. "Please, just watch him."

"I'm his nurse. That's what we do." Gone was the friendly tone. She snatched the IVs and started dabbing at the bleeding wounds with a clean gauze, any further conversation clearly at an end.

I looked once more at Charlie before obeying Laurie's unspoken command by slinking away. As I retreated down the corridor I peered into each room, hopeful that something might distract me from my burning shame. I'd burned another bridge, dammit. My heart skipped as I passed Bed 28, as if some invisible vapor from Anthony Richman's horrible death still lingered. Something in that cubicle caught my eyes. A patient in a gown lay huddled on the floor. Bed 28's patient must have fallen out of the bed. Where were the alarms? Why had he remained unnoticed on the floor in the middle of a damn ICU?

I entered the room and approached the patient. He was facing away from me, gown askew, IV tubing trailing from his arms. Where were the nurses? "Hey! Hey, are you okay?" He didn't turn around. I approached cautiously, unwilling to frighten him any more than he already must be. The coppery odor of blood, the unmistakable smell of loosened bowels hit me. I shivered as cold wrapped around me. He turned around to face me even before I reached out to help him up.

I recoiled and stumbled backwards several steps as empty bleeding eye sockets fixed me in a sightless gaze. A ventilator tube jutted from his mouth, and his legs were swathed in bloody bandages. Anthony

Richman's corpse, or soul, or *something*, opened its mouth around the tube, as if screaming. My mouth dried to cotton. I tried to yell out, but could only whisper a grunt. I backed out of the room and stumbled out through the ICU doors, not daring to look back for fear those horrible sockets would never release me.

CHAPTER 14

It was as if I'd never left for a weekend of respite. Mainly because I *had* never left after coming in to look at Timmy and Charlie. I wished I hadn't. Timmy's parents hated me. The ICU nurses probably marked me as some Angel of Death intern. Charlie was going to die in a place where the dead didn't stay dead. That last vision of Richman, or the thing that used to be Richman. . . souls, or spirits lingered all around me. Snatched from a peaceful afterlife, and at least one of them hated me for it. Why me? Why was I the only one who could see them, or was haunted by them? Never mind my only support came from a disgraced bitter ex-doctor rotting away in a nursing home.

"Lindmark!" Bethany's bark stole my last shred of confidence. He grabbed my arm as we walked towards the next patient. "You're the reason I'm on this team with you, *again*. The powers that be felt you needed special supervision, after you almost killed one of your patients." His glare spoke of disgust as much as did his tone. "Poor supervision, according to Mr. Strickland, which means *me*." His complexion had turned that worrisome volcanic shade of red as he bit off his words. "So you better have all the labs. All the *right* labs. And don't do anything without running it by me first."

I wanted to sink through the floor. I couldn't look anyone in the eye, afraid of what I'd see. But as we went from patient to patient on rounds, shame gave way to something else. Bethany was now the last word on my actions, which meant that Bethany could do whatever he wanted with what I ordered and with the labs I saw. I still didn't know how those labs on Timmy had been so wrong, but I knew what I had seen. Someone must have altered those labs. Easy enough to do, if you knew about the hospital's electronic records system and knew about medicine. Bethany knew both. And now he could change whatever he wanted to change, and I'd never know. But because they were my orders, anything that happened would be blamed on me.

I was not going to go the way of Travis. Bethany was the firefighter who set blazes only to look the hero as he arrived first on the scene. And now he had made it even easier to set me up as the obvious arsonist. For all I knew, he somehow was doctoring my food to explain the hallucinations. With each patient we rounded on I became more angry at being set up as Bethany's patsy, and even more angry for the next possible victim of that bearded toxic narcissist. I resolved to look over the computerized records again, very carefully. I'd keep watching him, keep searching for proof.

"Doc, how you been doing? You here for a taste from the Marinara-Man, or you gonna play doctor?" The raspy voice jolted me out of my thoughts. I'd been sleepwalking through several patients until coming to Aaron Shirkey. He'd been ready for discharge when he'd started throwing up blood and had been sent for emergency surgery to repair a deep oozing stomach ulcer. Despite his original heart attack and kidney failure, the self-proclaimed Marinara King had survived. His chart was becoming as thick as Shirkey himself.

"Not bad, Mr. Shirkey," I said. "Probably a little better than how you've been."

His swollen eyes crinkled as a huge smile crossed his sallow features. It was an expression of genuine friendliness. At least one person in the hospital still regarded me fondly. "Yeah, well, I'm like the pizza from my competitor's restaurant. You can't keep me down." He started to laugh, but clutched at his belly incision in pain. "And it's Aaron, Doc. Call me Aaron. You've seen parts of my body that my wife doesn't even know exist. The least you can do is cut out the 'Mister' stuff."

"Dr. Lindmark, what the hell is that?" Bethany asked. I followed his gaze and saw red liquid filling the bag connected to Shirkey's feeding tube.

The attempt at an answer caught in my throat under a surge of panic. Some other way to kill patients? Not just through the IVs, but now by pumping toxin into a patient's stomach? "It, ah, looks like new tube feedings," I replied doubtfully, scanning the bag up and down to find a clue as to whatever poison it contained.

"I know it's tube feedings, Lindmark. Call Pharmacy and find out what the hell—"

"It's okay, Doc," Shirkey interrupted. "No one told you about it?"

Bethany looked at him, eyes squinting with suspicion. "Told us about what, Mr. Shirkey?"

"That's the new red sauce I came up with right before I got sick. It's lighter on the oregano, with two different garlic types. If I reveal my secret ingredient, I'd have to kill you. Had to take the meatballs out, of course, but—"

Bethany's cheeks darkened. "You mixed your own sauce in with your prescribed hospital tube feedings?"

"Hell no, Doc, I didn't mix anything with it. The whole bag is filled with my sauce. I asked the surgeons. They said it was okay. Probably has lots of antioxidants, whatever they are."

Typical surgeons, I thought to myself.

Bethany exhaled his irritation. "As long as it's not going to erode through the sutures, Mr. Shirkey."

I focused on a more obvious issue. "Mr. Shirkey, you can't taste it. What good does having flavored red sauce drip directly into your stomach through the tube in your nose?"

"Doc, I can't taste *any* of the stuff you say is good for me, dripping into my veins. My new red sauce is better than all that. It's got them anti-accidents, remember? So whether it's dripping into my veins, my stomach, or my mouth, it's gotta be helping."

His logic was impeccable, if not a bit medically unsound.

"Maybe a little more attention to his lab work, Dr. Lindmark?" Bethany held out his hand. I surrendered my iPad to him. He looked over the labs and handed it back to me. Then gazed for a long time at Shirkey, eyes narrowed. "Blood count's stable, Dr. Lindmark. Keep an eye on it. In your case, use both eyes. *Don't* order anything without running it by me first." Then to the patient, "Please try to stay out of trouble, Mr. Shirkey. I think your restaurant needs you more than we do." A twitch of a smile betrayed the attempt at humor his tone lacked. He turned back to me. "Let's move on," he said curtly.

Something nagged at me as I looked over Shirkey's room one more time.

"Lindmark! *That's* the patient you've decided to pay attention to? A little late, don't you think?"

Shirkey was on the mend, but still had an IV. "No, Dr. Bethany. I just, I'll be right there." Of course he needed an IV. He'd had a major bleed. How long ago had I been about to make Aaron Shirkey a "Do Not Resuscitate" because some hallucinated voice told me to? That ICU rotation seemed like years ago, but every word of Bethany's objection surfaced as if he were repeating them now. *Should* he be a No Code *now*, only days away from getting out of this place probably healthier than he had been in years? I shook my head that I could even consider such a ridiculous move.

I jammed my iPad into a pocket as if it were hot and hurried after the team. We made our way through several other remaining patients, all of whom were under the care of my fellow intern on the team, Frank Bannister. I barely listened to Frank's rendition of lab values and diagnoses.

"Lindmark!" Bethany's tone pulled me to attention. "Rounds are over. Dr. Sorenson wanted to meet you briefly for lunch. Go meet with him, then come back so we can see some of the new admissions."

Dr. Sorenson wanted to eat lunch with me? What could our supervising attending physician, a high and mighty neurologist, want with a lowly intern? I headed toward the dining hall, walking towards the unknown from *both* sides of the grave.

Three minutes after sitting across from Dr. Sorenson, it became obvious that eating lunch had never been on the agenda. "Harry, I just wanted to make sure things were on track. I also want you to know that putting you on probation has been done with the utmost attention to confidentiality."

Probation? I was on probation so confidential even I hadn't been informed?

Sorenson continued with composed smoothness, oblivious to the turmoil his words had set in motion. "I'm sure you understand it's our responsibility to make sure patients aren't endangered and to uphold medical care to our highest standard. Sometimes interns and residents get somewhat, ah, stressed under the strain. Sometimes to the point of seeing or hearing things, losing concentration, making terrible mistakes. Our lawyers have assured me they will hold off any action as long as you are handled appropriately with help, not punishment. We don't want to lose anyone. Patients *or* doctors." His smile was more of a twitch that came and went without a trace of humor. "Not enough people coming out of medical schools to fill the vacancies. I hope we're clear on everything, Harry?"

Clear? I had just dined with a shark as it circled about me, waiting patiently until I turned my back before attacking. Only the threat was clear—one more mistake and probation would give way to termination. Meantime, humiliating babysitting would be enforced as I tried to complete my internship.

I shuffled through the hallways with my head down, avoiding what I was sure were looks of pity and ridicule. More disdain greeted me when I caught up with Bethany for afternoon rounds. He'd known what lunch was about. I'd become the scapegoat he'd needed to get away with the killing. But I would not turn into Leland Travis, an outcast deemed crazy or dangerous. I just had to somehow be as cunning, as smart, as

Bethany. I swallowed down a sudden sour taste in my mouth. Yeah, good luck with that.

"So, Dr. Bannister, what's with all those bubbles?" I'd followed Bethany with the rest of the team into Room 458. My fellow intern was standing at the bedside of a man in his forties. A contraption hung at the foot of his bed, connected to him by a long rubber tube inserted into his chest between ribs. Another tube connected to a suction outlet in the wall. A continuous stream of bubbles stirred water in one of the chambers with enough force to shake the entire contraption.

"They're air bubbles, Dr. Bethany," Frank replied.

Bethany eyed him. "That's very insightful, Dr. Bannister. I hadn't been entirely sure what those bubbles were filled with until your explanation. Now that we've cleared up that mystery, could you fill me in on where they're coming from and what that apparatus does?"

Frank's eyes widened as he cleared his throat several times. "This is Mr. Tobin. He came in with nodules in his lungs. Radiology put in a needle into one of them to get a biopsy and his lung collapsed. He has had a large air leak since then and had to be admitted."

"So those air bubbles are escaping from his lung?"

Frank glanced at the bubbles, then looked at the patient. I knew exactly what was going through his mind. Was this a trick question or just an unusually easy one? He swallowed several times. That bowtie was going to leave bruises. "Um, yes, they're escaping from where the needle punctured his lung." His voice rose at the end.

"Exactly Dr. Bannister. It's a large leak, judging from those bubbles." Bethany turned his glare on me. "Lindmark, he's hooked up to suction through a chest tube inserted between his lung and ribs. Without that, all the air you see escaping would build up in his chest and could become lethal very quickly."

Roland Tobin looked up at Bethany, eyes rounded in fear. Bethany's furrowed brows relaxed and his grim expression softened. "Not to worry, Mr. Tobin, you're safe. That leak will seal, and the results came back benign, so all good news. You may be in for lying around at the end of a suction tube, but boredom in a hospital is definitely better than excitement." He darted a glare at me. "Right, Dr. Lindmark?"

I flushed but kept quiet.

After rounding on Frank's other patients Bethany gave him a list of things to do and sent him off. Bethany and I saw the rest of the patients on my list, all of whom were hospitalized with routine problems. I was obviously not to be trusted with anyone who might possibly pose a risk for complications. But my night on call was looming, with all that I knew lurked around me. "Routine" suddenly didn't sound so bad. I'd even settle for "boring" if it meant both I and my patients would survive another night in this place.

CHAPTER 15

"Dammit, Charlie, why did they have to get *you*?"

The old man lay on the bed, eyes closed, breathing in rhythm to the metronome hissing of the ventilator. Of course he didn't react to my words. I just needed to talk without fear of judgment or interruption. Talking to someone in a coma certainly qualified. Besides, we'd been told that people in a coma might still take comfort from someone speaking to them. I sat with Charlie for a few moments before my call night began, not sure if it was to comfort him, or if I was seeking comfort *from* him. Either way, I'd forced myself through the ICU doors, looking from side to side for the Richman-vision or for some other failure of survival in the ICU to emerge and gape at me.

"You knew, Charlie, you and Travis. I believe you now. You knew from that first day you saw me in the tunnels. And now I'll never get the chance to tell you." I grasped his hand and wiped away the tears that stung my eyes. "I don't know what to do, Charlie. I don't know how to help you or my patients." Richman's dead, gaping face loomed in my thoughts. "What if it's not Bethany? What if it's like Travis was saying? You agreed with him. What if it *is* the dead, Charlie? What the hell do I do now?"

The old man lay still, the ventilator's implacable hissing the only answer. I took some solace in the peace that had relaxed all the crevices and wrinkles on his face. Only that smooth dent marking the metal plate in his skull disrupted his features. Something about that plate.

Then it hit me. Laurie's words surfaced in my mind, about how that brain wave test had convinced Charlie's doctors to take him off life support. "Every single lead showed the same thing. . . " she'd said. But that metal plate covered part of Charlie's brain. Some of those brain wave leads would have shown only electrical artifact, or nothing at all.

It had to have been someone else's brain wave. Someone else in this ICU was brain dead, or close to it. Not Charlie. It couldn't have been Bethany. He had nothing against Charlie. No other living person had any grudge against Charlie. So who would have wanted Charlie taken off life support to die? The dead. Morrow was trying to finish off what the electrocution had failed to accomplish. And once again, that ghoul had let us doctors do the work for him, just like with me and Timmy's sodium levels. Simple keystrokes re-naming another patient's brain wave test, and Charlie became no longer worth keeping alive. Timmy had a high sodium, and Richman needed insulin–all because the medical records said so.

They could interact with the physical world just enough to command a keyboard.

They didn't need to lift, or stab, or strangle, or overcome impossible barriers between the physical and the afterlife. They only needed to manage simple keystrokes from beyond. The computers that controlled doctors did the rest. We had all abdicated medical skills in the name of modern technology. Maybe Charlie hadn't awakened yet. That didn't mean he wouldn't. But if the doctors here in the ICU took him off the breathing machine before he was ready, he'd die.

Fear churned a sickening feeling in my gut. Fear of what could happen to anyone in this place. Fear of things long dead that could *never* die, things that lingered and seethed and waited on their side of the grave. It was all Morrow. He'd carried his medical genius and his hatred and a need to avenge his horrible death with him beyond the grave. I gripped Charlie's arm and leaned close to him.

"I'll tell you why it's happening again now, Charlie." I whispered. "Back when Travis was having all his troubles, somehow the dead could cross over and interact with the physical world. But that became too obvious and backfired, right? Revenge on the living only caused panic and concern and closed everything down, didn't it? But now? Now all they need to do is punch a few keys on computers, enter new information that becomes gospel, and let us do their work for them. All it took was Morrow's genius from the other side, and trust in the computers from *this* side of death. Nothing gets done unless the computer says it's done. Morrow has made slaves of us living doctors. Because he knows *we* are slaves to our computers."

I grasped Charlie's hand. "You'll get better," I said to him, keeping my voice low. "They're wrong. I'll tell them, Charlie." Was that a squeeze of his hand around mine? He lay still, no twitch of expression.

"What the hell you doing here, Harry? We're on call tonight, you know?"

I dropped Charlie's hand and whirled around. Lincoln Tanner was standing at the opening of the cubicle.

"Yeah, Dr. Tanner, I was just following up on a few patients that were on my service. This one—"

"First, call me Linc. Second," He darted a glance at Charlie. "Seems like you're in for a one-sided conversation." I'd run into Lincoln Tanner a few times before. The residents alternated call nights, and it was apparently Bethany's night off, thank God. Interns and residents rarely coordinated call nights. Interns could receive many more points of view about medical practice from different resident doctors. I wasn't sure how many new teaching points I would pick up, though. Lincoln Tanner was as tall as my beanpole co-intern Frank, but with triple the waist size. His hair was speckled with premature gray, as was the bushy unkempt mustache that curled under his upper lip. Tanner always looked dull and disinterested, usually appearing more the spectator when I'd seen him on the wards instead of an active participant in medical care.

He glanced down at Charlie. "Friend of yours?" I nodded. Saying anything would erupt the tears I was fighting to hold back. Tanner shrugged. "Yeah, well, he's not on your service, and you're on call with me. Visit later." He gazed down at Charlie's still form, a thoughtful expression replacing the blankness of disinterest. "Not brain-dead yet, is he?" Tanner's bluntness was shocking, talking about Charlie as if he were nothing more than a case study on an exam. Anger gripped me when Tanner actually grinned. *Grinned.* "This can still be teachable, even though he's not your patient. You should probably read about brain-death. It's always tough to explain brain-death to families. They see the ventilator going and see the heart monitor blinking, so they can't accept that their loved one is dead. I'll tell Bethany to go over it with you."

I remained silent, this time to keep from yelling at him instead of avoiding tears.

"He will definitely ask you about it."

Shut up, Tanner, just shut up. That's *Charlie.*

"Listen, I'll help you out," Tanner added in a conspiratorial tone. "He'll probably ask you what else can mimic brain-death. He loves asking that. He'll ask what you need to check before declaring someone brain-dead. Know what it is?"

I shook my head.

Tanner winked knowingly. "If someone's been given a paralyzing drug, they can look every bit like they're brain-dead. They don't appear to respond to voice or even pain, they don't breathe on their own, and they'll die right after life support is taken away. They can be screaming on the inside with absolute terror at not being able to move, but no one will know because they can't move a muscle." The terrible story about Dr. Morrow's death poked into my thoughts. "An EEG, you know, a brain-wave test, can tell you what's really going on. So now you're prepared. Bethany always asks that. The rest you'll have to read on your own. I've gotta go and check on how your partner's doing with his admission."

I shook my head again as he shuffled out of the room. Tanner talked about Charlie like he was describing last night's ball game. I sighed and swiped at the tears that I could no longer stop. This ancient uneducated man had become more than a friend. He was my goddam protector in this place of death and un-death. And he'd had years, decades, to learn about what really went on in here. He believed. I needed to know more but Charlie wasn't talking anymore thanks to the dead that he believed in, the dead he had been afraid of but fighting against for so many years. Now he couldn't reveal the secrets he'd held in for so long.

I squeezed his hand one more time, rubbed my eyes, and hurried out of the ICU towards the refuge of the call room. I rounded a corner and almost ran into someone. "Sorry," I muttered, still gazing down at the floor. "I'm in a little hurry, if you don't—"

I looked up, directly into the cold gaze of Timmy Strickland. Up walking around at night? "Timmy. Are you okay?"

Timmy stood motionless. I cleared my throat and said, "Let's go back to your room, Timmy. Your—"

"Tim."

"What?"

"Tim. My name is Tim."

"Sure, okay." I tried smiling to generate a little warmth between us. "What are you doing, wandering around here at night?"

"Don't know."

His reply left little room for any more small talk. I cleared my throat again. "Anyway, Timmy, um, Tim, your parents are probably wondering where you are. Let's go back to your room. And we need to hurry, because—"

"No."

I huffed in frustration. "Yes, Tim. You're a patient in a hospital, and you need to be in your room. With your parents." I pulled on his arm and started walking towards the elevator, but he jerked his arm out of my grasp.

"He said, NO!" a deep voice suddenly hissed at me. I glanced back and forth, but couldn't see who had spoken. The hallway was empty except for Timmy and me. A cold dread wormed its way up from my stomach. I looked back at Timmy and was relieved to see two nurses walking towards us from behind him.

"Hey, you two, I'm going to need a little help with this patient. He's a little. . . confused. If you both could help me direct him back to his room?" I reached out for Timmy again as the nurses came up on either side to help.

"No." Timmy's eyes looked through me as he repeated that single word. The nurses faded as they drew near, replaced by images of withered patients in hanging tattered gowns. The one on Timmy's right sharpened from blurriness into an old gray man, mournful eyes staring at me, a large catheter hanging loosely from a large vein in his neck. His drooping gown exposed the circular burn mark of a resuscitation paddle. The other figure was definitely not a nurse. Coming out of her, then *becoming her*, emerged a woman. Gray throughout but somehow blurred around the edges, like the wisps of fog melting into a coming day. She reached out her arms towards me, not towards Timmy. A large breathing tube protruded obscenely from her mouth. Faded crimson stained her gown from a stitched incision. Frigid invisible tendrils gusted around my arms and legs. I staggered away from the approaching visions.

Timmy stood there, immobile. His eyes veered to the ceiling, then rolled back and forth to look at the two vaporous things surrounding him. I stood, frozen in place, as he turned those cold distant eyes to me. "Not Timmy." The voice was Timmy's marbly thick mutter, but coated with venom instead of Timmy's singsong lightness. "Not Tim. Finally." The tone was icy and distant. Timmy turned and walked away down the hallway. The things on either side, wavering gray decayed features, advanced without sound or emotion. Cold deepened around me and sharpened the terror that choked off my breath. I threw my arms up over my face and squeezed my eyes shut. My heart stuttered, the air in my lungs froze into a block of ice.

Only seconds passed until I dared open my eyes and look from side to side. I turned completely around, but the hallway was empty. Timmy was gone. I breathed a long sigh of relief. They were all gone, thank God.

I was alive.

I didn't remember walking down hallways and up stairwells. I punched the combination of the call room with shaking hands. My mind raced as the room's isolation silenced distractions. The calming memory of Charlie's Cheshire grin lasted only seconds before surrendering to the image of the plastic breathing tube violating his features. Unbeckoned, Timmy's stony visage crowded out that vision of Charlie. I shivered at the memory of its voice uttered with frost that wasn't heard as much as felt, as if he had been standing in front of a freezer.

A sudden suspicion pushed me to the computer. If it was too ridiculous to even consider, why the sweat dripping into my eyes? What had that old man Frazier said at the nursing home? Turley. He'd croaked out that name at Charlie. This time I didn't need to widen the search dates. TURLEY, JOSEPH populated the search window. Admitted four years previous, just prior to Bethany coming on as an intern. Aged fifty-six, definitely not "one of the young ones." Died only one day after an admission for what should have been an uncomplicated hernia repair. But something happened on the operating table. He had coded right there in the OR, and never responded to resuscitation attempts. Given the unexpected death the case had been sent for an autopsy, which showed an excessive amount of anesthetic in the blood, but never confirmed 'error.' Something in Turley's demographic information caught my eye.

MEMBER, BOARD OF DIRECTORS. NARRAGANSETT GENERAL HOSPITAL. Joseph Turley had been a big shot, a VIP, at the hospital he'd died in. Did that mean that his soul had been sentenced to a life in limbo like so many lesser patients? He must have been as important after death as he had been alive, to go to the front of the line for . . . a body.

I slumped back in my chair, unable to keep my hands from shaking. Disturbing images and memories invaded my thoughts, as if some hidden spigot had been turned and had released its bottled poison into my head. Voices whispering to me. Phantom things all around me, killing my patients. I didn't know how they came to be, didn't know why I was the only one experiencing it all, but I realized now what those souls were doing. They were waiting. They were souls waiting for

Richman, and Timmy, and Frazier, and anyone else who had the youth and hope they had surrendered with their untimely deaths. The young ones, *just like Travis had said.* The more my recent actions crowded into my mind, the more I realized what all the things around me were doing. Morrow and all these lingering phantoms weren't killing my patients. They weren't exacting revenge on the living. They were waiting, but not to kill.

"They were escaping."

My voice broke the silence of the room. I'd uttered the words without realizing it. I ground my hands against my eyes, trying to rub away everything I had seen.

A noise in the room pierced my thoughts. I looked up, but no gaping apparition leered back at me. The room remained still and empty. The noise came from the keyboard in front of me, followed by chattering from the computer as it grinded through its hard drive. The screen lit up and glowed back at me. A cloying sweet aroma of suntan lotion filled the air. The computer screen flickered. Images of old handwritten medical notes scrolled across the screen. A fruity nostalgic smell of old-fashioned crayons wafted in and out of the suntan lotion scent. New letters glowed in the search window. I leaned forward and squinted at the name.

Travis, Kevin.

CHAPTER 16

"Dr. Morrow's waiting. He's going to be next, now that he's finally succeeded with others in here."

I whirled around in my chair. It was the boy wandering lost in the tunnel, but he wasn't lost anymore. He'd found *me*. His edges were fuzzy, like he was unraveling into the air. I backed away from him as he spread twig-thin arms to either side. He was dead, like all the rest. "I didn't do anything. Stay away from me. Stay away. All of you." My words whispered past a throat closed down. Acid boiled up and soured my mouth. My chair bumped against the desk, preventing further retreat.

"Please don't go," a voice spoke inside the room. *His* voice. "Don't be scared." I dared to look at him. "Everything you've seen around here, and you're afraid of *me*?"

I swallowed against a mouth gone painfully dry until I could speak in more than a whisper. "Who are you?" I finally managed to utter, trying to keep control of my voice. "*What* are you?"

A wisp of a smile lightened his ghostly features. "I used to live around here. Actually, I used to just live."

"What's that supposed to mean?" I asked.

"I've passed over." He paused. "I'm not one of *them*." The teenage thing gazed at me with eyes so pale I could almost look through them. I was talking with something dead. Or talking to myself, through a hallucination? Neither thought was comforting at the moment. I went with "dead."

"You *are* one of them." Visions of Richman and Charlie filled my thoughts, igniting an anger that stiffened the dread penetrating me. "You're killing people. Innocent people only trying to get better." I looked at the specter. "Please, just leave us, leave *me* alone."

The boy looked almost sad. "Listen to me. I can't hurt you. I don't want to hurt you, or anyone, so just listen."

Something dead sounded urgent. I listened.

"Some go in peace. I don't know why some of us are left behind. I think when you're pulled from life so quick, sometimes you're just left. . . in-between. It hurts so bad to be left here." He faded from a gray boy to a wispy presence, a cold void frosting the room's gloom. "I've seen it all over the years. The way you are in life, well, somehow you get more like that after you die. At least here, in-between. I won't hurt anyone, I can't hurt anyone, just to escape from this place. I'm *not* one of them."

His voice wasn't a voice. It was a wisp of sound, a whispering tone that circled around me like coils of smoke. The boy wavered in and out of focus while peering around the room as if he were expecting something to appear. He resumed, "Dr. Morrow, I don't think he was a bad person, really. But my dad didn't trust him. I think Dr. Morrow needed to be important. Maybe dying when he shouldn't have made him so bad. The longer he's been here, the more he needs to leave. Escape back with the living, where he was. . . big."

"They're stealing into bodies, stealing back into life." Saying those words out loud didn't make them any more believable. I felt like I was role-playing, telling ghost stories around a campfire. Except I still couldn't help looking around nervously, expecting horrible ghastly things bearing the scars of failed resuscitations to emerge from the dark of the room.

"Don't be afraid, Dr. Lindmark. They can't steal from the living. Your soul owns your body as long as you're alive. When you die, your soul departs, leaving your body open. . . for the taking." The cold deepened. So did the smell of suntan lotion, and buttery popcorn, then a calming aroma of chocolate. "I've seen these things." The blur of his pale face could not hide the odd lack of any expression. "Dr. Morrow won't kill to just kill. If he did that, he'd only have useless bodies that can't be brought back to life. He wants out, like all of us want to leave this side. They can steal a body in the moment its soul leaves, but they can't bring someone back to life." The specter shrugged its small shoulders. "They need doctors on your side to bring that body back to life. That can only happen in hospitals, with bodies that die so they can be, you know, saved back to life."

"And the person who died? I mean, the one whose soul was there first?" I whispered.

"They can't return. They have nowhere to return to. They stay here, in-between."

I didn't know if my shivering was from the cold, from those words, or because I was alone in a room with a dead teenager. It didn't matter. Everything was making certain horrible sense.

"Do you understand now? Dr. Morrow, all of them, they need the people in here. They need their bodies. Then they need to kill them in the right way. They don't want people with living wills who are allowed to die, because they won't be brought back to life by doctors."

"You told me to write 'No Code Blue' in Shirkey's chart, didn't you? To protect him."

Whatever used to be Kevin Travis nodded. "They can't escape from here in a body that's not going to be revived." Cold still wrapped around me, but smells exploded as the boy's voice became stronger. Hot chocolate, freshly-cut grass, old-fashioned glue flavored the frigid air.

That terrifying insight left me breathless. I muttered more to myself than to the apparition hovering before me. "Morrow. Only a doctor would know how to kill but leave the corpse viable enough to allow resuscitation. Sylvester Morrow is a genius on both sides of the grave. But he needed time until we doctors on this side could do it for him. Because the dead can only physically change our world so much, right?"

The Kevin-soul, or specter, or whatever he was, stayed silent, piercing me with those orbs. "Computers are perfect. So little contact needed from the other side, my side. Slaves to Morrow's bidding. Just like you doctors."

The wispy vision breathed utterances that filled my ears and pushed in on my brain. "So many people have died in here. People who just wanted to get better, get cured. It got bad after Dr. Morrow died. Most of them were my dad's patients. It was Morrow. After he died, he just didn't know enough. He didn't have the drugs, and the machines, and all the stuff he can use now to make death easier to be revived from. He just had his anger. So those patients he tried to steal, they just wound up dying. Couldn't be revived."

The boy's form faded. His eyes were only shimmering wells where eyes should have been. Hazy gauzy spaces in his head. "They all died while my dad was here, on call. I think because Morrow knew my dad was the only one smart enough to bring those patients back, with new souls. A way out from this in-between."

"He saw Morrow, and the others, right? He believed, but couldn't get anyone else to believe him."

"My dad warned everyone that the ghosts were doing it after he saw Morrow. They thought he was crazy. After what happened to me, I don't think my dad really cared about anything, anyway. Except how much he hated Morrow for what he did to me." His gaze captured mine no matter how much I tried to look away. "And now Morrow's gotten better. He's had all these years to learn. Just as I have."

I smelled buttery popcorn, so strong and thick I could almost taste it. "There's no more time. Souls have left this pain, this in-between, thanks to what Morrow has made you doctors think, and do."

Silence. The vision was gone. The room was lit only by the computer's glow. His voice came at me from everywhere. "But you knew that, didn't you? You and the other doctors, the red one, almost let Dr. Morrow steal that boy, the one with all the injuries. I'd never heard Dr. Morrow scream so loud than when that boy died." Was he talking about Anthony Richman? "His soul is here, with us. Dr. Morrow almost did it that night. But not even the smart doctor could bring him back." It *was* Richman. Was it my imagination, or did that rustling murmur coming at me from everywhere and nowhere take on a more accusing sharpness?

The sweet scent of apples filled the silence.

"What do I do? How do I kill what's already dead?"

The aromas faded. The air warmed around me. I slumped back in the chair, trying to swallow down the churn of nausea. Dead things were talking to me. This hospital held more trapped souls than it did living ones. I'd seen them, now I'd talked with them. I shook in my chair with a sudden involuntary shiver as other unspeakable revelations fell into place. Those disabled wrecks that haunted the Sylvester Morrow Convalescence Center with their wheelchairs and oxygen tanks must be both dead and alive at the same time. . . warehoused back to a different painful oblivion after resuscitations had left them ruined survivors of Morrow's efforts to find a way back. Joseph Turley must have escaped first, but the resuscitation hadn't gone so well. The soul of the big-shot VIP Turley had wound up escaping into a prison of the living, his new body disabled and twisted despite the best efforts of medicine. There were others there, too. All hateful testaments to their resurrections gone awry, all just existing until they finally passed on naturally, mercifully.

But Morrow must have learned from those failures. He'd chosen a better human to do his work. Bethany had stepped in with a seamless resuscitation of Timmy. It was all so awfully clear. I'd started saving Timmy *before* he'd died. That's why Morrow had stopped me. Bethany finished once Timmy's soul had departed. Timmy was not just some miracle rewiring of brain circuitry after surviving a Code Blue. Timmy wasn't Timmy. Timmy was someone else, back from *somewhere* else.

Jesus.

CHAPTER 17

Morning rounds seemed like the quiet after the storm, until Timmy. His seizures and mental status were improving, his swollen gums and misshapen features were the last remaining hints of physical disability. His behavior had become the problem. The Stricklands pleaded with us to do something.

"We're afraid," Norma confided, looking down at the floor. Her shame was obvious. "We're afraid of our own son."

I was also afraid of their son, because I knew he no longer *was* their son.

Bethany promised to come back and formalize plans for a psychiatric evaluation, but I could tell it was halfhearted. Dr. Sorenson had accompanied us on rounds, maybe to keep an eye on me. Living up to expectations of a learned physician at the top of the academic food chain, he peppered Frank and me with questions about possible neurologic explanations for Timmy's recovery.

"Those people should be thankful for the gift they've been given," he murmured after giving us his own explanation. "Their son was an eighteen-year-old in diapers, and now he might be able to actually pay taxes." I had the feeling he'd be willing to suffocate every intellectually disabled patient in his clinic hoping to reproduce Timmy's miracle.

Most of the other patients swam in and out of focus as rounds progressed. Their illnesses and lab reports paled compared to everything I'd seen and heard. Aaron Shirkey had abandoned his tube feedings and was now taking in his special sauce by mouth, which also allowed him to ingest the stuffed shells that hadn't fit through the tube. Roland Tobin's air leak was still bubbling away. Sorenson's insistence that he now be sent for surgical correction registered as if from a distance, as did Bethany's argument for further observation alone. An older patient with cancer, and a young woman with out-of-control diabetes, all went by in a blur.

At last the final order was written, the last problem foisted on the intern on call for that night. I was finally able to leave the scene of the crime, which is how I'd come to view everything I'd experienced in Narragansett General. The mundane drive home offered little diversion from the realities that tortured my thoughts. Launched from medical school naïveté into internship, I'd barely been prepared for all the disease and death that nature caused. But no amount of lectures or hands-on education could have prepared me for the horrors beyond death. There was nothing natural about that hospital. Or probably for any hospital that housed so much disease and dying. Who could I go to for help? What textbook could I read for the right guideline? Who was next? The thoughts terrified me.

A night of sleep dulled my terror to a distracting unease. I'd intended to sneak out of the house before Connie awakened, dressing quickly and quietly. I didn't trust myself to keep from babbling to her about all I had seen, because she still considered me a sane and reliable partner in life if a little overworked. But her side of the bed was empty when I woke up. She greeted me with a cup of black coffee and a dark expression. Another bad night of nightmares and tears? Another day of loneliness I'd done nothing to ease?

She answered my thoughts before I could open my mouth. "I'm on my way to the hospital too, Harry. I'm glad you're up."

"Are you okay? Is something wrong?" I couldn't take anything happening to Connie. She shook her head. "Did you change your aquatic therapy hours? Starting earlier?"

"No, Harry. I'm going to the pediatric wing to help Denise."

"Help Denise do what?"

"Help Denise cope, Harry. Audrey was admitted to the pediatric ward today. Remember that cough she had?" How could I forget? I'd never seen a child wracked so hard by coughing the last time they'd come over. "She probably had pneumonia even then. She's just so stoic, you know? She didn't complain to Denise until she woke up last night with trouble breathing. Her pediatrician admitted her today. Denise is beside herself."

"That's terrible, Connie," I offered. "But children her age, well, they usually recover without too much of a problem. Really."

Her eyes erupted with tears. "Really, Harry? Even children with cerebral palsy?" The tears patterned crooked grooves in her makeup.

I wrapped by arms around her, trying to absorb her anguish as the sobs wracked both of us. "I really don't know, Connie. I just don't know." My voice faded as I realized I couldn't even pretend enough knowledge to be supportive. "How is Denise doing?"

"She's a mess. I had an afternoon of patients at the therapy pool scheduled, but I found another aquatic therapist to take over for me. I couldn't leave Denise and Audrey alone." Her voice tightened. "Audrey's awfully sick. And so fragile, you know?"

I thought of the little girl's twisted frame, the limp dangling legs. "Yeah Connie, I know."

I had to see Charlie before rounds. Something was different about his cubicle. It was less cluttered. His face was peaceful, unmarred by bandages and the breathing tube. The ventilator had been removed. I approached the bed cautiously, remembering what I'd seen the last time I'd looked in on him. No apparition appeared, no icy gust froze me.

"Charlie?" I spoke softly. He didn't move or even blink. "Charlie?" I repeated more loudly. Still no response.

"He really got fried, didn't he?" a voice behind me broke into my thoughts.

I jumped at the unexpected intrusion and spun around to see Rose, one of the older nurses. "Sorry?" I responded.

"Still can't believe how it happened. Weirdest thing I've ever heard of. I sure did like old Washington, too. Real shame. Are you going to pick him up on your service?"

"No, just thought I'd stop in and see how he was doing."

"Oh, okay," she replied, her tone halting as if I'd answered in a foreign language. "You're, uh, just visiting Charlie? Because we'll probably be transferring him out in the morning. Maybe to you. I figured you wanted to look over the chart."

"He's getting transferred out? Doesn't he still need intensive monitoring? He's still at risk of so many things happening. How can he be transferred?"

Rose shrugged. "I guess that's the point, Harry." Not Dr. Lindmark, or even Doctor, just 'Harry.' "The last brain wave reading was pretty dismal. Every single brain wave lead they put on his head showed the same thing. Just a slow, meaningless squiggle. Not quite brain dead, but next to it. That's why he was taken off the ventilator. No family or power of attorney."

"Charlie was taken off the ventilator to *die*?" I asked in disbelief. "Not because he'd *improved*?"

"Sorry, Harry. I thought you knew."

"No. I didn't know." Charlie had never hurt anyone. "But you didn't die," I muttered. The message of Charlie's EEG bore into me. *You didn't die because that wasn't your brain wave, Charlie. Maybe Morrow did get them to disconnect the breathing machine early with that brain wave test, so you could be killed more easily.* "You're not going to die, either." Charlie didn't move, nothing to indicate any of my words registered at all. "Thanks Rose," I said as I brushed my way past her. "I'll look in on him tomorrow. And Rose," I stopped and tried to sound nonchalant.

"Why not call his intern and ask about taking his IV out? You know, might as well make him as comfortable as possible."

"I don't know, Dr. Lindmark," she said, suddenly on a more formal basis. She eyed me almost suspiciously. "I heard you had some problems with Washington's IV one other time you were in here. You really don't like intravenous catheters, do you?"

I looked down at the old wrinkled man. This place could give life or take it away. In this hospital, a simple intravenous catheter could become an executioner's tool. I breathed deeply, trying to place what I knew into the setting of everyone else's reality. I was *not* going to go the way of Travis. "You know Rose, you're right. Just tell him I stopped by. Take good care of him."

I walked out of Charlie's room, pushed open the heavy double doors, and headed back into the fray.

CHAPTER 18

"So nice of you to join us, Doctor," Bethany greeted me outside the call room. Sorenson hadn't arrived, but Frank was already standing at attention. A medical student stood at his side, but was so nondescript and withdrawn she faded into the background. Frank's current bowtie sported pictures of stethoscopes, doctor's bags, and hypodermic needles on a muted silver background.

"I had to see some patients before rounds started, Dr. Bethany," I explained. It wasn't exactly untrue. Charlie *was* a patient, just not *my* patient.

Bethany's surly expression relaxed a little. "Good, then rounds should be efficient today. I certainly hope so, because Sorenson said I could get off this service and go on elective." Even under his beefy jowls and beard, I could see his jaw muscles clench. "Apparently they've become satisfied my patient care doesn't need supervision any longer. And you, Dr. Bannister, will be going to the ICU tomorrow to start a rotation there."

I felt my face flush with embarrassment. He'd said nothing about me. "I, uh, I—"

Bethany fixed his eyes on me. "I don't know about you," he said. "You'll have to talk to Dr. Sorenson yourself." I could think of about fifty million other things I'd rather do than have a one-on-one with my attending physician.

"Meantime," Bethany said, "We need to start rounds." He looked over his shoulder at the clicking sound of approaching footsteps. "Morning, Dr. Sorenson."

"Doctors," Sorenson responded with his usual severe reserve. "We're already late, so let's get going."

Dr. Sorenson maintained a brisk pace through the rest of rounds. Teaching at the expense of patients was thankfully cut down to a bare minimum as well. Timmy Strickland, of course, did capture Sorenson's undivided attention. All three Stricklands were in the room as we walked in. Timmy's parents were dressed in their usual threadbare cornfield chic. Timmy sat by himself in a chair against the wall.

"Doctors," he greeted us formally. "How are you all doing today?" I glared at that Tim-thing with all the silent accusation I could muster.

"We're all fine, *Tim*," Bethany answered with pointed emphasis. "Looks like you're feeling pretty well." He looked pleased with Timmy's miraculous physical and cognitive changes, as if he were personally responsible for a medical miracle.

"I am, Dr. Bethany," Timmy replied. "No reason not to go home, right? Right, Mom? Dad?" Did he seem to choke on those names, or was it just my imagination? I was amazed how cooperative he'd become.

His parents glanced at each other, then they returned Timmy's look with bewildered smiles. "You have a good point there, Timmy. Um, Tim," Mr. Strickland answered. He turned in my direction and smiled. "I guess we would like to take our son home," he declared, favoring his son with a fond expression. "We need to get back to the crops. And I need to work on his swing." He held up the wooden Louisville Slugger he'd shown me before. "I think a few good hits will do more for him than any more hospital tests will. So how about it, doctors? Home runs instead of more brain wave tests?" I smiled inwardly at the man's words. He sounded too corny to be believed, except it was obvious how genuine his sentiment was. I glanced over at Timmy. His sneer revealed still-swollen gums and misshapen teeth.

Sorenson shrugged. "Certainly some loose ends left, but I would agree there are no longer any indications for hospitalization." He looked at Bethany. "Go ahead and discharge him, but I'd like him scheduled back to my clinic. Better have home health make daily visits until we're assured of stability."

"Thank you all so much for the care you took of Timmy," Mrs. Strickland spoke up. Her voice was still trembling and uncertain. I noticed she kept several feet away from her son. "We promise we'll be careful with all the medication dosing."

We murmured our "Goodbyes" and "Good lucks" to the family, then walked out. I took one more look at Timmy as we left. The friendly expression had hardened into a cold glare.

"How many more patients left, Dr. Bethany?" Sorenson asked as we walked down the hall.

Bethany looked down at a stack of cards. "Just two more," he answered. "Both are Frank's, uh, Dr. Bannister's patients."

"Perfect," Dr. Sorenson replied. He looked at Bethany. "I'll have Dr. Lindmark back with you shortly." Bethany shrugged and walked away with Frank. Sorenson directed his gaze at me. I shrank inwardly under the intensity of his eyes, certain that something bad was coming my way. "I understand you've something to do with a patient in the ICU," he said to me.

My heart raced. Were they finally getting around to blaming me for Richman? Or for Timmy? Or both? Was Sorenson at this very moment getting prepared to meet with the hospital's lawyers as they tried to kick me out of the program as gracefully and as quietly as possible, in exchange for lawsuits being dropped? I opened my mouth to confess all when the neurologist spoke again.

"Some of the nurses have voiced concerns over how inappropriate your actions may have been in terms of a certain patient... " He glanced down at a flash card in his hand. "A Charles Washington. One of our own employees, I understand. Pulling out IVs on someone not even your patient?" His manicured eyebrows drew together. "I have to admit, Dr. Lindmark, I'm having trouble keeping up with your interactions. Was this medical or personal?"

"He's just a friend, Dr. Sorensen," I muttered. "I was just trying to keep him comfortable."

Sorenson held his stare for what seemed like years, his eyes boring into mine until I felt they'd hit gray matter if the glare lasted any longer. "If that's how you treat your friends. . . " His pause needed no words to complete his thoughts. "It looks bad for a program to drop one of its doctors. You're pushing the limits of that, Dr. Lindmark." I could only nod, realizing that spewing my fears of disembodied souls circling my patients would not be particularly helpful at the moment. After several long moments of silence, Sorenson broke his stare. "Stay with Dr. Bethany," he abruptly snapped, then wheeled away without another word. I exhaled my anxiety almost explosively, grabbed a quick snack from the cafeteria, and walked back to meet with Bethany.

I bumped into him in a crowded hallway of patient rooms. "Glad you're back, Lindmark," he greeted me gruffly. "You've got a lot to do before the weekend."

The weekend? I hadn't even remembered it was Friday.

Thankfully, none of the other patients needed any procedures. Bethany didn't call with any new admissions, which allowed me to tie up as many loose ends as possible before the weekend. Two hours later, I'd written all the notes, ordered tests, and had signed out to the intern who would be covering over the weekend. The week was finally over. I stopped by the call room to pick up my backpack and was about to head for home when that last image of Timmy struck me. I knew the truth behind that sneer. For the thousandth time I thought back on Timmy's resuscitation. I sighed, sat in front of the computer and opened up Patient Records.

And sat there. What the hell was I supposed to look for? I focused on what I'd heard when I'd failed so miserably during Timmy's code.

'. . .too far gone. . .'

It hadn't been Bethany. I knew that now. At least, it hadn't been Bethany who'd hissed those words during Timmy's code. Morrow?

That goddam apparition had been playing with me, torturing me, setting me up to fail with Timmy. I closed my eyes and focused on that code. What had I really heard? Far. . . gone? I stared at the computer screen and in desperation typed "Far gone" into the main search window. I'd only typed in 'Far' before a list prepopulated. Farbain, Farley, Farlow, Farrow…the list went on. Something registered. I scrolled back up through the list. Faragon. I clicked on the name.

FARAGON, TRUMAN filled the patient name window.

I peered more closely, amazed. Truman Faragon. "Too far gone?" Could that be what I'd heard whispered, hissed at me in all that chaos? There actually had been such a person hospitalized here. I opened up the medical records. He'd been admitted with a stroke. Maybe that's why I'd heard the name. A patient named Faragon had probably needed something while Timmy had been coding. I must have heard the loudspeaker or someone's phone. It made sense. Timmy had been admitted to a neurology floor with his seizures. That floor would also treat patients with strokes. I scrolled down. Truman Faragon had been given a blood-thinner, and then died? Brain hemorrhage. Oh my God. Same damn day as Timmy had coded. Someone had committed one of the most dreaded of medical sins–giving a stroke patient a blood thinner without getting a head CT first, and had caused fatal bleeding into his head. Jesus.

Then I stopped scrolling. It couldn't be. I clicked through multiple other pages. It wasn't a data error. Had someone fooled with the records to cover up that fatal mistake? But why do that? It didn't make sense. I collapsed back in the chair. These records were scanned copies of actual handwritten records. They were genuine and had to be real. Truman Faragon had been admitted, then had died, in 1984. *More than thirty years ago.*

I peered more closely at the scrawled notes from decades earlier. Truman had been thirty-two years old, dropped off in front of the emergency room intoxicated with slurring speech. He was still slurring his speech even after the alcohol wore off, so a stroke was suspected. I scrolled to the typed document detailing the autopsy results.

My heart quickened and my hands slickened on the keys as the words came into view. SUBDURAL HEMATOMA with ACUTE INTRACRANIAL BLEED. Below: *Contusions Consistent With Blunt Head Trauma.* Separated from such a disaster by more than two decades, and I still couldn't stop the nauseating roil in my stomach. They had given a blood thinner to a drunk who was slurring his speech from a blood clot after a blow to the head, probably a bar fight. Like throwing fuel on a fire, the doctors had turned a treatable clot in a lethal bleed.

Truman Faragon had come in angry and had died even angrier. And that anger had then festered for years and years, deepened by the pain of the in-between in which he'd been imprisoned. Until Morrow had set him free. Morrow had finally been successful. Now Truman Faragon was back from the in-between, exchanging eternity in afterlife limbo for doting parents and Norman Rockwell afternoons on homemade baseball diamonds. All the comfort and happiness Timmy Strickland had loved, Truman Faragon, ex-drunk and bar fighter, would chafe under if not hate.

I shook my head at the screen. It still didn't make sense. Why wouldn't Morrow free himself, instead of helping some angry drunk escape back to the living? I scrolled back through the records, squinting as if only more only more focus would reveal the answer. I stopped when a single line appeared. Below the name of the resident who had managed Sparks' admission to the ER that day was the signature of the supervising physician who had overseen all the care.

Sylvester Morrow MD.

I slumped back as it became clear. Back then Morrow had been a young physician probably fresh out of his own Chief Residency. No doubt smart and talented, but without the years of experience that would have graduated him from smart to genius. He had supervised one of the only tragic mistakes in his illustrious career, when ego had trumped experience. Probably covered it up as well, with the power he'd held even back then. That's why he'd sent Faragon's trapped soul on. He'd put him in the in-between, he owed escape to him. Even beyond the grave, debt and blame mattered.

The pungent, sun-cooked aroma of suntan lotion hit me a second before I felt the numbing cold breeze. I bolted up in the chair and whirled around. He hovered close to the wall, his white face still as flat and still as a statue. The lost boy. The dead boy. Kevin Travis.

"What do you want?" I heard my voice shaking. I breathed in the warm suntan lotions, then inhaled a pleasing cut-grass smell. My fear ebbed as if those scents wrapped me in calm. "Why do I always smell those things whenever you appear?" I asked. "The others, like Morrow, it's always just the cold. But with you, I smell things."

A puzzled look crossed his shimmering features. "What smells?" he asked.

"I smell suntan lotion and cut grass. And sometimes flowers. I've smelled popcorn, and burnt hot dogs. They're not bad smells, but it's weird." I looked at him cautiously, hoping I hadn't said anything to make him angry. "Weird on top of weird."

As I watched, a sad smile curled around his mouth. "Do you smell anything else?" he asked.

I thought about the times he'd come upon me. "All sorts of things," I answered. "One time I smelled pine trees. Made me think of Christmas. A lot of those outdoors smells, like the grass. And then one time I thought Doc Tra-" I looked at him carefully. "I thought your father was around, because it was the same cologne I smelled in his room at the nursing home."

As I watched him, the boy flickered in and out of transparency in rhythm to his words. "All that's my life," he said, his tone still so eerily hollow. "*Was* my life. I don't know how or why, but each one is a memory I can see every day I've been here. They've kept me company. My dad and I always had a great time. He'd always take me to the playground. Sometimes we'd just sit in our front yard, right after the lawn had been mowed, and just do nothing. I always loved that smell. The sun would shine down, the clouds just floated by, everything seemed so safe." His eye sockets sharpened into pale blue eyes complete with irises, pupils, the whole thing. His pale expression turned wistful. "He'd make sure to take me to at least one baseball game a year, and when it got boring, he'd just stuff me with more popcorn and hot dogs."

I nodded. It was all I could think of doing.

He hugged himself with skinny arms. One of his elbows seemed frozen, leaving that forearm sticking out at an odd angle. "My dad would save one Saturday in the winter to go out and pick out a Christmas tree with me. It would take all day, and I think it tired him out more than me. It was always one of the smaller trees, missing needles. That way he could carry it." A wan smile tugged at the corners of his mouth. "He called it a Kevin-tree, because it was small, like me." His features blurred. "Whenever I came across one of those smells, it would always take me back to the good memory. I guess I took all that with me."

I looked down at the legs that remained warped and contracted under his floating form. Baggy blue jeans with rolled up cuffs draped over large black orthopedic shoes, unable to hide the pathetic uselessness of those limbs. "What did you do after you became, uh, when you couldn't walk anymore?" I ventured.

He gazed down at me. "I was never able to walk," he answered in a matter-of-fact tone. "I almost died when I was born because I was so weak."

"But then, how did you do all that? What—"

"My dad either carried me or pushed me in my wheelchair. That's why the tree had to be so small. He carried me in one arm and held the tree with the other. I think that's why it was so great just sitting in our front yard. Because there was nobody to steer around, and nobody to stare at us."

I pictured his father. Gruff, unshaven, unkempt, mentally undone. He had to be talking about someone else. What the hell had happened to Leland Travis?

Neither of us said anything for a few long seconds. Kevin Travis looked around the room as if expecting someone to appear. "I needed to warn you," he said. "There's something not right in here. I could hear Morrow screaming in pain. After what happened with that boy, Richman. You and the smart red one couldn't revive him and released Morrow back here. He'd never been that close to escaping in such a young person. Now he's brought out another soul. It worked. I feel something is wrong here." Those pale eyes fixed on me. "Please get out of here now."

I was not going to argue. But I needed more. "Look, just tell me—why is this all happening around here? To me? Why are *my* patients dying? I'll go, I promise. But can't you just tell me why? How the hell is it only me that sees you, and the others?"

Kevin Travis hovered in cold, ominous silence. It became so unbearable I heaved out of the chair and edged my way towards the door.

Kevin seemed to sigh, lifting his frail translucent chest and shoulders up and down weakly. "Maybe because you're always here." He looked down. "Just like my dad, *you* get blamed for all the accidents and mistakes Morrow has learned to create. Things that you doctors just *assumed* were accidents or medical mistakes, but tipped those patients over just enough to kill them. If doctors like the smart one could bring back that spark of life, Morrow and the rest would be there, to claim that body." He paused, his features a detached impassive mask throwing a glow into the room. "The smart one, the red one. . . he's special. To those here with me."

"Bethany? Dr Bethany?" A small shrug of withered shoulders. "But—"

"Why *are* you here so much, Dr. Lindmark?" the boy asked. "You have a family, right?"

"I just, you know, I just want to get the work done." I thought of the empty nursery collecting cobwebs in my home. Up the stairs to the right, just like we'd planned. I clenched my jaws. But we hadn't planned *everything*, like finally giving birth after so many miscarriages, only to have our baby die. Frustration had gradually hardened into anger.

And now, Kevin's guileless questions exposed what I'd probably known but refused to admit–I wasn't consumed with duty and caring for patients. I was using internship to avoid the house, the empty nursery, and even Connie. Because all that brought more pain than the death, violence, and creepiness that infected Narragansett General.

Popcorn and hot dogs encircled me in tendrils of invisible aroma. In the next moment, the ghostly vision in front of me darkened as it focused with sockets gone hazy. The delicious air around me soured and dissolved into a more pungent odor of blood and antiseptic soap. "You have a connection, Dr. Lindmark. To us. That's why it's been you, only you, more than all the others. You've touched death, haven't you? Death close to *you*, not a patient. I think, maybe, that is your connection to our side."

"No. I did not. I mean, no. Never." I did not want to summon those memories of holding my baby. Not now, not ever. But they forced their way into my brain from the crypt I'd kept them buried in. "My son was born with a fatal heart condition. Hypoplastic left ventricle. Whatever. One of those 'blue babies.' They took him away from us right after he was born, whisked him off to the Neonatal ICU. We never even got to touch him. The first time we were able to hold our son was to comfort him as he died. I held him as he just stopped breathing." I thought I'd run out of tears long ago. My eyes burned as that vision squeezed them out. "Yeah," I mumbled, more to myself than to the boy. "I've been close to death. I've *held* death." Was my reward a connection to the restless imprisoned dead?

"Go home, Dr. Lindmark," Kevin intoned, his withered form almost gone.

"It just takes so much effort to be at home."

"Please go home, Dr. Lindmark," he said. "Get out. Something is very wrong here."

I felt an almost uncontrollable urge to laugh and scream at the same time. Death and loneliness in one place, sadness and loneliness in another place. Too many places to run away from. I had run out of places to run away *to*. And I'd run out of people to confide my fears to, at the risk of being labeled a crazy psychotic fool. I was in my car, pulling out of the lot, when I realized there *was* one place, one person, I could count on. But God help me.

CHAPTER 19

The nursing station was a beacon of light guiding me out of the murky gloom of the nursing home hallways. Morrow had populated this place that bore his epitaph with the wrecks of his failed attempts to escape. They were patients he had selected at the beginning, who had been so easy to kill but so hard to bring back. They *had* been brought back, stolen by souls yearning to escape the in-between Kevin had spoken of. I was sure of that. Those souls *had* found new bodies back with the living, but each one a prison every bit as bad as the in-between. I hoped I wouldn't run into one of those human remnants again, because I wasn't sure who they would hate more–Morrow, or those of us still enjoying life.

One of the nurses was sleeping with her head tilted back and feet resting on the counter, while another was concentrating on a needlepoint pattern.

"I'm Dr. Lindmark, here to visit Leland Travis," I declared to the one nurse still awake.

She sat up straighter, pushed her needlepoint into a bag on the counter, and started organizing papers scattered in front of her.

"Is he in his room?" I asked.

"Well, yes, Dr. Lindmark. He's there every evening. Most every day, too."

I hadn't remembered how far Travis's room was down a long empty hallway. "Dr. Travis?" I said, arriving at one of the few rooms still leaking light into the corridor.

A form stirred on the bed. "Who's there?" a gravelly voice demanded.

"It's me. Dr. Lindmark."

"Lindmark? The intern?"

"Yes sir."

"What the hell are you doing here? Is someone sick? Am *I* sick?"

"No, no, Dr. Travis, everything's fine. Well, not fine, that's why I'm here."

"What the hell are you talking about? Why the hell are you in my room?"

I swallowed and tried to steady my voice. "I just came to visit."

The bed rustled and creaked as the old man struggled upright. He pulled a frayed robe tightly around his shoulders and fixed me with a sharp stare. "It's evening, Lindmark. Friday evening, I think. I have absolutely nothing to do during every day, and nobody visits. As soon as I have something important to occupy my time with, like sleeping, you decide to make a house call."

"I'm sorry, Dr. Travis, but I had to talk with you. I think you'll want to know what's gone on at the hospital."

"The only thing I want to know about that place is that I'm not in it. And you're just an unwelcome reminder of it. So you can just—"

"They almost killed Charlie, Dr. Travis," I said. "Did you know that?"

A long silence, finally broken by a husky tone. "Washington's dead?"

"Almost. He's close to brain-dead. Or at least that's what the tests show. I know he's not brain-dead, but he's still in a coma, still pretty bad. Morrow did it, Leland. Morrow and the rest of those things that are all around that place."

Travis just looked at me. It seemed as if the entire building had stopped to listen to my words. The quiet draped around us like a shroud.

"There's more, Leland. This is why I really had to see you. I talked to one of them. He stood–well, not stood. He just *was*. Not three feet away from me, and talked to me. I swear to God. It's happened a couple times. He helped me, Leland."

"It helped you?"

"Yeah, I think so. No, he did. He's not like Morrow. He doesn't hate, he doesn't want to hurt anyone. He didn't seem to want to hurt me, anyway."

"Stay away from all those things," Travis spat as he looked back and forth around the room. "Of course they all want to hurt us. They're dead, goddam it, and they want revenge. Stay away from them, Lindmark, I'm telling you. They ruined my life, they'll ruin you, or kill you. Should have expected Morrow would come for Charlie." His head dropped as he stared down at the dirty linoleum. "I'll never see old Washington again, thanks to Morrow. Just like I'll never see my son, thanks to Morrow when he was alive. Alive or dead, he's out for all of us, Lindmark. Goddam it."

I looked at this crazed, disheveled old man. "Look, Leland, I mean Dr. Travis. I'm here on Friday evening. I didn't go home to my wife, or collapse in my bed like I wanted. I came here to talk to you. I believe you. I just needed to hear someone say they believe *me*. And to tell you about Charlie."

"I had a son once, you know." No sign he'd heard me. I felt as if he had retreated into himself instead of talking to me. Should I tell him about Kevin? That the soul he'd warned me about was the son that probably occupied his every waking moment?

"Dr. Travis, I need—"

He straightened up in his bed, leaned forward, and gripped my arm with that same talon he'd used when I'd first met him. "Be careful, Lindmark," he muttered. "They've shown themselves to you. That's not good. Charlie's good as gone. *I'm* good as gone. They'll get you and everyone you love. Take a good look at me, Lindmark. Is this what you want to become?" He coughed and loudly spat a glob of something into a napkin.

I resisted the urge to run to the nearest sink and scrub my hands and arms raw. Instead, I pushed on. "You were right. They *are* trying to kill people in there. I've seen them. I can't do this anymore by myself. For all I know, they're coming after *me*. Your son warned me of that." My words were rushing by in a babble of nervousness, but I couldn't stop. "I just don't know—"

Travis' grip tightened. I looked down and saw his bony knuckles turning white.

"What did you just say?" he said. "What did you say about 'my son?'"

I'd been planning to tell him, but I'd wanted to prepare him first. Damn. "Your son, Kevin. I've seen him. I, I've talked to him." I told him everything I'd seen, everything his son's soul had told me. He bolted from the bed and pushed his face inches from mine. A faint scent of aftershave was overwhelmed by the sudden assault of foul breath and a pungent odor of urine.

"Stop now. Stop it! I don't know who put you up to this, or why. I thought you were better than the rest. You think I'm crazy, fine. Talk about me behind my back like I know everyone else does. But DO NOT dishonor my son." His voice had risen to an angry growl. "Now get out, damn you, before I throw you out."

I scrambled over to the door before turning back around to face him. "Leland, I—"

"Get OUT!"

I backed out the door into the hall as he stomped towards me. I had one last chance. "Leland. It must have been pretty hard, lifting both the Christmas tree and Kevin, especially in the snow. Lying on the grass just looking up at the sky was so much easier, right?"

He stopped in mid-stride and fixed me with an unwavering stare. It was not a look of fury, but of wonder and amazement. Seconds later, his features sagged with undisguised sadness. "How do you know that?" he whispered.

"His soul, um, his spirit, didn't die with him. He talks to me. A lot of them are caught in that place. They died the way they weren't supposed to. He's still here."

The old man looked at me in slack-jawed disbelief. "Kevin. . . Kevin. . . " he whispered. "How can it be, it can't. . . " He cleared his throat. "You're crazy. Like me. Now they've chosen you, Lindmark. Like they chose me all those years ago."

The distant clattering of rickety wheels echoed from somewhere deep in the building.

"I never should have told people what I was seeing," he continued. "Should've just kept trying to save as many of them as I could. But everyone started thinking Kevin's death had just pushed me over, that I couldn't handle things anymore. Hell, who does 'handle' a child's death?" The word 'handle' dripped with scorn. "They're doin' the same thing to you, ain't they, Lindmark? First killing your patients, then killing your reputation, then going after your sanity." His voice dropped. "All except my son. He can't be one of them."

"He's not, Leland," I assured him. "But there're others besides him. They've shown themselves to both of us. They've *chosen* us, like you said. We've both touched death, you and me. Our children. We're connected. That has to be it. *You*, I think they needed. *Me*," I gritted my teeth. "Me, I'm just a handy scapegoat for the bad things happening to people in there." My own words hit me. Morrow had needed Leland for his skill at resuscitating. Morrow still needed someone like that. Someone like that. . . I knew who it had to be. But why? Why was Martin Bethany helping the dead? A terrible, grotesque answer wormed its way into my thoughts.

"I don't know, Lindmark," Travis said slowly. "There are a lot of people who have been with their dying loved ones right before death. Hell, it happens all the time in a hospital. You know that. But I never heard anyone screaming about seeing dead people. Except us, Lindmark. There has to be more."

I couldn't argue. I just knew all that I had seen and experienced wasn't imagined. I wasn't here for metaphysical debate, so I pushed on. "Your son made it sound like it's still not safe. That's why I need your help. I need someone else who—"

"Forget it, Lindmark. I appreciate what you've told me. There's still a part of me thinks you're crazy enough to have hallucinated all of this, and another part of me that knows *I'm* crazy enough to believe it." A grim smile creased his stubbled cheeks. "But what you told me about Kevin, about talking with him, I'll think about that for a long time. And I won't give a damn if it's real or imagined."

"But—"

He cut me off. "That's why I need to go back to that hospital. I need to see my Kevin after all these years. I need to talk to him."

"They won't let you just walk out of here and visit the hospital, Leland."

"Of course they won't," he replied. "That's why I'm not going as a visitor. I'm going as a patient."

"But—"

"Do you have any idea how easy it is for nursing home patients to get transferred to a hospital? Hell, you get a cough, a fever, or a little low blood pressure, and you're in the ER before they can put a fresh pair of Depends on you."

A shudder ran through me at his plans. "Listen to me, Leland," I told him. "They're like vultures circling over dying animals. Waiting and planning for the next patient to die and get resuscitated. All these wrecks in here? Like that man Frazier? Those are the ones with new souls, but ruined bodies. But Morrow's gotten so much better."

"Goddam it, Lindmark, that's what I was telling you. But I thought he was only getting better at killing. Didn't know about all that other stuff. It's all evil, Lindmark. Evil."

The silence went on for several long moments before Travis shuffled back towards the bed, then collapsed onto it. "Look, Lindmark, they're driving you over the edge, ain't they? They haven't killed you. .

. yet. They're making you look crazy, like they did to me. Be careful, Lindmark. You better not tell anyone else."

"But—"

"Thanks for coming, Lindmark." I was dismissed. "I'm going back to my son. Don't interfere. Just let me have a little peace after all these years."

I sighed. The only person I'd counted on was lost in a past he'd never really left for decades. I couldn't do this alone. I was about to plead one more time when the clattering and squealing I'd heard before echoed outside the room. I poked my head out into the hallway. It was empty in both directions.

"Probably Frazier," Travis spoke up from behind me. "Sometimes he rattles around the halls until the nurses settle him down."

Fear seized me as I thought of the stooped-over wheezing gnome who'd accosted me when I'd come before. Frazier was one of *them*, those ruined failures of Morrow's early attempts to come back. Human guinea pigs for things beyond the grave. Of course they hated. Morrow had learned from those failures, learned to find better patients who could survive death, then resuscitation. Someone like Timmy, who was no more. Now a hate-filled Truman Faragon had escaped, thanks to Morrow.

I needed help.

Travis rolled over on the bed and huddled into a fetal position. "Go home, Lindmark," he said to the wall he was facing. "Don't come back here. Don't go back to that place."

It was the second time I'd been told to go home. This time from someone alive wishing he were dead. The other time from his son Kevin, someone dead acting very much alive. I shook my head. It was all too much.

I turned without another word and quickened my pace out of the Sylvester Morrow Convalescent Center, but couldn't outrun a sense of foreboding.

CHAPTER 20

The weekend had been too short. I had stayed in the house almost the entire time, reveling in the beauty of its quiet boring routine. I tried not to think about Travis, Kevin, Charlie or about the need to go back on Monday. Connie and I ate meals together each day, and talked. We didn't embrace, we didn't give in to pent-up lust despite the hours of private opportunity. We didn't go upstairs and visit The Room together. We just talked. I heard about the aquatic therapy sessions she managed in the pediatric wing of the hospital. She described each child's difficulties as if he or she was the only child she'd worked with that day. I'd watched her several times during her sessions. None of the other therapists seemed to hold, stretch, and cradle their clients like Connie did, as if they were her own.

It had been too long since we'd shared unhurried moments with each other. As I listened without interrupting, I realized how reversed our roles were at that moment. I'd been the one relating all the weird, troubling, exciting events of my life at work, away from her. Now at last *she* was revealing all that had kept her going through the loneliness and the grief. I swallowed down the sudden saltiness in the back of my throat and resolved that I would take time out and visit Connie more during her aquatic therapy sessions. It might mean facing the wrath of Bethany or Northrup, and even staying late to complete my intern to-do list. But at that moment either outcome seemed more tolerable than nursing the guilt that had grown like a tumor.

Our time together was ironically interrupted only by *her* need to go to the hospital instead of mine. Audrey was still hospitalized, still battling the infection that had settled into her lungs and was apparently getting the best of Audrey's weakened cough muscles. I made a note to visit Audrey as well, if my own parade of struggling adult patients would ever permit.

Which is why I drove in even earlier than I needed to when Monday arrived. I didn't know if I was paying honor to Audrey, or if I was paying honor to my wife and finally behaving like a husband instead of a boarder in my own house. I didn't care. I knew the burdens of my intern work day would swallow me up and never spit me out. I had to get a start on my mission of mercy before the workload ever started.

I'd never walked over to the pediatric wing. The trek was long and winding through hallways sparsely populated at that early hour. I finally reached the room and peered around the door. Denise was sitting on a chair at her daughter's bedside. She was bent over at the waist, her head resting on the bed. A hand clutched one of Audrey's. I crept into the room quietly, and saw Denise was sleeping, her hair spilling over onto the sheets.

As I crept into the room, a cough erupted as Audrey's breath wheezed in and out. The little girl herself stared serenely at the TV screen in rapt attention. I realized at once what drew me to her, and I smiled. Audrey didn't work to triumph over her condition. It never occurred to her to rise above her limitations. Her limitations didn't occur to her, *period*. Instead, she enjoyed the thrill of a new dirty word, being first in line at the new movie release, or waking up to an unexpected TV rerun.

"Dr. Lindmark!" Her words broke into my thoughts. "What are you doing here?"

"Just wanted to see how you were doing, Audrey. But I don't want you to talk, okay?"

"Guess what's on TV, Dr. Lindmark?" she asked. Her voice was more slurred than usual, but maybe it was the oxygen mask over her face. She didn't wait for an answer. "I can't believe they have movie channels in here. My mom won't let me have it at home. They're showing 'We're The Millers.' Have you seen the part—" Wracking coughs cut off the rest of her sentence. She worked to take in more breaths, then considered me with clear, earnest eyes. "Hey Dr. Lindmark, will you swear not to tell my mom what I'm watching? She thinks it's inappropriate."

I smiled. "Your secret's safe with me, Audrey," I promised. "But only if I get to watch it with you sometime." Her crooked smile was answer enough. I wanted to leave remembering that smile instead of her struggles to breathe. "Gotta go, Audrey," I added in a whisper. "I'm not allowed to watch these kinds of movies." She smiled again. "Make sure you tell your mother I came by." She waved and went back to watching the screen. The wheezing had quieted.

I couldn't get Audrey out of my mind. I thought of the IVs running into her, the oxygen mask, the jungle of devices. Everything meant to save a *child*, but not a *childhood*. Leland's warnings lurched into my head. Morrow may not want such a disabled body for escape, but that ghoul could still satisfy his hatred of me by killing that little girl. Maybe. Hell, why was I trying to fasten logic and reason onto things beyond death? I couldn't take the chance.

I hurried towards the nursing station and asked for Audrey's chart. "I'm both a family friend and a doctor here," I explained. "I just had a talk with Mom. She feels like her daughter's been through enough, and Audrey is actually mature enough to agree. She does not want her daughter to suffer on life support if she gets worse. Obviously, everything should be done up to that point. Poor little girl. Can't say that I disagree. I'm going to go ahead and write it in the chart. Her poor mom, Denise, just wanted to stay at her bedside."

"I guess. . . sure, Doctor," the nurse stammered. "That must have been so hard for them." I agreed with a token nod while writing my note in the chart. I couldn't, of course, write the actual Do Not Resuscitate order, but I could make sure that anyone, living or not living, would know that Audrey was not to be resuscitated if anything happened. Which meant she would never be regarded as prey, as an escape for those denied peace after their own deaths.

"Well, I wrote a note detailing our discussion," I announced to the nurse as I snapped Audrey's chart closed. "I'd appreciate it if you could put the appropriate sticker on the chart, just so everyone will know until the attending physician can write the order."

"Thank you for telling us, Doctor," the nurse replied.

I couldn't get over how simple that had been.

I walked back towards the adult hospital, immensely relieved. I'd been able to do something good, something positive, for Audrey and Denise. The dead boy had told me they wouldn't kill the ones who insisted on dying with dignity, without resuscitation. Audrey was safe, at least from the evil around her. But her breathing. If only she could conquer her cough and the pneumonia as easily.

The only thing worse than starting another week faced with a mountain of work, was looking forward to being on call the night *after* slogging through that mountain of work. The more I progressed through my internship year, the more I considered myself a modern-day Sisyphus. I inspected labs, performed procedures, took in discussions, admitted new patients, discharged others, only to find the same amount of work waiting for me the following day. I couldn't suppress a rueful smile at what was becoming increasingly obvious: the entire hospital had become a Darwinian struggle of survival for both interns and patients alike. Physical survival for the patients, emotional survival for interns. And always lingering in the background, things unseen trying to thin the herd of both groups.

A doctor at the end of the crowded hallway caught my eye. He was standing alone, moving slowly away from me. He wasn't jostled. He didn't sidestep or move to avoid anyone. His white coat barely moved even as his pace quickened. I watched this strange doctor until he stopped and turned around slowly, as if standing on a turning pedestal.

From the distance, his eyes bore into mine. A goatee framed thin lips that twisted into a snarl. I couldn't tear my eyes away. His entire face melted into a sneer that terrified me. Then he turned around again and walked away. I watched, frozen in place amidst the hallway bustle, as that white-coated form blended in with everyone else and faded from view.

I had been looking into death. I had been looking into the same eyes that had glared out at me at Timmy's disaster. Morrow's unearthly eyes. I whirled back and forth. Nurses were discussing patient charts, a receptionist was talking on the phone, no one was dying or running or even looking frightened. I peered down the hallway again. He was gone. But it had been Morrow. As I stood frozen, the hallway filled with staring apparitions. Patients. *Dead* patients. Open wounds, electrode marks, tubes from every gaping orifice. A rustling, whispering murmur closed in on me.

I couldn't move. Kevin's words ". . .something's not right. . ." echoed in my mind. Terror broke my paralysis and I stumbled through the halls into the intern call room and collapsed in the chair, shivering uncontrollably. I popped open a small bottle with shaking hands and dry-swallowed a Xanax, resolving that I would never leave the refuge of the room.

My phone sounded several times as I hid from the dead. I was able to dispatch those requests over the phone, but I knew that eventually I would need to emerge and actually take care of patients. I cowered behind the locked call room door, no better than a child hiding from the monster in the closet by burrowing under his covers.

I jerked awake and looked around the call room. How long had I been asleep? I glanced at my watch. Only 20 minutes had gone by, but I still felt guilty. Giving in to Xanax-induced sleep in the middle of the day was not only stupid, but was probably grounds for dismissal if I'd been discovered. I looked around again. The computer was off, the room still offering its quiet, undisturbed sanctuary. So what had awakened me? The wail of the code horn answered through the closed door, at the same time as I felt my phone's vibration. I looked down at the texted message.

CODE BLUE
ROOM 420

I looked fearfully at the door. That code horn wasn't just signaling that death was coming for some poor patient. I had known more death would be coming as soon as I had seen that awful specter in the halls. That siren was the scream from Morrow that all could hear, but that only I could understand. It was a cry of rage and revenge from beyond the grave. I was not going out there.

CODE BLUE
ROOM 420

The vibration would not stop. I slammed my fists on the desk, jumped out of the chair, and pounded my fear and frustration against the door before hurling it open and walking into the corridor.

The code horn sounded again. 420 was two floors up. I climbed two stairs at a time until emerging onto the fourth floor, where ordered chaos reigned. Therapists and nurses were running towards a room with a flashing red light over the door. A red crash cart stood outside the door. I ran with the others but stopped short when I saw something past the crash cart. Other nurses were running from that direction, but something stood out in their midst. Something that wasn't moving at all. I squinted and saw Kevin. He stood, or hovered, and locked his filmy orbs onto my eyes. He lifted one thin arm and beckoned for me to come. That eerie lonely vision then turned and drifted into a different patient room past 420.

"Dr. Lindmark! Dr. Bethany's already there. He's been calling you. Where the hell you been?" The sweating respiratory therapist didn't wait for an answer. He rushed by me and joined everyone else rushing into room 420. I threw one more glance down the hallway. The boy wasn't there. My one thought was that only a dead soul could offer protection against other dead souls. Kevin hadn't hurt me before, and he wanted me now. Without any more thought, I hurried past 420 towards the room Kevin had entered.

A young nurse almost ran into me on her way to the code. "I need you to come with me, um," I looked down at her name tag. "Christie. I need your help."

"But Doctor, this is the patient who's coding. The other one can wait, don't you think?" She didn't look old enough to be a babysitter, much less a nurse.

"Look, I don't have time to argue," I hissed. Surprise replaced her expression of uncertainty. "The other patient's, well, he's almost coding too."

"How do you know that?" She peered in the direction I'd been heading. "There's no code light, no message, no one—"

This was taking too long. "Another intern called me. His patient in room. . . " I looked down at the room Kevin had entered. "Room 458. He saw an abnormal rhythm on a monitor, but he's tied up with someone else. Now come on." I became more and more certain that something in room 458 was not right. I pulled on her arm as I rushed past the crash cart and the commotion of 420.

Christie glanced back over my shoulder at the frenzy of nurses and therapists, pulling back on my grip. "Okay, Dr. Lindmark, but I could get in a lot of trouble if—"

"Yeah, me too," I muttered as I pulled her along behind me.

"Lindmark? Lindmark! Where the hell are you going? The code's in here." Bethany's voice erupted from the room and chased us down the hall. He must have seen me through the crowd outside the door. "Where the hell's he going?" A pause, then, "I've got V fib here. Charge the paddles to 200 joules. Get ready to intubate." Bethany's voice faded among a rising babble of other voices.

I continued my grim advance towards the other room. If we arrived and found a peaceful sleeping patient, life as I knew it would be officially over. I'd deserted a coding patient in front of everyone. I'd ignored my senior resident's orders.

I shook my head and pushed open the door of 458. *A man lay peacefully on the bed.* He looked somehow familiar. I stared for a moment longer, then it came to me: the man with the spots in his lungs, who'd had the air leak after the biopsy. Frank's patient. . . Tobin, that was his name. I'd barely given him a second thought since rounds. Very straightforward, easy, not a good Teaching Case. He was supposed to go to surgery, because the air leak had never healed.

"He's not wearing any monitor at all, Dr. Lindmark," Christie said as she walked in behind me. "How could someone see any 'abnormal rhythm?'"

The sinking feeling in my chest grew into a stone. "Mr. Tobin?" I whispered, leaning over his sleeping form. He didn't stir. I gently shook a shoulder. "Mr. Tobin?" I repeated more loudly. "Are you okay?"

"He's sleeping, Dr. Lindmark. I would say that means he's okay," Christie said. "We need to go back *now*."

I shook Tobin harder. His mouth opened, and he drew in a strangled, wheezing breath. "Mr. Tobin," I persisted, trying to breathe against the pounding in my chest. His head lolled to one side. I spidered my fingertips over the side of his neck, searching for a pulse but feeling no reassuring throb of life. I threw off his covers and felt for a pulse over the large femoral artery in his groin. Still nothing.

"Christie, he's got no pulses," I snapped. "Call for help, quick!" She reached for the phone while I stood over the young man, frozen. I *was* the help, suddenly in charge of a young man close to dying right in front of me. Something in this room was different than it had been on rounds. Think, think, THINK! I screamed to myself. No pulses. Jesus, not even a sound in this room that someone was dying in. CPR, ventilation, all the actions that had been drilled into us during that class jittered through my mind.

"Christie, start compressions." It sounded more like a suggestion than a command. Christie kept talking on the phone. I was just about to start pumping on Tobin's chest when it struck me. *No sound.* I looked at the plastic contraption at the foot of the bed. The one that had been vibrating with all the bubbles when we had been on rounds. That's what was so different. The room was deathly quiet. Every morning on rounds, that contraption had been bubbling and vibrating like a burst pipe. All the air that had been escaping before, wasn't escaping now. Why? WHY? I searched around the device and followed one coiled stretch of tubing until I saw it disappear under the bed. I lifted the sheets covering it. The tubing was kinked under one of the bed's wheels. I tried rolling it off, but someone had locked the wheels. The pedal locking the wheel in its death grip wouldn't budge.

I straightened up, snatched the phone out of Christie's hands, and threw it onto the floor. "Help me push the bed off the tubing," I snapped.

"But—"

"Now!"

She hurried to the bed and together we pushed. I looked down at the unmoving young patient lying motionless. Terror at the thought that he might already be dead erupted sweat that stung my eyes. That thought hit me like a hammer. *Already dead.* I stopped pushing and pulled Christie from the bed.

"*Doctor*, what the hell are you doing? I was only doing what you told me to do."

"I have to check on him first, Christie," I muttered. "Stay away from the bed."

"But you said. . ."

Her words faded behind the rush of adrenaline that pushed me to the head of the bed. I looked around the room in all directions and saw nothing except Christie cowering against a wall. The code siren from the other code still pulsed into the room. I lifted Tobin's eyelids. His eyes were glazed and unfocused but his pupils responded immediately to the light flooding in. I saw no fury, no swirling hatred. Was I too late, or too early? Was this now Morrow, or was this body in front of me still unclaimed? Was I helping Morrow to escape?

I hurled myself against the bed with renewed effort. "Christie, help me," I grunted.

She rushed over and pushed with me. The bed squealed several feet across the floor, releasing the trapped tubing. It jumped and twisted as pent-up air exploded into it, boiled down its length, and erupted into the suction contraption. Under the sound of the bubbling, I thought I heard a faint eerie wail, or screech. Christie and I stared at each other, wide-eyed. What had we done? I stood still a moment longer, then reached with shaking hands to search for a pulse. Of course, I felt nothing. He'd died while I had wasted precious time worrying about things already dead instead of trying to prevent someone from joining them. Rage at my own stupidity overtook me. I deserved the shame and desertion I had coming. How many more patients would I—

A faint beat lifted my fingertips, then another. As I pressed deeper on to the man's neck, the pulses started coming faster, and stronger, until I could easily feel a steady throb of heartbeats. "Christie, do you. . . "

"I feel it too, Dr. Lindmark. He's got a good strong pulse back," she said excitedly.

"Try and measure a blood pressure." As I hovered over the bed, Tobin moaned and rolled slightly to one side. "Roland?" He moaned again and fluttered his eyelids open.

Bethany burst into the room, followed by a crowd of nurses and therapists. "What the hell are you doing in here?" he shouted. "That's it, Lindmark. You run away from a code? What the hell were you thinking?"

"Dr. Bethany, I—"

"Once again you've almost cost a patient his life, Lindmark. I want you out of here. Now."

"Look, I—"

"Dr. Bethany?" Christie interrupted. Bethany glared at her. His features had gone combustible. "Dr. Lindmark, he knew the patient was in trouble. When we got here, he didn't have a blood pressure or pulse, and he wouldn't respond. There'd been no warning at all. That's why he left the other room."

The flush in Bethany's pudgy face faded several degrees. "What do you mean? No one told me about any other emergency."

"It just now happened, Doctor. While you were coding that other patient. We found this patient unresponsive but Dr. Lindmark figured it out. His chest tube had gotten blocked. He—"

"I think he almost died of a tension pneumothorax," I said.

"We just moved the bed off the tube, and all the air came out." Christie walked over to the bed and joined several of the other nurses attending to Tobin. "He's doing much better now, Dr. Lindmark. His pressure is stable." She'd reported that update to me, not Bethany.

"You really left to take care of him?" Bethany asked, each word still bitten off. "How the hell did you know? And how did you think of looking under the bed to see if the tube was blocked?" His eyes narrowed. "Unless you put it like that in the first place." I saw Christie's head jerk up. She backed several steps away from me. Shit. Bethany had turned the tables on me. As usual, I was playing checkers with Bethany playing chess.

And my only response? *A lost boy no longer on this earth told me about it. Then he vanished, Dr. Bethany.* Right.

"I thought I heard, um, heard him struggling to breathe, so I rushed down here. I'm sorry I had to leave you. How did he do?"

"That other patient? He died. I think it was merciful, given what his quality of life had become. He should have been a No Code." Bethany looked over at Roland Tobin, who was starting to sit up. "Make sure that tubing is secured this time," he said to Christie, then turned to me. "I'll write up the other code." His suspicious squint bore into me. "Go back to bed, at least until something else happens. It usually does, when we're on call."

I stared back into his eyes, almost buried under the furrowed red brows and angry frown of his indignant expression. Who, or what, was behind that anger? I felt under siege by the souls yearning to return from beyond the grave, but refused to voice what I knew. Instead, I turned away and focused on the patient still sitting up groggily. I'd saved a life and prevented one of the hungry dead from claiming that life for its own. I was sure of it. Tobin would have died a very reversible death. Wouldn't even have needed much of a resuscitation. Just unplugging that tube and allowing air out and oxygen in. Bethany would have known immediately.

That realization struck me like a slap. I looked down at the bed, at the wheel that had been locked. The dead might invade the physical world to push keystrokes, but never move a heavy bed. That would take a human. Of course Bethany would have come in and saved the day. Because he must have moved the bed in the first place. Morrow was a genius. Bethany was a genius. It had been Morrow who had screeched away. As I trudged back to the call room, something nagged at me. Many things nagged at me, not the least of which was the certainty that Martin Bethany was in lockstep with the dead. But one other thing, *something*, was just wrong.

I had no time to ponder it further. The drama and heroics of Tobin's code quickly succumbed to the mind-numbing routine of a call night. Requests to deal with shortness of breath, the heartbreak of midnight constipation, the desperation of insomnia, all demanded my attention for the next several hours. As the night turned endless, I resolved to myself that in the morning I would leave this internship and never return to the living under threat of death and from the dead trying to live.

The calls finally stopped. I trudged towards the call room, hoping for at least an hour of uninterrupted sleep, when my phone vibrated at the same time the code siren again blared overhead. I gritted my teeth against the noise and looked at the text.

CODE BLUE

ROOM 143

Not 420 or 428. All I wanted to do was rest. Actually, I wanted to leave this house of horrors and just share a comforting embrace with Connie. But I was, of course, still imprisoned by my night on call. I scrolled through the list of patients under my care. None of the red-flagged patients of my fellow interns were in Room 143. I looked over my own list. None of my patients were listed in 143.

My mouth went dry, and I felt lightheaded when I saw it. Way down on the list, because there hadn't been any active problems in Room 143. No problems at all, in fact, except to finish up the discharge home. I raced the remaining distance into Room 143.

A shocking déjà vu greeted me when I skidded into the room. Nurses, therapists, several other residents were surrounding the bed or ferrying IV bags, syringes, tubing, and catheters. An uncomfortable blast of *hot* air hit me, not the frigid blast I'd dreaded. I noted with horror that people who had been working over the bed came away with bloody gloves and crimson-dotted gowns. Words jittered around and around in my head in anguished desperation. *Please not Mr. Shirkey, please not Mr. Shirkey. . .*

I elbowed my way through the crush of people sardined into the small room, almost choking on my panic.

"Dr. Lindmark!" a voice spoke from behind me.

I recognized the nurse who had helped me with the Tobin woman's incident. "Christie! What's going on here?"

"It's Aaron! Aaron Shirkey! Nancy found him about 15 minutes ago. His blood pressure kept dropping, then he, well, I just don't know what's going on. We've been coding him ever since."

I turned back around and shouldered my way to the bed. What I saw made me wish I hadn't.

Aaron Shirkey's large form lay on a bed of red-soaked sheets. His fleshy folds quivered under the force of chest compressions from the burly nurse heaving up and down over him. My eyes were drawn to his belly. All the sutures were gone. The edges of the massive incision had come apart, allowing the wound to gape open. It must have separated the entire way through, because the gash had filled with blood and with what looked like intestines. Each heavy compression on his chest resulted in a small eruption of blood and coiling bloated abdominal contents. As I stood and watched, the slippery mess overflowed the edges of the incision and started sliding down Shirkey's belly.

A strident voice I'd never heard before drew my attention from the awful sight before me. "Open up the fluids wide, and let me know how many IV sites we have. Any pulses with compressions? And will someone turn the damn heat down in here?" A surgical resident had arrived before me. Sweat dotted her forehead and ran in rivers down her face. Her blue scrubs were blotched with dampness. The temperature in the room was literally stifling. Why the hell was it so hot?

"Everyone, make sure you're wearing gloves and face shields," she commanded. As if to underscore the point, a spray of blood spattered up at the people around the bed. "Will someone try to wrap those abdominal contents in sterile gauze? And have the lab type and cross him for two units of packed red blood cells stat. You! Nancy! Call the OR desk. Get someone here ASAP. And someone call his wife."

I watched as nurses, respiratory therapists, and technicians danced around the bed in frenzied attempts to head off Aaron Shirkey's death. The surgical resident stood at the monitor, her face set in grim determination. The chaos that had become all too familiar suddenly became unfamiliar in one important respect. Bethany. Where the hell was Bethany?

"What can I do to help?" I asked.

"Hold compressions," she commanded the turmoil around the bed instead of answering me. "Any pulses?"

Several nurses shook their heads or murmured denials.

"Goddam it." She turned to me. "Medical resident?" I nodded, feeling uneasy with a battlefield promotion from intern to resident. "I shouldn't have to be doing this," she continued. "Our part was done. He was healing. I do incisions, not Code Blues." She looked at the crowd around the bed. "Resume compressions. I want the fluids opened wide. Give him an amp of epinephrine now. And you, bag him a little faster. He's probably acidotic."

Nurses pounded on Shirkey's chest, dislodging more blood from the gaping belly wound. The respiratory therapist was squeezing oxygen as fast as possible through the endotracheal tube. All I saw, though, was Shirkey's distended ruined belly.

The surgeon allowed several more interminable minutes of organized frenzy then barked, "Hold compressions again and check for pulses. Has he gotten an amp of bicarb yet? Yes? No? Give him two amps now."

"No carotid pulse," one of the nurses announced, her probing fingers pressed into Shirkey's thick neck.

"No femoral pulse," another one said, her tone as detached as if she were simply announcing the time.

Where was Bethany? He had been at Tobin's code hours before. Hell, he somehow made it to *all* fucking codes, almost ahead of time. I couldn't tear my eyes from Aaron Shirkey's belly. Distended puffy loops of bloated intestines poked up out of the wrapping. The room was still stifling. Had the sutures been removed too early? I hadn't done it, thank God. It must have been a surgical resident. But hadn't Shirkey been sutured up the last time we'd rounded on him? His belly had felt fine. We'd inspected those sutures, right?

The surgical resident looked down at the monitor. "He has no rhythm. No pulses, no cardiac activity, most of his intestines are on the floor instead of in his abdomen. He's been recuperating from horrendous illness for weeks, he's a diabetic. Of course he wouldn't heal well. It's hopeless." She looked around the room, her eyes above the facemask darting from one person to Shirkey to another person until she'd circled the room. "I'm calling it, unless anyone has any objections." Each person around the bed remained frozen. I heard the surgical resident sigh, then snap off each of her gloves. "That's it. Time of death 3:30 a.m."

One day away from Aaron-ara the Marinara Man finally going home. One damn day away.

A woman's choking voice caught my attention. A nurse, still sobbing and sniffing, was talking to another nurse. "He rang for me around midnight. Said he was hot and that he was bloated and cramping. I walked in, and almost passed out from the heat. The thermostat was turned up off the scale. I should have known he was a little confused. Anyway, I gave him some pain medicine for the cramps." Her voice trembled. "He called again an hour later. I remember saying that for someone going home in the morning, he sure was complaining a lot. I walked in, and he must have turned the heat up again. He was holding his stomach and moaning, then he looked at me. I'll never forget it. His eyes were bulging wide open. 'They're cutting on me. . .' he said. Poor man. I've seen medications do that to patients, but they've usually been older. He must have thought his belly pain was someone operating again. I tried calming him down and offered him more pain medicine. Stupid, stupid, stupid! I should have called the intern."

I hung on each word.

"He kept asking me not to leave. I felt so bad for him. The poor man just needed to get home. I gave him a shot to relax him, and he finally quieted down. I just wanted him more comfortable."

She started weeping again. The other nurse put an arm around her shoulders and eased her out of the room. She really *should* have called someone. Thank God I hadn't been there. I felt sorry for Nancy. Unlike with residents and attending doctors, people were much less forgiving when nurses made a mistake. She wouldn't get the second chances I'd received.

The more I thought about what Nancy had said, the more it chilled me. Those sutures had been in. I remembered how they'd felt as I'd examined him on rounds the day before. Had he watched as those sutures somehow unraveled? What had Shirkey seen during those moments?

I was about to surrender to the urge to vomit when the temperature around me dropped. It was a welcome relief until it became uncomfortably cold. Very cold. Frigid wind swirled in around me, then breezed away.

A ghastly shriek penetrated the room, rising and falling as if that cold swirling wind had come to life with a sound of its own. The very air in the room seemed to vibrate. The sound was coming from everywhere, rumbling up from Shirkey's gaping mouth, from the floor, from the walls. It rose in volume and pitch until it became a scream, a silent scream, boring into my head. I covered my ears and looked around the room. No one else seemed to hear anything. They were all just staring down at Shirkey's still form. The shriek cut off suddenly, leaving the entire room silent. The monitor had stopped beeping long ago.

The mass of intestines, shaken loose from the gauze wrap, oozed down Shirkey's naked belly, slid over onto the bed and plopped onto the floor. I finally vomited into the trash can.

Morrow was raging. I quaked in the dark of the call room, collecting my thoughts, trying to keep my hands from shaking. The calls had finally slowed, but the rest of the call night still loomed. I'd managed to make it back to a call room that offered no refuge. Images battered my brain and prevented even the briefest of dozing. Tobin's dead eyes looking up at me as his chest filled with trapped air. Morrow had been there, hungering for that body to release its soul, its owner. I'd stopped it, relieving the tube obstruction just before Tobin's body had surrendered to death, and to the dead.

I glanced around the empty room. "Kevin?" Of course there was no answer. I pounded my fist against the desk. Might as well go to the hospital chapel and call out to God for help. Or, I considered wryly, do what the average emotionally stable human being would do and go to a superior for help. Like Bethany.

Right. His Bearded Majesty would know just what to do. Report me for the final time and make sure I would take my visions and ghosts and body-snatching souls out the door as fast as the elderly security guards could escort me. I ground my hands against my eyes but couldn't quash the memories. Shirkey. Poor Aaron Shirkey. Somehow disemboweled by the dead. I knew that heat hadn't been turned up by Shirkey. Nothing in this place happened by accident. I'd been thinking about the whole scene since leaving my dinner in the trash can. The heat in that room must have expanded the air in his intestines, making sure they pushed out through that wound.

What did that surgical resident say? "With diabetes, of course he wouldn't heal well." Those bloated coils of intestines, pushing up through sutures weakened from obesity and diabetes. Maybe by scissors? It was diabolical. Only someone, or *something*, with medical knowledge would have known how that would happen. Like Morrow. And where had Bethany been prior to that code? Where had he been *during* Shirkey's failed resuscitation? Why hadn't he been there? Almost as if he had just let it happen. No, I considered, it hadn't been a failed resuscitation. This one had been a murder.

I couldn't stop shivering. Morrow had been behind Tobin. Another way to kill but leave resuscitation easy, he'd still failed over and over to achieve his own escape because of me. Now he was exacting his revenge. It was all happening as it had years earlier with Leland. Morrow had rampaged then, killing without reason, killing to release his rage. He'd hated Travis then, he hated me now. Aaron Shirkey was only the first. I looked at the door, half-expecting it to come crashing open, revealing a scowling cowled vision of Death holding a scythe.

The young ones. The babies and the children.

I looked around to see who had whispered those words. The room was empty, silent. Those words had been my own, released with little control as a terrible fear pierced me. *The young ones.* Audrey was still in the hospital. Morrow wouldn't *kill* me, he'd make me suffer by killing people I cared about. He'd already started making me pay. Morrow didn't want Audrey's little twisted body for his own. He would simply kill her.

A realization even more sickening seized me. I'd written that order in Audrey's chart, the No Code Blue order, to make sure she would never be used by those things to escape. But that ghoul wouldn't kill to resuscitate, he'd use her as revenge on me. Now I'd *God in Heaven* made sure she wouldn't be resuscitated when he came for her, making

Audrey's "accidental" death so much easier. What the hell had I done? I'd tried to outsmart the dead and had failed.

The rest of the call night could look out for itself.

I was breathless when I arrived on Audrey's floor in the pediatric wing. Running towards Audrey's room I was surrounded by a crush of hospital workers and pushed down the hall as if carried on a current of frenzied doctors, nurses, and therapists. All heading to the room I'd been desperate to reach.

I squeezed with everyone else into Audrey's room and forced my way to the front. A small form lay on top of disheveled sheets, the face covered by a large plastic mask pressed down tightly by a pediatric resident. The furry Teddy bear dangling from his stethoscope made a mockery of the tragedy on the bed. Gloved hands searched for some thread of a pulse or a glimmer of response. They pushed the small gown up rudely, and my worst fears were realized. It was a girl. A girl with thin wasted legs. I couldn't keep a moan from escaping. *Morrow had won.*

"This has got to end soon," the resident muttered as he continued to pump air into Audrey's lungs. He glanced over at a nurse who was hovering by the bed. "You say she suddenly spiked a temp last night, and became less responsive?"

The nurse nodded, eyes wide open and jaws clamped shut in obvious terror. The resident raised his eyebrows at a young Asian woman wearing surgical scrubs under an immaculate sharply-creased white coat. "She's gotta be septic, Dr. Tung," he stated. His authoritative tone couldn't disguise tight anxiety. "It was a matter of time, you know," he continued. "She was a mess from the beginning. With her disease, an overwhelming infection was always just around the corner."

The resignation in his voice infuriated me. "She is a full code, you know," I blurted. "That order wasn't meant for her. Her mother wants everything done."

He glared at me. "I know that. Her mother was very firm about that."

Then do something more than just talk about her, I wanted to scream.

"And her mother will know that we worked on her. But I am not going to let this little girl linger on life support, only to die of leukemia anyway." He turned to the crowd around the bed. "Make sure the fluids are opened wide. Still a sinus rhythm?"

One of the other nurses nodded. A burly man with a plastic shield over his face looked at the resident managing the resuscitation. "Gonna intubate her, Doctor?"

I barely heard, concentrating instead on the resident's words. Leukemia? Didn't he even know his own patients? Audrey didn't have leukemia. I peered more closely at the little girl's head and noticed for the first time the thin wisps of dark hairs that covered the pillow. Each time the back of her head rubbed against the pillow, it loosened a few more tufts.

I grabbed the arm of the nurse who was watching the monitor. "Where's the girl who was in this bed? Audrey. Cerebral palsy, pneumonia? Audrey Schlager? Where is she?"

She looked at me with a shocked expression. "Don't snap at me, Doctor," she answered in a severe tone. "We're all a little stressed here. In fact—"

"Where. Is. She?"

Her lips pouted together as if she were about to erupt when the resident's voice cut through the turmoil. "Marge, where's Tricia's mother? I need to talk to her mother. Where is she?" His voice took on an almost desperate tone.

I must have been nose-to-nose with "Marge," because the imposing nurse in front of me turned at his words. "I'll go find her, Doctor," she answered, then looked back at me. "We moved that girl one room down. She had pneumonia, and this little girl couldn't be exposed to anyone with any sort of infection. Exactly who—"

I raced out of the room and veered into the next open door. Audrey lay in the bed. A large oxygen mask was covering her face loosely. The twisted legs and contorted upper body were unmistakable. A chair had been pulled up to the side of the bed and still had Denise's cashmere sweater draped over the back. Relief eased the pounding in my chest. "Audrey?" I asked. The little girl didn't awaken. "Audrey? Where'd your mom go?"

She didn't answer or even look at me. I looked down at her more closely. Her sunken chest was barely moving, and her swollen lips had a bluish tinge. Her face had *changed*, no longer looking so gaunt and thin. Her eyes were almost swollen shut. I shook her shoulder, first gently, then more vigorously. "Audrey, wake up now," I commanded. A strangled wheeze erupted from her throat, a horrible sound of air leaking out through a pinhole.

"Is everything okay?" I looked behind me. A pediatric nurse had followed me into the room. My first thought was to slap the Teddy Bear off her stethoscope. "I'm not sure," I answered. "Audrey!" Her eyes stayed closed. "Jesus Christ," I muttered, fumbling with the tubing, the covers, anything that came within reach of my hands. Ugly red blotches patterned her arms and chest. I looked over at the only other living person witnessing this horror. "You. Listen to me. She's not breathing. Damn. Damn! Get me an ambu bag. Get help."

The nurse stepped up to the bed beside me. "They're all busy. Next door, with the little girl who's coding in there. This little girl, I think she's a No Code. I think that's what was signed out to me—"

"She's *not* a goddam No Code. She's a child. I don't care what the chart said." I looked around the room, not exactly sure what I was looking for. I leaned back over Audrey, my head pounding in rhythm to my pulse as my heart threatened to explode. "Audrey?" Her head lolled to one side, her face was more swollen than it had been moments before. She puffed out useless small breaths between lips resembling small balloons. I'd never seen it but the words from the Advanced Life Support Class we'd all taken pushed their way into the frenzy of thoughts racing in my head.

"Nurse. Whatever your name is. She's. . . it's an acute allergic reaction. Gotta be it. Look at her. Swelling, rash, she's in anaphylactic shock. Is she allergic to anything?" I looked up at the IV bag dripping her antibiotic into a vein. The label read 'Zosyn.' A powerful antibiotic used for severe infections, related to penicillin.

She scurried over to the room's computer. I waited an agonizing several seconds before she looked up, eyes wide. "Nothing, Doctor. No allergies." I shook my head in frustration. The flesh-and-blood nightmare before me with her red raised rashes and swelling screamed out a silent message more believable than any sterile computerized response. "Garbage in, garbage out," I snapped. "Maybe no one ever bothered to even ask about allergies. Whatever." I pressed on Audrey's thin neck and felt a rapid thready pulse. A list of medications, treatments, and labs broke through the cloud of panic and flooded my thoughts. "I need epinephrine and one hundred milligrams of hydrocortisone. Add fifty milligrams of Benadryl. Hell, bring in the whole damn crash cart. Now. Please, now!"

"Right away, Doctor." As she scurried out of the room, I leaned over Audrey again. She looked *dead*. Oh God. . . I cradled her head. "Audrey, wake up. Please, hang on, Audrey." I needed to think. I had to *think*.

I reached up and turned off the intravenous drip, then hurried over to the wall and turned up the oxygen as high as it would go. Turning back to the bed, Audrey's eyes stared glassily, unseeing, back at me. The certainty of the little girl's death hit me like a physical slap. "Hey! Help in here!" I called out. Where was that nurse? Where was anybody? "I need an ambu bag now. *Now!*"

I collapsed onto a chair in a corner of the pediatric wing's waiting room, weighed down by the horrors of the last twenty-four hours. I'd seen four codes with two children, all in one horrible night. Morrow was going to keep rampaging until everybody I cared about was dead. I did nothing to stop the tears from overflowing down my cheeks.

"Harry, is that you?" Denise walked towards me. Her eyes were red, her face was swollen and blotchy.

"Denise, I. . . " What words could possibly sound right? She kept on walking and threw her arms around me. I embraced her awkwardly and absorbed her sobs, wiping at my own tears at the same time.

After what seemed like an eternity she broke away and wiped a hand across her eyes. "Harry, I'd only left for two minutes to go to the bathroom. I'd been right beside her, the whole time. Our nurse came in, hung Audrey's antibiotics, told me to take a break so I did." Her words babbled out faster and faster until they tripped over themselves and ran into a wall of choking sobs. "Two goddam minutes, Harry, that was all."

I didn't know what to say, so I embraced her again. "They told me what you did, Harry. Said you just showed up." Her lip trembled. She pulled away and looked at me. Her eyes were red, swollen, and angry. "Of *course* she was allergic to penicillin, Harry. *Deathly* allergic." She stared at me, bloodshot eyes raccooned with smeared mascara. "That was the first thing I told the nurse, because I knew she'd need antibiotics. I watched her type that in. The nursing supervisor looked into it. The electronic medical records show 'No Allergies.' Gone, Harry. One simple instruction erased, or whatever, and my Audrey almost died. 'Computer error,' I was told. Computer error? *My daughter is not a goddam error*. Everyone around here is up in arms over this. They sure as hell *better* be up in arms." She sank against me, still shaking.

The longer I held her and tried to comfort her, the more guilty I felt. It was all my fault. The dead were raging through the living. Even worse, I'd been complicit. No one had been watching Audrey closely, because she'd been a No Code, *thanks to me*. I hadn't deleted that penicillin allergy warning, but I didn't deserve to be the one providing comfort. "Denise, I've got to go. I'll have Connie stay with you." I pried myself out of her grasp and offered a reassuring last squeeze on her arm, but couldn't look her in the eye.

Plodding back to the adult hospital, I wondered when Morrow was going to wreak more horror. I felt physically sick as I thought of what little Audrey had gone through, and of how I'd failed her. She'd deserved better. Could I ever forgive myself for that?

CHAPTER 21

As if I hadn't already been through enough, now this. "I'm glad you called me," I glanced at the nurse's name tag. "Valerie. I'll take care of this. You can go on and take care of your other patients. Just close the door behind you."

Valerie crossed her arms and glared at me. "This isn't my patient. One of the younger nurses got scared and called me. I only called you because your name came up a few times in all his babbling. Now I *will* call security unless you get some control. I will not have my floor disrupted like this." Valerie spun on her heels with military precision and stalked from the room.

I turned back towards the patient standing on the bed. "Leland, what are you doing?" I asked the old man.

He looked down at me with an annoyed expression. "Get out, Lindmark."

"Leland, can you get down? You're in here with a heart attack. You should not be climbing on beds and waving your arms."

The bed squeaked as he turned and tried to keep his balance. His flimsy gown had come undone in back and was gaping open. "It's no heart attack, Lindmark," he said. "I told you I was going to come back in here. All an old wreck like me has to do is mutter about having more chest pain."

"Why are you standing on the bed, Leland?"

He fixed me with a stare so intense it almost burned. "I want him to know I'm here. I want him to see me. *I* want to see *him*."

"Who, Leland?"

"My son. I need to see Kevin. You said he was here." He tilted his head up towards the ceiling and strutted around on the bed, waving his arms wildly. I wasn't sure if he was trying to get his balance or signaling to his dead son. Either way, this was not a good look for a patient admitted with chest pain. Especially one admitted to Captain Valerie's MASH unit.

"Kevin! Kevin. I'm here, son. I need to talk to you." His voice rose, then started to crack with emotion. "Kevin. . . " he wailed. "Kevin, I'm here." He sounded psychotic.

"Your son hears you, Dr. Travis. Now, can you lie back down on the bed? Please?"

I wanted to believe it was my calming bedside manner, but it was most likely simple exhaustion that made him stop waving and collapse back down on the bed. "This damn IV," he muttered. "I didn't want any IVs, do you hear me?"

"Yeah, I know, Leland, no IV catheters." I instantly regretted my sarcastic tone. "But you're in with chest pain," I added in what I hoped was a more gentle voice. "All possible heart attack victims need at least an IV. You know that, right? Can I give you a pill to swallow, just to relax you a little bit?"

"What if he comes?" he asked. "What if Kevin comes, and I'm too medicated, huh?"

"Leland, Kevin's always here. He's always *been* here. He's not about to leave now."

Travis collapsed on the bed like a deflated balloon and closed his eyes. I opened the door. Valerie stood sentry only several feet away. "Dr. Travis is feeling a little better now," I said. "I think one milligram of Xanax would do him a world of good." I put a hand on her arm gently. "Let's also keep this confidential, okay Valerie? I think this may have resulted from some of the medications he was given. Dr. Travis, well, he's been through enough, don't you think?"

"Some of the nurses who admitted him last night warned me about him. He's been here before. Always crazy, but never this crazy," Valerie said. "It's not the medications, Doctor. He needs a psych consult, or something."

"Just get him the medication, Valerie." All I needed was for Travis to pour his heart out to some psychiatrist about wanting to see the long-dead son I had assured him was floating around the hospital.

I made it without further incident to the cardiology conference right before lunch. I'd returned to the hospital after that awful call night only because it had been my turn to rotate off the wards and go on to elective, where I would see patients from an educational distance. Three days had passed since that awful call night without any more patient deaths or ghostly specters. I no longer crept through the hallways as if they were minefields, wondering when the next code horn would sound or when the next innocent patient would be poisoned, electrocuted, or suffocated. They were still here, I knew it, Morrow and his desperate dead. Each day of calm was a sign that I had defeated them at every turn. But always, Audrey was never far from my thoughts. What she had been put through, and what I had caused, pulled at me whenever I had a spare moment.

When I wasn't thinking about that little girl, my thoughts went back to someone much more unpleasant. Where had Bethany been, during Shirkey's code? He'd always been there to grab up the glory, but Dr. Bethany had been a no-show in Shirley's room. He had been on call with me, responsible for supervising interns like me. I hadn't seen him since that night. Had he left the hospital? Had administration finally marked him as the real Angel of Death? Which was it—human evil in the form of a bearded belligerent narcissist, or revenge from long-dead souls never allowed to pass on? Or, God help me, all just my overactive imagination ignited by the stress of seeing what happens to very sick people always on the edge of catastrophe?

"Hey, Harry," a voice interrupted my wandering. "You love cardiology that much, or did you fall asleep? Conference is over, man.

We're rounding with Ganz in a couple minutes." I looked up at the intern who had been sitting next to me.

"Yeah, sure," I answered, shaking away the fog. "And no, I don't like cardiology that much."

Endless lectures and three new consults eventually dulled the uneasiness that wouldn't release its grip on me. That uneasiness turned to outright anxiety when we approached our last patient on rounds as the afternoon wound down. Fortunately, Leland Travis was sitting quietly in a drug-induced calm when we entered his room.

"How are you feeling, Mr. Travis?" Dr. Ganz, this month's teaching cardiologist, asked as we gathered around the old man's bed.

"Still having that pain, Doctor," Travis answered. "It's not there all the time, but when it comes, it's a sort of squeezing pain that radiates right down my left arm."

"His enzymes and EKG are all negative, Dr. Ganz," the resident on the team, Nicole Something-or-other, spoke up. "He could probably go back to the nursing home and complete a work-up as an outpatient."

"That may be, but you can't really ignore those symptoms. They're almost textbook for angina," Ganz responded. He turned to Travis. "You may need to stay here a little longer, Mr. Travis," he said. "In fact, I'm going to talk about scheduling you for a possible catheterization, if that's okay. Nothing else speaks for significant coronary disease except your symptoms, and I can't ignore them."

"That's *Doctor* Travis," Leland corrected. "And yes, that's OK. Of course, I'll have to miss the big black tie affair at the nursing home, but there'll be others."

Ganz shrugged and walked out of the room without another word. Just outside the door he stopped and turned back around with a puzzled look on his face. He eyed Travis suspiciously. "What happened to your IV, Doctor Travis?" he asked.

"I took it out," Travis answered belligerently. "You can always replace it if it's suddenly needed."

"I'm afraid that's not acceptable, Dr. Travis," Ganz answered. "With chest pain, and an upcoming cath—"

The same nurse who had witnessed the morning behavior interrupted with a whispered murmur in his ear.

"All right, Dr. Travis, I can see you have, ah, issues. And I can't have you upset in the middle of a hospitalization for chest pain. So I'll tell you what. We'll leave the IV out for now, but you will definitely need it for your catheterization." The man spun around and strode out of the room without waiting for an answer.

Leland Travis grabbed my arm as I followed Ganz out. "Of course it was a textbook description of angina," Travis whispered. "I *read* that same textbook. I'm going to do whatever I need to do to stay here until I see my son. Can you help me, Lindmark?"

"You're also here with Morrow and all the others. The ones you always thought wanted you dead."

"I'm going to see Kevin," he said. "And now I don't care if I have to die to do it. Because when I see Kevin, I'll know there's something better waiting for me. Better than the crap I've been wallowing in for the last who knows how many years." He let go of my arm and collapsed back onto the bed. "Why the hell does he come to you, and not to me?" His tone told of defeat and sorrow far more than did his words.

"Dr. Lindmark, are you coming?" Ganz's voice asked sharply from the hall.

I looked around one more time, but saw nothing, hateful *or* friendly. A damp smell of leaves interrupted my thoughts as I walked out after rounds had finished. "Dr. Lindmark?" Kevin's hollow voice whispered in my ear. I looked around as nonchalantly as possible, but saw only the usual hospital denizens hurrying by.

"Where are you, Kevin?" I muttered under my breath.

"I'm sorry about the little girl, Dr. Lindmark. She didn't deserve that. No one does, but especially not her."

I looked around furtively. Nobody else was nearby. "Kevin, where were you when your father was calling? He looked like, well, like a crazy old man. Because of what I'd told him."

The corridor remained empty. "I miss my dad. I miss the way he was, and I miss that we can't ever be together." I could almost picture the shrug of those small withered shoulders. "It won't happen, with him. It's only you who can hear and see. I don't make the rules, Dr. Lindmark. I just live them." I shook my head at the irony of those words. "And I hate it, just like the others on this side. It hurts being here."

It had always gnawed at me. Scared the crap out of me. Why me? Why *me*? "What if he needs protection in here?" I asked. "What if *I* do?"

The air warmed around me. "Kevin?" I asked the empty hospital corridor.

Silence answered me back. Not a calming relief from visions of people long dead and souls denied a peaceful transition. The air thickened into a blanket of menace so oppressive I felt like clawing it away, as if I'd become entangled in an invisible clinging cobweb. Something I'd heard, somewhere, nagged at a corner of my thoughts, offering a way to comfort. That vague hopeful memory dissolved as dread consumed me.

CHAPTER 22

I used a different entrance each morning the following week, my first full week on the cardiology elective, avoiding the tunnels and using only well-populated hallways. Abnormal heart rhythms, the newest drugs for heart attacks, treatment of heart failure, besieged me daily. But all those lectures were merciful tangible lifelines to normal reality. Several of the other interns actually came up to me and asked what it had been like to manage a code on my own. I'd been at more resuscitations than most of my fellow interns had experienced put together. I should have felt relieved; instead, I couldn't help wondering if I'd simply surrendered my sanity to the all the disease and responsibility I clearly wasn't ready for.

Certain things, though, were out of place. Men in suits walked around and asked questions of nurses, therapists, and, of course, the doctors. I was sure it was about the sudden rash of codes and near-deaths. I could sense that my days were numbered. Maybe the hospital's days were numbered as well.

"Dr. Lindmark?" Dr. Ganz was standing with a wearied expression on his face. "Could you please keep up? We only have so much time to cover all these patients."

My face burned with embarrassment. We walked quickly through several patients, all of whom were in various stages of recovery from bypass operations. Leland Travis was always our last patient. He looked much different from the agitated crazed old man on that first disheveled day. He'd become withdrawn, morose, and totally uninterested in anything.

"Dr. Pierson, I understand Mr. Travis' cath was negative?" Ganz started off as we neared the end of another day's rounds.

"*Doctor* Travis," Travis mumbled while looking down at the bed.

"Yes sir, his coronaries were clean," Nicole answered, ignoring Travis' correction.

"Good news, Mr. Travis," Ganz said almost jovially. "I guess you'll be getting out of here soon."

"Still having chest pain, *Mister* Ganz." His belligerent tone was the first sign of animation I'd seen.

Ganz ignored the insult, or simply didn't recognize it. "Well, whatever it is, we know it's not dangerous. I think you could be worked up as an outpatient, don't you think?"

"Normally I wouldn't care whether it's dangerous or not. But I'm not going back to that nursing home until I really feel better. They don't take care of you there." Bloodshot eyes stared down Ganz. "I need to stay in here."

"We'll discuss it with your doctors," Ganz responded. I'd have to remember that phrase. It had come in handy for Ganz with almost every patient, as if he *weren't* one of the doctors. He strode out of the room, the rest of us in pursuit. As I was passing by the bed, Travis grabbed me.

"Lindmark, wait."

I looked over my shoulder at the rest of the team. "Look, Leland, I can come back."

The claw tightened. "My son, Lindmark. You told me he was here. I want to see him. I can't make up any more reasons for them to keep me here." His glare softened, eyes becoming glassy with tears.

"His soul is here. I swear it," I muttered under my breath.

"You know what the worst part of it is, Lindmark?" He swiped a hand across his eyes. "First, I thought you were just crazier than the rest of them. That made me feel better, because that meant I wasn't the only doctor who'd cracked up under the strain of being here. Then I thought you were better than the rest of them. Now I know you're just *like* the rest of them. Just sneakier."

"Leland, I—"

"But you know what the goddam *worst* part is?" he asked. "The worst part is that makin' fun of me like this, stringing me along, desecrates Kevin's memory. Like kicking over his headstone. Now get the hell out of here, before you miss out on a chance to impress your friends."

His son's name triggered what had been nagging at me out of memory's reach. "Leland. Dr. Travis, wait. What was that you said before? Something about waiting here to see your son?"

"Screw you, Bismark."

"Leland, please. I'm trying to help here."

He glared at me, eyes more alert and penetrating than I'd seen. "I said, I'm going to see my son and I don't care if I have to die to do it. Until I realized it was just a bunch of shit. I don't know how you found out about what we did, all the private stuff Kevin and I did, but I just don't care anymore. Now get the hell out."

He rolled until his back was facing me. And just like that, I'd lost the trust of an old man lost in his own past, the only ally I'd had after Charlie. But he'd given me a possible answer to what had been plaguing me almost since day one.

"Dr. Lindmark, *please*," I heard from the hall.

Finally, teaching rounds were over. I ducked into a bathroom and allowed all my earlier thoughts to release in the quiet privacy of a stall. *I don't care if I have to die to do it.* Leland's words. I rubbed the scar on the front of my throat. The scar of the tracheostomy I'd needed from years before. The scar I'd always tried to ignore, because the memories of that time never failed to paralyze me in post-traumatic terror.

I'd died. I'd been pulled under by currents while swimming off a beach in that long-ago vacation. Drowned, I was told. Resuscitated by the resort's lifeguard, but required an emergency tracheostomy because of seaweed and sand blocking my airway. I'd had to coax the details from my reluctant parents, who eventually gave in and told me the awful story of how their son had been without pulses or life before that tracheostomy.

I'd died. *That's* what separated me not only from Travis, but from Bethany, Connie, practically everyone else who never saw or heard what came from the other side. I'd *been* on that other side and somehow had carried that connection back. I didn't need to consult a medium, or priest, or textbook about near-death experiences to know why only I'd been burdened, literally haunted, by a bond to the world beyond death that had never closed. Kevin had taken all the smells of his life with him into death, his own connection between worlds. I had been burdened with my own private terrible connection to the world beyond.

Relief washed over me in the silence of that stall. Relief that I wasn't psychotic or crazy. There was an explanation. In the next instant, a stab of dread slithered up and poisoned the brief sense of calm. Was seeing and hearing the souls of the dead really so much better than suffering from mental illness?

That question haunted me from the moment I exited the bathroom onward. Each day progressed uneventfully, save for my inner turmoil, until the last day of the week. Men in suits prowled through the halls daily, invading the nursing stations and peering uninvited at computer screens. They even distracted me from thinking about little Audrey and everything else that came with that episode. I went the entire week without running into Connie, even though I knew she had increased her aquatic therapy classes to three times a week. Guilt dragged me down like a stone around my neck, as my promise to visit her aquatic therapy slipped by unfulfilled. Yet internship never released its grip on me and my time, no matter how much I tried to find just a few spare minutes. I loved my wife. I just couldn't find any damn way to show it.

The last day of the week, we were told that attendance at Grand Rounds was required for every intern and resident unless they were actively involved in a life-threatening patient crisis. The auditorium was crowded when I entered, so I took a seat in the back. Our Chief Resident walked up to the podium, looking as lean and hungry as ever. I knew a Chief Resident had completed the year of internship and two years of residency, but then had chosen to pursue one additional year of being in charge of the residency program before venturing out into private practice. It was typically reserved for the most hard charging and intelligent resident in his or her class. Dr. Martin Bethany seemed to be in line for coronation next year.

"I'll get right to the point," he began. "The strangers you may have encountered in the hospital are from the state Department of Health. Apparently, our hospital has had more than its share of, ah, patient incidents." His words seemed rushed and almost flippant, but his angular jaw was set, his expression grim. "We have nothing to hide, and if something needs correcting, we want to make those corrections. Actually, I'd like to reassure everyone. Most of the incidents were unavoidable outcomes in patients who were already near death. Unfortunately, some of them were associated with medical errors. We've spoken about this before, in this very room."

His tone became more animated. "As you would expect, errors with morphine, blood-thinners, and insulin have occurred most frequently here. Unnecessary allergic reactions to medications made the list as well."

He gripped the edges of the podium. I was gripping my own armrests just as tightly. Morphine and blood-thinners and insulin. . . lions and tigers and bears. . . morphine and blood-thinners and insulin. . . the words ran through my mind in a chilling mantra. I was hanging on his every word, waiting for him to suddenly look up, point an accusing finger at me, and proclaim, *"Unfortunately Dr. Harrison Lindmark was the chink in our armor, responsible for the errors that all the supervision we have here couldn't stop!" I would stand up, the Accused, and announce the souls of long-dead patients were killing, not me. Then I would be jabbed full of anti-psychotic medication, drummed out of the residency program, and be deposited in the nearest secure psychiatric ward as quietly as possible.*

"Therefore," he continued, "I am confident that we've taken the proper steps to assure the best and safest patient care. By the time we've finished, our electronic medical record system will have been completely upgraded. Virtually every aspect of patient care, from charts to labs to radiology, will be on-line and protected. We've already received a vote of confidence from the inspectors. I hope everyone will remain patient as we build this institution into one of the leading hospitals in this region." He smiled triumphantly as applause erupted.

I didn't applaud. The message chilled me. More trust in the computers–just greasing the skids for easier ways to kill. I thought back to what had happened to Travis years before. The rampage of patient deaths, the hospital closing down at the peak of the deaths. The hospital must be on the verge of doing the same thing now as it had been forced to do years before. Any more unexplained catastrophes and the state would be forced to do more than just send in investigators. They would suspend doctors and nurses, close off floors, possibly even suspend the hospital's license. Trapping Morrow in even more of a prison, without patients providing escape. That was the only thing the dead could be afraid of: never leaving the agony of the in-between.

I had time. They wouldn't kill now. Morrow had seen his rage backfire once. Travis was safe for now. Hell, all the patients were safe, at least for a while. Now I just had to find out how to stop any future horror. What else would the dead fear? They were *dead*. Wrenched away from their earthly bodies, trapped, sentenced to endlessly haunt a place without peace. What else could I threaten that was worse than that?

The last meeting of the week with the cardiology team finally loomed. As I organized the papers on my clipboard, readying for Dr. Ganz and his questions, I saw a familiar woman weaving in and out of the crowd in the hallway. Norma Strickland? I hadn't seen her since Timmy had been discharged for the second time. She hadn't changed. She was even wearing the same frayed wallpaper dress.

"Mrs. Strickland?" I greeted her as I reached out an arm and steadied her shaky gait.

She seemed to force herself to focus on my face, then recognition lit up the blankness. "Dr. Lindmark?" I nodded. "Dr. Lindmark," she repeated. "He's in the emergency room. Can you go there and see him? It's my husband, Norm, in there."

"Your husband? Not Timmy?" I glanced at my watch. Ganz didn't strike me as being all that understanding if one of his interns was late for a lecture. "What's wrong with Mr. Strickland?"

"He was trying to teach Timmy baseball again, but Timmy hated playing after he came home. Or maybe he just hated coming home." Her eyes started to water, and her lower lip trembled. "But my Norm kept at it, bless him. He stopped putting Timmy's bear at first base like he used to, but he'd still take him outside and pitch to him."

"Mrs. Strickland, what happened to your husband?" I prodded. "And where is Timmy?"

"I looked outside and saw, oh God, I saw Timmy standing over Norm, h-holding the bat, and Norm bleeding on the ground. The bat, it had blood on it."

I laid a hand on her shaking shoulder.

"And then, as I kept watching, Timmy started having another seizure. I think he'd stopped his medication again. I called the ambulance for both of them, and I've been in the emergency room ever since. Nobody's told me anything."

"They're *both* in the hospital?"

She looked up at me, hope brightening the lined weariness of her face. "Can you find out what's going on, Dr. Lindmark? Please, can you?"

My phone went off. The cardiology conference. "You know, Mrs. Strickland, it might be best to just let the guys in the ER work on them without a lot of distractions. Those guys know what they're doing, believe me."

"I just want to know how my boys are doing. I need to talk to them before they're taken off somewhere."

I backed away, getting more anxious about the impatience that must be awaiting me around that conference table. "Mrs. Strickland, they are not going to do anything without informing you first."

The grip around my arm actually hurt. "Are you sure they'll call me?"

"Definitely, Mrs. Strickland. Definitely." I hoped my smile would reassure even a little. "I will definitely be back to check on them. Okay?"

My attention faded through the remainder of the final conference until Ganz pushed away from the table with the satisfied air of a man who has just feasted on a large many-course meal. "Excellent work," he remarked to the rest of us. "I do hope you all have learned something this week. So when you face your own patient complaining of chest pain and palpitations in your busy office, you'll know what to do."

Yeah, I wanted to retort. *I'd call for someone as smart as you, stat.*

I left the conference room as quickly as I could. The weekend had finally arrived, but there was one more thing I had to do before going home.

"Hey Harry," a young nurse greeted me as I walked into the emergency department's usual controlled bedlam. "You're not working here tonight, are you?"

"No, just here to check up on a patient," I answered. "Timmy Strickland? Or Norm Strickland? Do you know which bay they're in? I promised I'd come here and check up on them."

I could swear she paled. "Which one do you want, Harry?" she asked. "Norm Strickland? Or Timothy?"

"Does it matter?" I asked. How far apart could they be?

"Actually, Harry, it does. Timothy, the younger one, he came in dead. He seized at home, apparently right after eating. Somewhere out there, he vomited and then aspirated. We worked on him for a long time, but it was hopeless from the beginning. He was dead when he arrived. His medication levels were zero, if that makes any difference."

"Looks like he put everything in his mouth *except* his seizure meds," a voice broke in from behind us. I turned around to face Martin Bethany. His face was grim behind the ruddy pudginess and beard. "His mother told us he just refused to take his medications, or spat them out when he thought they weren't looking. And what he did eat went into his lungs at the end. I'll probably have to write down the 'Cause of Death' as 'pepperoni and cheese,' you know?" He wasn't smiling or smirking. His words were as blunt and brutal as Timmy's death must have been.

I stared at Bethany. "What about his father?" I asked, afraid of the answer.

"Came in with a skull fracture, but he's alive," Bethany said. "Timmy clubbed him pretty good with that bat, right before that final seizure." He reached behind the counter and pulled out a long wooden object. An old Louisville Slugger, the end discolored in crimson. "Had to actually pry this out of the kid's hands," he said. "Seizing, drowning in vomit, pretty much dead, but still holding the bat he'd clubbed his father with."

"Have you seen Mrs. Strickland, Dr. Bethany? Did she—"

"Yeah, of course I saw her, Lindmark," he answered. "I ran the code on her son. Which means I had to be the one to tell her Timmy had died."

"Did you, did Timmy's mother get a chance to see him? Before he died?"

Bethany's face crinkled in puzzlement. "No, Harry. We were just a little busy with him, trying to save his life."

He glanced over my shoulder. I turned around and saw Norma Strickland standing silently several feet away.

"He died, Dr. Lindmark. I wasn't there for my Timmy. I'd always been there for him. Guess you didn't get a chance to come down here either, before. . . " She clutched a tattered stuffed bear in one trembling hand. "I brought this with me, to give to him," she said, holding the bear out to me. "He doesn't need it anymore."

She stumbled towards us, arms outstretched. I rushed over and lowered her into a chair as slowly as possible. I wasn't sure what to do with the bear, so I stuffed it into a pocket of my white coat.

"Where's my husband?" she asked after several moments. I noticed she was looking at Bethany, directly away from me.

"Over behind those curtains," Bethany answered.

"Can I see *him*?" Each word thrown out with deliberate emphasis. Her bony knuckles whitened on the armrests of her chair. I noticed the emphasis on that last word. It had to be directed at me.

"Of course, Mrs. Strickland." Bethany eased her out of the chair and escorted her towards the curtained-off area. She turned once and looked at me with blank eyes. Then she resumed her stumbling walk, all the time leaning into Bethany.

Once again, I'd let down the family I wanted so much to help. I quickened my walk away from the ER and from Norma Strickland's accusing eyes. I had to get out of this place. Away from all the deaths. Especially the last one, Timmy.

I bumped and apologized my way down the corridors, never looking up from the floor. As I walked, the regret and sadness faded, slowly replaced by an odd apprehension. Families, orderlies, white-coated doctors crowded past me. Each group of rushing people seemed to leave in its wake a breeze that wrapped me in foreboding. I felt as if the very hospital was on edge. The sense of imminent doom pressed down on me until I found myself almost running towards the exit. Something was coming, I knew it. That premonition continued to gnaw at me even after I'd reached the refuge of my car. I clutched the wheel with damp hands as I made my way home.

My eyes were drawn to the single white sheet of paper on top of the kitchen table that replaced my nameless premonition with the shock of certainty. Connie must have finally surrendered to the loneliness. She'd left the sadness and unfulfilled promise of a family behind, and me with it. My very own "Dear Harry" letter. I was the collateral damage of a motherhood deserved but never realized.

I picked up the paper with trembling hands. The note had only three or four sentences in Connie's rushed scribble. She'd gone to visit with Denise again, because Denise was still having a rough time. Relief flooded over me, knowing I still had a wife. At the top of the stairs I passed the nursery, The Room, and could not help looking in. Empty, quiet. The happy wallpaper of this useless nursery taunted me. I collapsed against the wall, sinking down to the floor under the weight of loneliness at home and torment from the dead at work. *Was it ever going to stop?* Too much reminder of death here, too much actual death in that hospital.

That hospital. . . Timmy's body must have given up its second soul when he'd died. That second one, Truman Faragon, was it still so angry? It had escaped the hell of the in-between, only to die again. What had happened to that angry soul? Really, this time, *too far gone* to return? Or had Timmy's death just added to the rage that infected the unseen unholy side of the hospital?

I jumped to my feet. Living people I cared about were still there, at the mercy of all that eternal wrath. I'd been wrong about that reprieve. Morrow had taken genius with him to the grave, but had left behind any vestige of human emotion except rage and hate. They weren't going to stop and wait out the chaos to recede, because rational human behavior deserted what was no longer human. They'd already given in to that hate, and wouldn't stop. I was probably already marked for death, but maybe it wasn't too late for the others.

CHAPTER 23

"Denise?" I laid a hand as gently as I could on her shoulder, but she still jumped with surprise.

"Sorry," I muttered as she spun around on the chair and faced me, tears overflowing her eyes.

"I'm not giving in. I'm not giving up on her." She tightened her grip on the little girl's contorted hand.

I forced myself to look closely at Audrey's still form. The white breathing tube going down into her lungs violated her face. She'd been lying in that bed on life support since the catastrophe with the allergic reaction, motionless. For an interminable week I'd been expecting Connie to tell me that Audrey had suddenly regained consciousness and ripped that tube out on her own, because she hadn't been without oxygen for that long. But had she? How long had she been like that before I'd arrived? Had she been ignored because of *my* No Code Blue order? That stupid, stupid order I'd written. . .

"No one is giving up, Denise," I said.

"Really?" she snapped. "Then why do the neurologists come in every day, shaking their heads and working on their sad expressions?"

"Because, well, because they're neurologists."

"So she's going to get better, do you think?"

"I'm not a pediatrician, Denise," I answered. She's *got* to get better, I wanted so much to say instead.

My words only squeezed more weeping as Denise slumped in her chair. I felt an overpowering urge to rip out the IVs, tear off the pads, do something about that terrible tube. I clenched my hands against that insane impulse and considered how far over the edge I'd been driven. Any of the medical tools we all trusted could be tools of Morrow's rage. They'd *all* become instruments of death. I couldn't rip away everything. At least, not before the hospital security staff would stop me and rip *me* away.

But at least I could make sure nothing else would happen to Audrey. It meant doing what I'd tried to keep hidden. It meant ruining what remained of my professional life. It meant there would never be any going back. My heart pounded as I considered what I was about to do. I'd ruin myself, but I'd also, just maybe, redeem myself at the same time. I breathed deeply and walked my own Green Mile towards the Emergency Department.

Martin Bethany was leaning up against the central work desk, rotund belly tucked comfortably under the edge of the large, cluttered counter. His white coat was rumpled and stained. I had to do it now, before the next heart attack or stroke pushed through the ambulance entrance.

"Dr. Bethany?" I greeted him. My mouth was so dry I had trouble forcing out the words.

He squinted back at me. "Lindmark. What are you doing here? Someone else come back who'd suffered the misfortune of your medical treatment?"

"Can we go somewhere and talk, Dr. Bethany?" I asked, ignoring the jab.

He squinted at me even harder. "Gosh, Harry," he said with mock emphasis. "The last time I heard those words, my girlfriend was about to break up with me. I'd never realized those long nights on call had meant so much to you." Someone snickered behind me.

Laugh it up now, Big Boy. Because I know what you are. And I'm going to expose you. You and all the rest. "It's important, Dr. Bethany," I said. "It will only take a few minutes."

He shrugged and beckoned me to follow him. "Take over for me a second, will you?" he asked a resident I'd never seen before.

Bethany walked me towards the ER on-call room and closed the call room door behind us. "So what's up, Harry?" His tone softened. "Is everything okay? Still having problems with what happened to Timmy and his dad?"

"Yes. I mean, yes, I feel bad about Timmy, but that's not what I need to talk about." I'd never been more scared of saying something. "I need your help."

"For what, Harry?"

"To help protect." My planned exposé against hungering souls died in my throat. Bethany tried to sneak a look at his watch. I didn't have much time. "Do you, uh, do you believe in ghosts, Dr. Bethany? I mean, life after death?" I forced a glare into his eyes, looking for some hint of what lurked inside. "Because I know who you are, Martin. Or who you are *now*. I know why you did it. I just need you to talk to those other spirits, or ghosts, or whatever they are that you left behind in that afterlife. Tell them to stop. Especially Audrey. She doesn't deserve any of this. Please."

His sympathetic expression hardened into a suspicious glower. "Lindmark, what the hell's going on? Are you okay?"

I practiced the calming breaths advocated by my therapist, which did nothing to quench my nervousness. I plunged ahead. "Dr. Bethany, I know why everything happens to *your* patients, on *your* call nights."

"As I recall, most of those disasters happened when I was on call with *you*."

"That's what I mean. They need *me* to make the mistakes, or at least need someone like me to blame. Then they need *you* to resuscitate those same patients. Because you're still one of them. Maybe now in the flesh, but you owe Morrow for your escape, don't you? I don't know if you were always this smart, or if whatever dead soul you are now was smart before, when he was living. It doesn't matter. Those codes happened on your call nights because they could count on your ability to *fix* mistakes, and on my ability to make them."

"They? Who are 'they,' Lindmark?" When I didn't answer, he went on. "Harry, we've all been too patient with you." He opened the door. "But now," he spoke his parting words to the hall in front of him as if he couldn't even stand the sight of me. "Now I think you do need help. Reality is always a good thing to be in touch with when you're dealing with patients. And you're not."

Desperation gripped me. "I'm going to stop them, Dr. Bethany. With or without your help. You can go ahead and report me. If I'm fired, I'll still come back. And I will keep researching, and looking into this, and I will find something to do. But if you do that, and the hospital comes down on me, they'll probably at least get you, too. For inadequate supervision at the least. For shared incompetence at the worst. Don't forget about that Code Blue on Aaron Shirkey you just ignored and didn't even bother showing up for. You ignored the code horns on purpose. You *wanted* him to die, didn't you?" I heard myself panting and realized only then that I hadn't taken a breath while spewing at my supervising resident.

He kept walking. That was it. I was done. My resident, one of *them*, would just go on until he released Morrow, and more. And innocents like Charlie and Audrey and whoever else fed their revenge would die. Then he would report me to the medical staff office, to Sorenson, to anyone in charge of medical training and physician competency. I slumped in my chair, wondering who would show up first–men in business coats with briefcases or men in white coats with straitjackets.

Bethany stopped in his tracks. He turned around slowly and walked back into the room, his gaze never leaving me. He closed the door behind him and advanced towards me, his eternally pugnacious expression thoughtful.

At that moment, I wasn't sure if he was going to attack me or talk to me. "First, I wasn't at Shirkey's code because I was at yet another disaster that night. That horrible night. You remember that surgical resident who was there?" I nodded, but refused to release my glare. "She was there because I called her, to help you. To hopefully save Shirkey when I couldn't be there. Why else would a surgical resident just show up for anything besides the chance to operate?" It was Bethany's turn to glare, but only seconds later his belligerence dissolved.

The Martin Bethany actually averted his gaze away, focusing instead on the floor. Seconds passed, then he cleared his throat. "I've been where you are, Harry." His voice held no trace of threat or anger. "Believe me, I understand. And if it will help get you through. . ." A deep sigh. "I'm going to tell you something that I've never told anyone. Because no one took the time to help me when I needed it. You can be a good doctor, unless you keep telling everyone about all the ghosts and dead people." He wiped his forehead and looked directly at me. "There are no ghosts. There are mistakes, Harry. Terrible medical mistakes. Do you know how many codes I'd been at before you ever got here?"

I actually did.

"You just can't stand that you can't save everybody. Or rather, you can't stand that anything bad would happen to patients on your watch. So you blame something else, *anything* else no matter how farfetched, for mistakes that you're afraid you may have permitted."

He averted his eyes downwards again and sat down heavily on the bed, springs squealing in protest. "You have no idea about a bad internship, Lindmark. Some of your patients have died and you don't even try to learn more and keep it from happening again. *You* come up with ghosts. Jesus, Lindmark. You want to know why I run codes the way I do? Why I show up to emergencies whether I'm called or not? Why my patients survive more often than with most of the other residents?"

His complexion blazed as crimson as his hair. I cowered back in my chair as Bethany practically spewed at me. "Because I vowed to make up for my own internship, Lindmark. Midway through my internship year, I admitted an old man on one call night. He was in heart failure. Fluid around both lungs, short of breath, but not critical. Remember that, Lindmark, not critical." He paused and swallowed noisily, as if that were supposed to mean something.

"We started him on oxygen and a diuretic, gave him some morphine to calm him and reduce the shortness of breath. He started to get more comfortable. Good old congestive heart failure treatment 101, and it was working."

He looked off to somewhere over my shoulder and seemed to shrink. The more he talked, the softer his voice sank, and the more his usual belligerence shriveled before my eyes. I felt as if I was watching Zeus coming down from Olympus using a walker instead of striding down with lightning bolts flashing.

"But that wasn't good enough for me. I needed experience, Lindmark. I needed to make internship truly a training year, so that I would be the best. I needed to practice draining fluid from around the lungs. So I called in the nurse, told that patient I would make him more comfortable because there was still so much fluid around his lungs. That nurse and I propped up that sedated, *already comfortable,* trusting patient into a sitting position. Then I tried to drain the fluid. Nothing came at first. With that needle still stuck in his back, and no fluid coming out, I realized I probably wasn't as good at doing procedures as I'd thought. I almost got sick when I saw the hub of that needle move up and down every time he breathed. Like it was *in* his lung, not in the fluid *around* his lung. It moved up and down, Lindmark, with his breathing. Up and down. Up and down." He stopped talking. Zeus was sounding increasingly un-godly. I shook my head as the man with the flaming hair and disposition to match shriveled before my eyes.

Bethany continued, "I took that drainage catheter out, then stuck it in a little lower down where there should have definitely been fluid. That time I got back some drops of blood. *Fresh* blood. The patient started to cry. 'It's starting to hurt, Doctor.' he said. 'Hold real still, and we'll be done real soon,' was all I could say. He wasn't so much trusting as he was still sedated from the morphine. I finally had to stop the whole thing. He was really hurting when we laid him back in bed, and his breathing was a lot worse. All I could think about was getting into trouble for what I'd done. The nurse asked if I wanted to get an X-ray, just to make sure. I told her we had better take care of the pain first. I knew that I'd probably collapsed his lung at best, and had probably started bleeding around his lung at worst. So I didn't order the X-ray because I didn't want proof. In today's world, that would be called 'a cover-up.' I gave him some more morphine, which at least did make him more comfortable." He exhaled a deep, husky sigh. "The next morning, I told his family he had passed away peacefully in the night. The nurse who had helped me had already left so I was really the only one who knew what had happened."

He bolted from the bed and jammed his fists deeper into his pockets. "What I'd really done, Lindmark, is give him terrifying pain and suffocation, and then allowed him to die. No, I'd probably *caused* him to die, because I'd wanted more experience. Then I lied about it. Nothing you've done, Harry, can match that. And as if I couldn't punish myself enough, about a month after that I fell asleep driving home from a night on call and ran off the road. I should have died with the kind of head trauma I had. Went through the damn windshield. After what I'd done, Lindmark, I probably deserved to die. Anyway, I was in the hospital or in rehab for the rest of my internship year. Know why I have this beard? Because red and bushy looks better than the scars under it. All I could think of, that whole time, was that I was being punished for what I'd done." His complexion reddened around suddenly bloodshot eyes.

He stepped towards me, regaining his inner Greek god with each step. "Maybe I've been so hard on you, and on everyone else, because all of your mistakes get in the way of the promise I'd made after that."

"Promise?"

"I promised no one else was going to die on my watch. Ever. Unless that death was deserved."

"Deserved?"

"Dammit, Lindmark, do I have to explain everything to you? Deserved, as in they deserved to no longer suffer from terminal painful cancer, shortness of breath, or any other disease that couldn't be cured. Otherwise, no one was going to die, especially from mistakes by interns like you. So own your mistakes and learn from them, Harry. You don't know what having a bad internship means. Honor your patients, dead and living. I've been trying to be better ever since. Hopefully, you will take my mistakes to heart. Forget the ghosts, Harry. I promise you, I'm as flesh-and-blood as you, trying to make up for something I can never really take back. You need to stay employed." He turned away and walked out the door.

Superhuman Dr. Bethany was only human after all. He was not one of *them*, taken over by something from the other side. He wasn't a ghoul hellbent on killing patients. I felt like laughing as relief washed over me. The chuckles died in my throat as an even more frightening realization gripped me. I was alone. My only chance at getting help was literally turning his back on me. Bethany may not be one of them, harboring a soul back from the dead, but patients were going to keep dying. The dead *were* real, even if Martin Bethany wasn't one of them. I needed someone as smart as Bethany to stay one step ahead of the things that refused to stay dead by using our own medicine against us. I now trusted he was a fellow member of humanity on this side of the grave, which meant he'd never believe in what I knew existed on the other side. But he might listen to science.

"They use the computers, you know," I blurted out. "The Electronic Medical Records of this place. The lab reports. We don't see patients, Dr. Bethany, we see computer records. The computers are closer to the patients than the doctors are. They give us numbers revealing metabolic catastrophes. But what if those numbers don't belong to the patient they're supposed to? Like Timmy, Dr. Bethany. They're going to keep killing, and they're getting better at it. Pretty soon *you* won't be so useful to them. And then you better hope you're gone from here." I stopped to take another deep breath. Bethany had stopped his retreat and had turned slowly to face me again.

"I'm not crazy, Dr. Bethany," I resumed. "Timmy was one of them. He didn't get a new brain, Dr. Bethany. He got a new soul. We all thought the Stricklands were rewarded with new meaning in their lives, because Timmy could talk to us the way *we* respected. Does it look like the Stricklands have more meaning in their lives, Dr. Bethany?"

Bethany stood and squinted down at me, his silence more ominous than any outburst I'd been previously battered with. "Even you can't explain everything that's gone on around here, right? Believe the science if you don't want to believe in anything else, Martin."

He held his hand up. "First, it's back to Dr. Bethany." His brows furrowed down over squinted eyes. "Have you told anyone else about this, Harry?" I shook my head. "Well, don't. I have never heard such bizarre stuff spoken with such passion since managing a schizophrenic patient who had gone off her medications for a week. But you are not psychotic. Maybe somehow you have stumbled on something that, well, is hard to explain. But don't tell anyone else who might not be looking out for you, if you know what I mean. I still don't believe you, but if there is any way to protect patients on my watch, I'll listen to you. Maybe even help you unless you ask me to beam up with you to the mother ship. In all seriousness—"

The door burst open. "Dr. Bethany, we've been looking all over for you," the nurse exclaimed. "We got a sixty-year-old obese male with chest pain, a blood pressure of 80 over 40, and heart failure in Bay 2. Cardiology's stuck in the ICU, and your resident is about to wet his pants in there."

"Norm Strickland's okay, isn't he?" I interrupted.

She eyed me curiously. "Yeah, sure, he's doing fine. I haven't checked in on him lately."

"I gotta go, Lindmark," he said slowly, deliberately. "We definitely need to talk more." He turned to the nurse. "I'll be right there. Get an EKG, make up an IV for the blood thinner, and start levophed at 5 micrograms per minute." He left the call room without a backward glance.

I exhaled long and hard, then walked out into the emergency department hallway. The usual cacophony of controlled medical pandemonium assaulted me immediately. Every monitor shriek, every shouted order, every IV pump beep was reassuringly human but dredged up unwanted familiarity at the same time. Something silent and intangible pressed in on me as I left the emergency department. It was a premonition of something coming, an uncomfortable shroud of dread that made me want to scratch it away from my body to keep from suffocating.

CHAPTER 24

There was no doubt my elective was definitely over from the moment I entered the hospital on Monday. I dared one more glance at the intimidating list of patients I'd inherited the night before. The countless duties and diagnoses raced through my thoughts, derailing the plans I'd so carefully put together the night before.

"Harry! Harry, do you hear me?"

I looked at the bespectacled, angular face peering at me. "I guess we're back on service together," Frank Bannister continued. "But I don't think I have as many patients as you seem to have."

I wasn't comforted. "Hi Frank," I responded. "Who's our resident?" Instead of answering, he swallowed hard several times, his bowtie bobbing up and down on top of his sharp Adam's apple. The sharp staccato clicks of heels answered my question.

Dr. Teresa Northrup strode down the corridor towards us. Her expression was still severe, her posture every bit as ramrod straight as it ever had been. Her jet-black hair pulled into a compact bun that stretched away every possible wrinkle and blemish.

"Dr. Lindmark, Dr. Bannister," she said, greeting more us as if she were addressing cadets instead of interns. "I guess we're it. I'm told that there were no students available for this rotation, so we can get started. I hope you both have had some time to review your patient lists." She motioned impatiently for Frank and me to follow as she clicked briskly down the hall. I mumbled my way through several of my patients until we came to Frank's third patient. "This fifty-four-year-old white male was admitted through the Emergency Room with a traumatic skull fracture," he began with medically correct grammar, in medically correct monotone. "He—"

"What's he doing on a medical instead of trauma service?" Northrup broke in.

Frank gulped audibly. That bow tie was definitely going to leave marks. "He's got diabetes, Dr. Northrup," he said. "Trauma team thought he'd be better off on a medical service."

Northrup breathed deeply, then shrugged. "So, a little elevated blood sugar trumps a life-threatening skull fracture? Go ahead, finish your presentation." I already knew the details, because the blackened eyes and reddened bandages couldn't hide his weathered cragginess. I wanted to reach out and shake Norm Strickland's shoulders until he opened those eyes and sat up. Because he had to get better.

"What's his prognosis, Frank?" I asked as we walked away from the bed.

"Well, the neurosurgeons said he'll live," Frank replied. "The trauma team thinks he'll probably regain most of his function, but they'd like to see evidence of sustained wakefulness." Frank blinked owlishly behind his lenses and continued. "But I don't know, Harry. I don't know whether waking up will be such a good thing. Right now, he doesn't know his son died. I'm not sure I'd want to wake up from a coma and have that as the first thing I'd hear."

I'd already considered that. At least Norm wasn't aware, under those bandages and his shaven splintered skull, that his own son was responsible. Or, I considered, what had *been* his son. I shivered involuntarily and looked long and hard at the intravenous tubing coiling over Strickland's arm and at the clear liquid dripping so innocently into his body. I couldn't just turn it off and rip it out of his arm. Norm Strickland and I were in the belly of the beast. I couldn't tell anyone, but I would watch him closely.

We reached a familiar room, but Northrup paused outside instead of striding in as usual. "Dr. Lindmark," she began, choosing her words carefully. "Dr. Ganz told me how Dr. Travis had previously asked that you not round on him when you were consulting with the cardiologists."

I waited for more humiliating criticism.

She continued primly, "I'm sure you'll be happy to hear that now he has requested *only* you to be his intern. Congratulations. May God be with you."

Travis had asked for me? Had Kevin finally appeared to his father?

Northrup added, "He spends all day talking to himself and crying." She laid one hand gently on my arm. "When you see him, Dr. Lindmark, please suggest that there's nothing more to do for him in the hospital. If he's even coherent enough to listen."

I opened the door slowly, wondering what sight would greet me.

The shriek of the code horn interrupted whatever lay in wait in Leland Travis's room. We all stopped and cocked our heads, waiting for the monotone announcement of where a patient was trying to die.

"Code Blue, Physical Therapy. Code Blue, Physical Therapy."

We looked at each other quizzically. Physical Therapy? I'd never heard a code called in Physical Therapy.

Dr. Northrup sighed heavily, then looked at Frank and me. "All right Harry, I want you to finish rounds, especially with Travis. We have to get him out of here. I don't know why everyone's so scared of pissing him off. Frank, you come with me to the code. You ever run a code?"

Frank shook his head.

"Then this would be a good time to learn. You'll be a resident sooner than you think." She glanced at me. "I know you've been in several codes already." Her tone was disdainful. "Frank, let's get going."

"Code Blue, Physical Therapy, Pediatrics. Code Blue, Physical Therapy, Pediatrics."

This was getting worse. Codes weren't supposed to happen to kids, for God's sake. The leukemic, Audrey, and now yet another poor child. My chest suddenly tightened.

Morrow…*The therapy pool was in pediatric physical therapy. Morrow had threatened to go after anyone I cared about.* First Charlie, then Audrey. . . now Connie?

I ran towards the pediatric physical therapy department and the pool. I thought I heard Northrup shout something from behind me, but it didn't matter. Nothing else mattered. Connie didn't deserve this, goddam it.

People jumped out of my way as I thudded down the maze of hallways towards the pediatric hospital. I was running towards something horrible, I was sure of it. Why else would there be a code in the therapy pool, of all places? The 'deep end' was only three feet deep, and Connie had said the therapists outnumbered the children at all times.

A crowd of people gathered outside a door ahead of me. Most were visitors in street clothes. Doctors and nurses mixed in among them. All of them were bent over, retching, coughing, or wheezing. Most were looking at the closed door with bulging eyes watering and bloodshot. Several children were lying limply on the floor, also coughing and sputtering. As I pushed into their midst an acrid odor overwhelmed me. Before I knew it I was bent over like the rest, trying to wheeze air into lungs suddenly burning and constricted. I could barely open my eyes against the stinging.

"Connie?" I called out desperately. "Has anyone here seen Connie Lindmark?" My shout came out as nothing more than a raspy whisper.

The entire mass of people started backing up. Panic swept over me as I saw a white mist bubbling out from under the door to the pool. *They're here.* I backed away with the rest of the crowd, unable to contain a moan of stark terror. The murky tendrils circled and eddied across the floor and wrapped around our legs. Seconds later my eyes started burning and watering all over again as the door burst open and several more coughing people raced out, enveloped in white clouds.

It was gas, poisonous gas of some sort. The murky fumes wafted closer. I was able to open my eyes just enough to see Connie among the group that had burst into our midst. I clutched at her blurred image. She was safe. Thank God. "Connie, what's happening?" I rasped.

She opened and closed her mouth with the gasping helplessness of a fish out of water, but no words came until she coughed out a phlegmy mixture of water and blood. "She's still in there," she whispered. "We. . . we were in the pool, in our therapy. This stuff started bubbling up out of the water. I tried to grab her, but my eyes were burning. I couldn't breathe. I couldn't *breathe*. I reached for her, honest. I reached for her, but someone pulled me out of the pool." A spasm of violent coughing wracked her body.

"Who, Connie? Who's in there?" I babbled frantically.

"Denise. . . Denise. . . still in there."

From somewhere behind me, I heard glass breaking. The bitter smoke swirled around us in a toxic stream as more of it was sucked through the open door. The crush of people screamed and stumbled away as the gas rushed out. I slitted my eyes open long enough to see Connie pulled away with the rest.

I had to get Denise. I dropped to my stomach and started crawling through the door. The air close to the mildewed tile was still foul but at least didn't choke and burn like the white clouds churning overhead. I made it to the pool and was surprised to see that most of those stifling clouds of gas had wafted out into the corridor. I crawled over several plastic bags, one of which was open and still leaking a thin stream of gray powder into the water. 'DANGER – CHLORINE' was inscribed on the sides of the bags. I stood and tried to keep going towards the pool. Wisps of gas hung over the water like fog. A blurry object became visible in the water. I squinted against the stinging. A woman floated face down in the pool.

Where the hell were the other doctors? Why weren't people already here? I tore off my white coat and jumped into the water. Another white cloud erupted in front of me. The cloud had a snarling mouth and blinding sockets. A chilling frost surrounded me as Morrow's face leered inches away. "Not yet," the thing hissed, smiling horribly within that dainty goatee. "Not yet."

I splashed away in panic. Pressed up against the side of the pool, I dared a look back at the shrouded water. Denise's body was bobbing up and down, shrouded in clutching tendrils of sour mist. The pool water felt like molasses as I tried moving forward on legs that refused to work, as invisible scratching things plucked at me. The picking became groping fingers or groping *claws*, trying to hold me back. I swatted at the clutching fingers but met only cold, frigid air.

"NOT YET," Morrow rumbled at me. More dead talons grasped at me and pulled me back. I watched in horror as Denise moved one hand and a second later jerked in the violent shudder of a seizure. She twitched once more, then remained still.

Morrow's face floated closer. "She's yours now, if you still want her." The vision dissolved into the last remaining currents of whitish chlorine gas. I squeezed my eyelids shut against the burning air. When I dared to open them again, I saw the limp form still floating motionlessly. I splashed over and lifted her up out of the pool.

Her eyes were wide open and staring. Lifeless. Blank. Dead.

"Denise?" I whispered. "*Denise*?" She remained flaccid and wilted in my arms. Grief washed over me, drowning out a small urgent voice pushing me to act, to start CPR, to do *something*. But it was too late. I knew it.

I don't know how long I'd been there when I heard voices and footsteps behind me. Nurses, pediatric residents, a red crash cart spilled through the doorway. People jumped into the water. Some were barking out orders, while others lifted Denise's body from my arms.

"What were you *doing*?" someone asked. I looked up into the face of someone in a white coat. "Don't you know CPR?" His voice was scolding.

"Hey Todd, we need you over here," someone else called. Todd threw me one last critical glance and splashed away. I felt numb, all thoughts frozen in a dense void. I was still standing in waist-deep water when a spasm of coughing broke my trance. I looked around the pool, but saw no one else. I'd been left alone. I staggered out of the pool and groped my way out of the door.

The hallway was in shambles, but no bodies living or dead littered the floor. A breeze wound past me. I followed it until I saw a shattered window. Something caught my eye as I glanced down at the broken shards crunching under my shoes. A baseball bat lay among the debris. I picked it up and squinted a closer inspection through eyes still burning. Norm's bat? Dark crimson stains discolored the grain. What the hell was it doing here? And where the hell had everyone gone?

Jumbled voices and scurrying footsteps answered my thoughts. I rushed towards the sound. The main corridor was in chaos. People were lined up against the wall and on the floor. Children with withered limbs and twisted swimsuits sprawled beside swim therapists and parents. All were coughing, gasping, and trying to gulp in air. Pediatric residents and interns darted among the victims.

I searched desperately for Connie–someone I could still protect. Firefighters in bulky coats and gas masks pushed through the crowd or were bent over prostrate victims. The last remaining wisps of deadly chlorine gas eddied away and vanished through the broken window.

More medical residents poured down the hall, barking out orders to the respiratory therapists hurrying among them with oxygen tanks and intubation kits. I saw Northrup bending over one of the parents. Frank hovered anxiously beside her, too blind behind fogged lenses to do anything other *than* hover.

Where was Connie? How the hell far could she have gone? I looked frantically at the turmoil. Northrup was arguing with someone standing next to Frank. Oh God, was she working on Connie? I stumbled in their direction. Northrup had summoned over one of the respiratory therapists, who was preparing a breathing tube for Northrup to insert. A bedraggled woman writhed on the floor in front of them, clutching her throat and wheezing air in and out with a strangled effort.

She looked up as I walked over. "Lindmark!" she snapped. "Just who I want. Your favorite patient seems to have wandered where he's not needed. And he wants to play doctor. Now get him out of here."

I stared at Leland Travis in disbelief. The old man had thrown on his tattered robe and must have followed all the noise in his confusion. I glanced down at the woman on the floor. A stranger, not my wife.

"Lindmark!" Northrup snapped again.

I put my arm gently around Travis's bony shoulders and tried pulling him out of harm's way. "What the hell are you doing here, Leland?"

"I'm a hell of a lot better off here than I would be in my room waiting for. . . " I waited. "Morrow," he breathed.

"Morrow's *here*, Leland," I hissed. "I saw him in there. Trying to kill my family." I strained to keep the tremble out of my voice. "This is *all* Morrow."

He grabbed me with his gnarled fingers and pulled me against the wall. "No, Lindmark. He was heading towards me. Listen to me," he murmured, his claw tightening around my arm. "He's coming for *us*. For anyone he wants dead."

Muttered curses interrupted him. Northrup had pulled the tube out of the woman's mouth and had straightened up. "Dammit!" she spat. All traces of poise and control had given way to panicked beads of sweat rolling off her. "I can't see her vocal cords. Too much swelling." She looked towards the respiratory therapist. "Bag her for a second," she commanded. I dared a glance at the woman lying on the floor. She was no longer writhing. All of her energy seemed focused on drawing in a breath. Her chest heaved and pulled, but only a tight strangled whistle made it past the pinpoint hole her throat must have closed down into. Northrup's eyes darted around wildly.

Travis pushed his way past Northrup, bent over the woman, and muttered, "We did these all the time. No specialists back then. I need a scalpel, Kelly clamps, and the smallest tracheostomy tube you have. If you can't find any, I'll take anything–large IV catheter, small urine catheter, even a fucking straw. Anything with a tube and a hole. Now!" Arthritic but gentle hands held the woman's head firm without palsy or hesitation.

Everything was becoming more surreal. I left Travis and Northrup, certain I would have nothing meaningful to offer to their frenzied efforts, and staggered away between and over the huddled clusters of poisoned swimmers and their rescuers. A child leaning up against the wall ahead of me shrieked and pointed at my side. I was still clutching the bloodstained baseball bat and must have looked like a crazed serial killer.

I stared at that screaming child, thinking only of another child somewhere in this building. *Someone else I cared about.*

I ran as best as I could through the disheveled corridor until coming on the check-in desk for the physical therapy department. I snatched up the phone and punched in the number of the pediatric ICU. "Let me speak to Audrey Schlager's nurse." I'd lost any trace of patience as I growled instead of spoke. Morrow had taken the only person who had ever watched out for Audrey, her mother. I'd be damned if he'd take anyone else. Connie had to be okay. She'd made it out with all the rest, I hoped. Safe somewhere in the crowd. But Audrey was left alone.

"She's busy right now," the voice on the other end sounded strained. "Can I have her—"

"This is Dr. Lindmark," I cut her off. "Is everything okay with Audrey Schlager?"

"Well, she. . . " I heard commotion in the background. The voice resumed, sounding distracted and edgy. "You know, they brought all the people from the pool in here all at once. All at once."

"What's going on?" I demanded.

"Well, the cuff somehow broke on her breathing tube. With everyone coming in suddenly, you know, we were all very busy. We don't know how long the tube had been that way when someone heard the alarm. Anyway, we had to take it out, because there was too big a leak. They're working on her now, and—"

I slammed down the phone and started towards the door in a panic.

"Dr. Lindmark?" someone called from behind me.

I turned impatiently. "What? *What?*"

"Were you, um, all finished with your bat?" A nurse held the bloodstained bat I must have dropped. I glared at her, but she remained serious without a hint of sarcasm.

"Norm Strickland. Over in the adult hospital. It's his. Run it over there and make sure you put it with all his belongings." I thought of the evil that surrounded us all, everywhere. "On second thought, lay it next to him in bed." I left her gape-mouthed as I sprinted past gagging bedraggled children and parents on a dead run towards Audrey.

I pushed open the Pediatric ICU doors and walked into chaos. Parents and staff clustered around almost every bed. An unpleasant metallic odor filled the air.

"Dr. Lindmark?" A disheveled nurse came up and looked at me through strands of dripping hair.

"Yeah, I'm Dr. Lindmark." I looked around the crowded bustling unit for a ventilator that might be attached to a curled-up little girl.

"She said you weren't coming, but I'm glad you were able to break away. I know she'd love to see you."

Audrey was alive? And already talking? It seemed almost too unbelievable to be true. But why not? Something finally had to go right in this wretched place. I followed the nurse as she wound her way through a jumbled maze of bassinets, wheezing parents, and disarrayed monitors. Oxygen tanks and exhausted interns alike lay strewn about the floor. Dangling IV lines swung from poles like translucent vines in a jungle. It was as if I'd walked into the remnants of some terrible natural disaster.

She'd love to see you. Morrow hadn't gotten to her yet, but I had to get to Audrey before he did. In the midst of all this, killing a little girl would be simple. He'd almost succeeded once. Oxygen turned off, wrong medications infused, too much of the right medications into those same little veins, I'd put nothing past Morrow's genius and rage.

We wormed our way into a quieter corner of the ICU. A small bed stood off on its own, a ventilator perched to one side with a nurse leaning over on the other side. The machine's implacable hissing rhythm announced that someone on the bed was living, but was not able to breathe on her own. How could Audrey have talked, if she were still on a ventilator? I rushed forward but stopped short as the nurse straightened up and bolted towards me.

Connie, not a nurse, slammed into me and embraced my chest in a hug almost painful. In the middle of chaotic din, we stood silent and unmoving, taking comfort in absorbing each other's desperation. She finally pulled away, as if unable to absorb any more emotion, and looked at me through eyes still reddened and swollen. I couldn't tell if they were inflamed from chlorine gas or from crying. Her expression was old, tired, and sad. It was Connie who had spoken to the nurse. It was Connie who would of course love to see me. I forced my gaze towards the bed. Audrey lay motionless, eyes closed, still violated by that hard plastic tube forced down into her lungs. I clutched one small, distorted hand and pulled Connie close with my other arm. I squeezed harder, our shared feelings battling against the helplessness that threatened to overwhelm us.

I had no idea how long we held each other. She finally lifted her head from my shoulder and looked at me. "I'm sorry, Harry. I'm sorry for all of us." Her voice faded off.

"I'm sorry, too," I whispered back. I didn't know what else to say. A slight movement drew my attention. I looked down and convinced myself it had been nothing. Until I felt it again.

Small fingers squeezing around my hand and holding it tight.

I'd seen it in some of my own patients. It couldn't be anything else. Sorenson had made sure to point it out when he'd run out of other teaching points on brain-damaged patients. Patients without a functioning brain cortex will involuntarily grasp anything put in their hand. Nothing more than a mindless reflex with no thought behind it. The grasp reflex, Sorenson had taught. It seemed as if the patient was following the command to squeeze, until he was asked to let go. The grasp would just continue without any thought behind it.

"Audrey?" I whispered.

The tiny fingers tightened.

"Audrey?" I said more loudly, unable to keep the hope out of my voice. I felt another feeble squeeze. I bent down closer. Her eyes snapped open. I almost jumped backwards, my heart pounding. The eyes that were really looking at me. They *knew* me. "Audrey?" I questioned one more time.

Fingers squeezed.

I dreaded what I knew had to be said next. "Audrey, let go. Let go of my hand, Audrey." Nothing happened. Her eyes blinked several times, but nothing else changed. Just another reflex. Of course it had been.

The little hand released my finger.

"Hold my hand, Audrey," I prompted shakily. "Now let go," I persisted softly.

The grip relaxed again. I looked back at her face. She was rolling her eyes.

Dr. Lindmark, enough with the squeeze, let go, squeeze, let go. Do you know any other great games? I could almost hear her saying those words.

She was more than just alive. She was *Audrey*, who'd survived Morrow again. He didn't have her, yet. But he would. He'd have everyone I knew or cared about. That unspeakable ghoul had won, even from the other side of death. I needed to take what was left of my life, which pretty much meant Connie, leave and start over.

My phone vibrated. I tried to focus on the text. Northrup wanted me. How long ago had I started rounding with her and Frank on all those patients? I'd left Northrup with Travis, who might be next. *Any* of us might be next.

An icy wind circled around me and literally blew me backwards, a frigid gusting mist out of which a gaunt ugly face loomed.

"You." It came from the face. The cold deepened around me. *Fine, I thought as blackness closed down around me. You've taken everything else, Dr. Morrow.* The face shimmered and bloated. *Go ahead, Morrow. Go ahead.* The dark didn't rush at me. It just closed in, like a coffin lid, and tightened down like a noose.

CHAPTER 25

"Lindmark?"

The voice rasped as if rising through dirt and gravel.

"Lindmark. Come on, dammit!"

I cracked open my eyes. A gaunt, unkempt face stared down at me. Travis's gaunt face. My head throbbed as I raised myself up and saw the spartan interior of the interns' call room surrounding me. The vise around my head gradually eased and the last wisps of fog cleared from my thoughts. The pool, and the fumes, and Audrey battered into my memory. Audrey with no mother. Morrow had been in that ICU, with the children. I struggled to sit upright, panic clutching at my throat as memory flooded back.

"Lindmark, relax," Travis commanded. "You passed out. Must've inhaled more chlorine than you thought. I knew you wouldn't make it. Followed you over there, saw you go down. ER's too full, so we brought you here to watch you."

Travis was bathed in a soft glow. The scent of freshly cut grass wafted gently around me.

A strange calm descended until the memories pushed their way back. "How long have I been here? I need to get back." I set my jaw as images of Connie, and of Denise's limp body, and of Audrey sharpened into focus. "I need to take care of—"

"Relax, Lindmark," Travis repeated. "If I hadn't almost broken my back getting you onto that stretcher, you'd still be lying passed out. So why don't you lie back a little while longer before the same thing happens again?" He must have seen the panic in my expression. "Don't worry. I paged Dr. Bethany. I told him what happened. He said he'd take care of things for you."

"Bethany? You talked to Dr. Bethany?"

Travis nodded.

"He listened to you?"

"Yeah. That pompous fat fire hydrant in a white coat didn't even argue with me. Asked if you were okay. Residency must be turning him all warm and fuzzy."

"All right, fine," I replied. "But you don't understand about Morrow. He's still here. He's not going to stop, you know."

Travis cleared his throat. "Morrow ain't so tough, Lindmark. I thought he was, but he ain't. I thought he'd taken my life away when he took Kevin's, and I've been afraid of him ever since. Afraid of him when he was alive, and afraid after he was dead. But he didn't take my life away, Lindmark. He's a pathetic blowhard on both sides of the grave." Leland Travis spoke with a vigor I hadn't previously heard.

The strange moment vanished as the door burst open. Bethany's face was more flushed than usual. "Travis said you were here, Harry." He looked at the older doctor. "Guess that should be *Doctor* Travis," he added. "Dr. Northrup told me what you did back there in the other hospital with that emergency tracheostomy. You must have been a hell of a doctor back in the Middle Ages." He turned to me. "Anyway, you're needed, Lindmark."

I'd never seen Martin Bethany look like this. "Everything's going to hell out there. That accident over in the pool must be spreading fumes all over both hospitals. We were pulled out of the ER to help out the rest of the hospital. Haven't you heard the code horns? If you don't get up and start helping us out there, more are going to die after they inhale that stuff." He directed his gaze at Leland. "We could probably use you too, Dr. Travis." He allowed a small smile to twitch inside his beard. "You seem better without a medical license than some of my colleagues who have one."

I took a deep breath. "The only place I'm going is the Pediatric ICU, to see Connie and Audrey. That ghoul won't stop until everyone I know and care about is dead. Whether they leave this hospital or stay." I swiped at the tears that suddenly burned my eyes. "It's not the chemicals, the fumes, the medications that are going to kill more patients, Dr. Bethany. They're just tools. It's *us*. Morrow and the rest are going to keep killing. It's the dead. They'll just keep killing everyone."

I shut my eyes against the sights I had just endured, then opened them. Travis and Bethany appeared blurred and indistinct through tears. "He knows how, don't you see? Morrow–he lived and died and practiced medicine in here, for God's sake. He uses our tools, our computers, everything we trust to kill and then to escape. I'm not so stupid, Dr. Bethany, and I'm not psychotic. Remember how hot it was in Shirkey's room? Of course you don't. You weren't there." I heard myself babbling but I couldn't shut off the words once they'd started rushing out. "Hot air expands. Gas in bowels expands. With those sutures holding together diseased diabetic skin, all it took was heat to expand his bowels like balloons through that wound. Charlie–electrocuted. That boy Richman–insulin shock. Poor Audrey Schlager–given the only medicine she was allergic to. Her mother, *dead*, goddam it. You want me to go on? I know what everyone thinks, that I'm a shit doctor. Maybe I did make mistakes. But I know what I've seen, on both sides of the grave. And maybe, just maybe, some of them weren't mistakes." I gave up trying to stop the tears and instead turned my head away.

"Just can't let it go, Harry? Look, just lie back, okay?" I'd never heard Bethany sound so gentle. In the next instant, his expression changed. "Grab your crucifix and garlic and whatever else you need, but don't forget your stethoscope and whatever modern medicine you can scrape together. Just get out there. Now."

I swiped a sleeve across my cheeks. "Didn't you hear what I just said? All the science in the world isn't going to cure this place of death.

It's Morrow." Aromas of popcorn, cut apples, and crayons suddenly wafted around me. My breathing slowed.

"I been saying the same damn thing for years, Lindmark," Travis said. "Unlike you, I don't care if people think I'm demented or psychotic." A crooked grin revealed teeth long deprived of meaningful hygiene. "I know my boy must be here. I believe you, Lindmark. Who cares what Dr. Ass-Hat thinks? But—"

"Let me finish. I'm not giving up. But I'm *not* going to protect the people I love with formulas and machines and medical algorithms. I'm going to give Morrow what he wants and put an end to all this."

A strange expression softened Bethany's features. I blinked and squinted up at my resident, but his expression remained inscrutable, almost stony. "Harry, I think those fumes may have done a job on you. I believe you about the dead. At least, I believe that you and Dr. Travis believe. I'll admit, with everything so out of control, I'll believe just about anything right now. So if the dead are here, I'm as scared shitless of them as you are. But we still need to be doctors, Harry." Bethany's tone was wary. "Now, we need to get going, *with* all those formulas and machines. Right?"

I sat up in the bed, swung my legs over the side and stood up. The room swam sickeningly for several moments, then steadied. "No, not right. It's not going to stop until Morrow gets what he wants. He knows he didn't deserve to die, especially to suffer like that. Being trapped in-between just prolongs he pain. I know this because. . . " I glanced at Travis and knew I could not torture the old man with more stories of his son. "I just know it. He'll keep finding bodies, *creating* bodies from people just trying to get better until someone, maybe *you* Dr. Bethany, can resuscitate one successfully and let him walk out like Timmy. But that trapped soul got tired of being babied, didn't it? It got tired of taking medications. That's one thing Morrow didn't count on. A new soul still has to answer to whatever illnesses remain in a used body. Like a seizure disorder, in Timmy's case. But Morrow is always learning, isn't he? *Isn't he?*"

"Calm down, Harry." Travis grabbed my arm as the room spun. "You're panting. No wonder you're dizzy." Travis released me as I landed back on the bed.

The unsteadiness cleared but the expressions on Travis and Bethany infuriated me. "He'll wait like he has been, even if they shut this place down for a while. You can't disinfect a hospital of souls. Hungry souls. All they got is time. So I'm going to give him someone. Me. My body. Because he's going to kill *me* one way or the other anyway. Or make me wish I were dead. At least no one else will have to die." I stared at Bethany, then at Travis. "You both are going to help me."

The pungency of cut grass weaved through the sweet scent of suntan lotion that perfumed the air. I breathed in deeply, but choked as icy wind slashed through the smells and burned its way into my lungs. I clutched at my throat, trying to tear open the blockage and let in air, but I couldn't pry away the vise of icy fingers that were squeezing, strangling. Redness clouded over my vision, then darkened to dried-blood crimson. The room started spinning again.

"Help me," I gasped out. I clawed one last time at my throat but couldn't open the pinhole that was tightening closed. The redness and blackness washed over me as I fell, *upwards, up* into the darkness.

"Dr. Lindmark?"

"Harry. Harry! Come on, Harry, you're okay, dammit."

The voices buzzed and nagged at me like flies.

"Dr. Lindmark, you better get up now." There it was again. So familiar. The smell hit me. It had to be Kevin. But the smell wasn't popcorn or sunny meadow flowers. It was foul and curdled, like—

"Jesus, I wish he'd stop passing out."

"I don't care if he passes out. I just wish he'd do it without throwing up first."

It was Bethany's voice. He was here with me. I became aware of something icy still wrapped around my throat, and more coldness shrouding my head. Had Bethany and I both died, and now we were on Morrow's side? Trapped with *him*, his icy fingers still wrapped around my throat?

I bolted upright.

"Watch it! He's going to throw up again." Bethany's voice. I felt hands grip me and gently push me back onto the bed. I managed to open my eyes and look around. No redness, no blackness. The call room looked. . . like the call room. Nothing dead leered at me. Just Bethany and Travis. They both looked very much alive, which meant I was alive, thank God. I reached for the cloying icy fingers that were locked around my neck–and grabbed a cold washcloth. A damp, cold cloth on my forehead dripped water down my cheeks..

"Take it easy, Lindmark," I heard Travis say. "Leave the washcloths there, or you might vomit again." Hands again pressed down on me firmly. I opened my eyes and tried to shake my head clear of the fog.

"Did you guys. . . what the hell happened?" I managed to ask. "I was choking. Morrow was killing me. Choking me. Did I die?" I saw Travis and Bethany look at each other.

"You passed out, Lindmark. You didn't die, for God's sake," Travis said. "One of the worst panic attacks I've ever seen."

"So what happened to the two of you? How come I was the only one who fainted?"

"Don't forget about throwing up, Lindmark," Bethany said. "You were the only one to do that, too."

"I have to leave," I snapped. "You don't need me, Dr. Bethany. If you really want someone who can help, take Leland. Dr. Travis." I looked at the old man. "You know what he can do. I've got to go." I flung open the door of the call room and swerved my way into the hospital's chaos.

I merged into the crowd and snaked my way through the throngs of nurses, scurrying families, and harried respiratory therapists. An occasional firefighter clomped by me, a strange vision so out of place in a hospital corridor. Word of the pool accident must have traveled quickly and spread panic. I shouldered my way upstream against the crowd, finally pushing through into near-deserted corridors. Acrid wisps still snaking through the halls finally disappeared as I stumbled into the Pediatric ICU.

"Harry!"

I turned and was almost crushed in an unexpected embrace so tight I could barely squeeze out words. "How is Audrey?"

Connie's arms relaxed from their death grip. "She's *good,* Harry. She *smiled* at me around that awful tube. She needs real close observation, but the doctors are pretty optimistic. They keep saying it's as close to a miracle as they've ever seen."

God, she'd smiled. I couldn't stop the tears. I broke from Connie's arms to walk to Audrey's bed. She peered up at me above that plastic tube, with eyes that *saw.*

She smiled.

We slept the entire night as close to that smile as possible, Connie on one side of the bed, I lay vigilant and trembling on the other. I dreaded when we'd have to do what life and disability and near-death couldn't do–finally kill that smile. Because we would need to tell her that the one constant in her life, her mother, was gone. Only Connie and I could tell her. I dreaded that. The death of that smile would be the death of me.

No, I considered as I lay trembling amidst the disarray of the ICU. My death would come from something far worse than a child's anguish, and it was coming soon. I knew what Connie didn't, that we offered little real protection for ourselves or for Audrey. Connie rested contentedly, secure in the comfort adults offer children against the darkness, against the imaginary shadows and monsters that always disappear in the morning. I couldn't rest so easily because I knew they weren't imaginary. They'd be waiting and hungering even in the morning. It was the first time I'd slept beside a child at night. It would also be the last time, because I was a condemned man.

The morning arrived peacefully, which was to me only a cruel illusion. Connie persuaded me to go home, to shower and change clothes before digging into the chaos of the hospital. If only she knew. The emptiness of my house wasn't lonely or threatening. The quiet was welcoming and safe. No code horns, no reek of disease or antiseptic or body fluids, no *dead*. I put on clean scrubs meticulously, slowly, stalling my return. I brushed my teeth carefully over and over again, using a*ny* mundane task to put off returning to that hospital.

The Room pulled at me. We should have made it into a study, I thought bitterly, not kept it a memorial. The sheets in the crib were crisp and pristine. Had Connie continued to change the sheets? Daily, or weekly, or monthly? Why? Why put herself through that? Was she punishing herself for nature's cruelty? Or was Connie just too stubborn to close the door on both the room and on the past, as I was only too willing to do?

Children's books lay carefully stacked in one corner. Many of the pages were dog-eared and worn. Connie's own books, probably. How often had she imagined reading them to her own child?

A small box caught my attention. "Tooth Fairy Treasure Chest" emblazoned the front in Connie's handwriting. I opened it up. Empty. I peered around a room I'd never really seen before. A baseball glove leaned against one of the crib's legs. The worn, faded baseball glove I'd shown to Connie one day, an eternity ago. *My old glove*, I'd declared to her proudly. *We need to make sure not to lose it*, I'd cautioned her. *Because a kid needed to learn how to catch even before he learned to walk. Because baseball players made good money, and because I'd need a playmate.* I'd forgotten all about that glove. Apparently Connie hadn't.

I almost succumbed to a sudden lightheadedness, steadying myself against a wall as I looked around a child's room. A room complete with everything for a childhood except a child. It was a testament, I realized. A testament to Connie's hopefulness and determination.

Where had my input been? I'd been the one with all the plans for baseball, and football, and games, and fun. I'd also been the one to dive headfirst into internship after our baby's painfully short life. All the while Connie had held on to vanishing hope that she could become pregnant again. Even if that happened, there was the likelihood the same genetic defect would sentence our next child to an early death. I shook my head at how saving lives as a doctor had become so much more important than creating lives as a husband. A bitter taste soured my mouth. I'd been too much of a coward to invest my feelings in a lost cause.

I glanced once more into The Room. I'd literally closed that door and never looked back on that room, and on Connie. I released a long, shaking breath. The disgust I felt, disgust for myself, overwhelmed the fear that had driven me from the hospital. It pressed in on me from the inside out and drove home the certainty of what I had to do. I had run away again, like the coward I was. First, I'd run away from Connie and from the pain of our loss. Now I'd run away from people who needed help. People I cared about, and people who I hadn't met yet. Anyone who was in that hospital. I felt angry and disgusted, but no longer afraid.

It was important to keep going. I *had* to keep going. The plans became reassuring in their complexity and logic as I collected my phone, hospital coat, and keys. A strange peace slowly replaced the frenetic urgency of my actions. Morrow wouldn't win. He wouldn't take Audrey, or the Stricklands or Connie or Bethany or—

Morrow wouldn't take any of them. Morrow and the dead would not win. Something I'd been told, an academic nugget tossed out at me, took hold and spurred the plans that now offered a small sense of calm. I *would* need Bethany and Travis. I would even need to rely on Morrow's evil. And I would need to do it before they shut the hospital down, or else Morrow and the dead would just wait and linger and yearn to escape that prison until the opportunity arose again with new patients, with better computers in a remodeled fail-safe hospital. *Yeah, right.* Fail-safe for the dead, as long as the living persisted at the mercy of numbers and pixels.

I reached for the door, but stopped just before grasping the knob. Wasn't this where I should get my affairs in order? Shouldn't I say or do any last meaningful things before the end, forever? I looked around the kitchen, then glanced one more time up the stairs to the bedrooms.

The emptiness turned on me. It was no longer comforting. The façade of refuge was now just a place empty of people, warmth, memories. No one to say last words to, no one to give witness to my last wishes.

I forced myself to keep moving. I had to keep moving.

CHAPTER 26

I called Bethany from the car and told him what I'd need. I even told him exactly where to go and hoped he wouldn't ask me how the hell I knew about it. He didn't. He paused for a long several seconds, then assured me in a quiet un-Bethany tone that he'd take care of it.

"You sure about this, Harry?"

"I'm sure, Dr. Bethany." The pounding in my chest betrayed the certainty of my voice.

"Call me Martin, okay?"

We both knew what was going on, but neither of us would say it. "Thanks. . . Martin," I said. "I'll call you when I get there."

Next, I called Travis's room from my cell phone. I was relieved when he answered. Morrow's next rampage could easily have started with Leland. He, too, said nothing after I'd explained what I needed. "That's it, then?" he asked.

"That's it," I assured him. "Do I have a choice?"

Maybe it was the guilt he'd endured every night for all those years. Guilt over that one time, the *only* time, he hadn't been there for Kevin. Maybe he needed a shot at revenge to ease that guilt.

"No, Lindmark," he rasped on the other end. "No choice. I understand."

I hung up and shook my head in disbelief. I'd just divulged the same incredible future to two people. One a well-respected doctor, the other a once-respected doctor, and they'd both agreed to join the conspiracy. They'd just accepted it.

Was I crazy, or were they?

We'd looked a ghoul in the face. We'd all faced a hatred so intense it had survived death. Psychotic breaks from reality weren't contagious. Morrow was real. My eyes burned with tears. Why *shouldn't* they both accept what I'd asked of them, if it meant both their lives and the lives of other innocents might be spared at the expense of mine?

The hospital rose into view as I drove to the visitor's lot of the children's wing. It looked more ancient and forbidding than it ever had. I couldn't afford to be stopped before going through the Pediatric ICU. It didn't matter where the hell I parked. It would be a one-way trip. I wasn't planning on leaving.

Two fire trucks were still stationed outside the doors, disconcerting reminders of yesterday's catastrophe. I forced myself past them and entered the hospital. A bitter smell still lingered in the corridors. Not everything had come back to normal overnight. Workers chipped and hammered at stained sections of the walls and ceilings. Official-looking men in dark suits prowled down the corridors with decontamination appliances held in front of them. A spider web of yellow tape crisscrossed in front of the hallway leading towards the therapy pool. It was probably only due to the massive logistical problems of moving so many patients, and interrupting critical care, that had prevented Narragansett General's immediate shut-down.

The doors to the ICU finally came into sight. I looked around until I saw Audrey's bed. The breathing tube had been removed. She was breathing on her own.

"Audrey?" I reached for her hand.

Round eyes fluttered open and peered up at me. Small fingers squeezed my hand weakly, as reassuring to me as a crushing iron grip would have felt. She lay in a limp tangle of wires and sterile hospital bedding, but breathing on her own. Weakly, each breath sucking in skin and muscle between protruding ribs, but breathing on her own.

"Hi, Dr. Lindmark!" Her voice was hoarse and strained from the breathing tube that had scraped her vocal cords raw on its way to saving her life.

"Hi there, Audrey," I grinned back. "I—"

"Could you move a little bit?" Her voice was an eerie mimic of Linda Blair's rasp in The Exorcist.

"Well sure, Audrey," I replied. "Is everything all right?"

"I'm okay, Dr. Lindmark." She smiled up at me through the opaque plastic of the oxygen mask. "I just talked them into putting one of my videos into the player, and now you're in the way." I turned around and saw Austin Powers fighting Doctor Evil in a submarine lair.

I had to grin at her. "Looks like you're pretty well plugged in, huh?"

"My throat hurts."

"It's the tube, Audrey. The one that—"

Frigid air whistled around my shoulders and snaked down around my legs. "He's here," Audrey whispered. "He said he'd come back. He's here."

I wanted to yell out that it was too early, that I would do what he wanted if he would just let us be for one last visit.

A pungent fragrance cut through the cold.

"Kevin. Hi, Kevin," Audrey warbled. "I told you he's here. Kevin-from-heaven. Kevin-from-heaven."

Kevin?

I didn't see him anywhere. Audrey's eyes were closed, but her crooked little lips widened into an even bigger smile. "Kevin?" I whispered.

The boy's whisper was far more chilling than the cold he'd dragged with him. "Go away from her. It's time."

"Is Morrow here?" I asked fearfully.

"He's not here, Dr. Lindmark. He's waiting for you. You don't want him to come here."

I leaned over Audrey and gazed at her face. Now *she* could hear and see Kevin. One more living person who could sense the dead, because she too had gone over to that side and had been brought back. She smiled up at me. I'd never get more friends for her birthdays, but I sure as hell would make sure she'd *have* more birthdays.

"You seen my mom, Dr. Lindmark?" she rasped. "She must have got lost. I think Mrs. Lindmark must be looking for her."

I couldn't stop my eyes from watering. "I'll be back, Audrey. I'll let you know." I'd copped out again, but it would be the last time I'd cop out. I squeezed her hand, then stumbled away. I looked around for Connie, but she'd left somewhere. I needed to see her, to tell her goodbye. Maybe it was for the best. She wouldn't believe me, or would try to stop me. Either way, I'd leave her safe.

I sighed, walked out the doors, and had almost reached the entrance to the adult hospital before it hit me. "Kevin?" I asked into the empty corridor. "Where am I supposed to go?"

"Down."

A jolt of fear twisted in me. "The tunnel? I'm not sure. . . "

"We can't be interrupted."

"But people use that tunnel. All the transporters use it. That's where—"

"No one now," Kevin answered. "Look."

We'd arrived at the faded metallic doorway to the stairwell. The same yellow police tape stretched from one side of the frame to the other, an official warning against opening the door. The cloying scent of suntan lotion drifted about and helped calm the dread that wormed through me. I tore the tape aside and pushed open the door leading to the tunnel.

Something moved in the corner of my vision. I turned and saw the small boy far down the hallway. Still a lost, frail teen. The spectral image of Kevin gazed at me.

"Just one more thing, Kevin. Please." Maybe I was stalling. But death was waiting for me in that tunnel. The Room rose in my thoughts, gnawed at me. Now, when it was too late to do anything, why was lost parenthood suddenly so important? I knew it somehow came back to this place. I had to know for sure, because I somehow knew that in this place lost parenthood would end with me, but it hadn't started with me.

I needed the answer to my last request and stopped before entering the yawning gloom of the stairwell. "Kevin, your dad, I know all about what happened. I've never heard either of you even mention your mother. Where is she?"

"This is important? Now?" He drifted closer, features still indistinct from the distance.

"It's important, Kevin." I glanced at the open doorway. The row of lights strung above the tunnel cast a feeble glow over the stairwell in front of me. "*Especially* now."

"You have to go. Soon. My mom, I think, tried her best with me, but I always knew I wasn't right for her. I think my mom kind of gave up on me. She always had something to do whenever my dad and I went places. Usually with her friends and their families. With *their* kids."

"Kevin—"

"My mom came up to see my dad one night while he was on call. After I died, my dad, well, my dad wasn't so good. I guess my mom didn't want to be with him anymore. So she came up to the hospital and met my dad down here, in this tunnel. He liked being down here by himself when he didn't have a patient to take care of. Talking to himself, down here. Sometimes he'd talk to Charlie."

Uneasy dread fingered icily down my spine.

"She said all sorts of things to him, Dr. Lindmark." His radiance dimmed. "She asked why he'd always ignored her and spent so much time on me, when he knew I'd only die anyway. And then she told him that he didn't even have a rep, a repo. . . "

"Reputation?" I finished quietly for him.

"Or the future she'd wanted. She told him that, Dr. Lindmark. She'd wanted a family, and she wanted everyone to be proud of them. She told my dad that now she didn't have either. He was an embarrassment. She said she wanted to start over and have another child. But she couldn't because they might have another child like me. She yelled that." His words hung in the air as ghostly as he himself was.

"Then she held up a knife. I think it's called a scalpel."

I could do nothing but nod.

"I watched my dad take a few steps back. My mom walked towards him."

A metallic coppery odor filled the air. "She made so many cuts across both of her wrists with that knife. Right in front of my dad. I saw blood everywhere, Dr. Lindmark. My dad did what he could, but there are no phones down here. No way to call for help. So he was in the tunnel trying to stop it with just his hands, until she died. But she never left. Like me. Because . . . I guess because it was so wrong how she died."

I'd walked down the stairs without realizing, so caught up in the words of a dead boy. The tunnel's walls loomed up on either side, resurrecting the terror I'd felt every time I was down here. Especially that one time when bloodied, contaminated medical waste had filled the tunnel with screaming death as it hurled at me. "I heard her, Kevin," I gasped out the sudden realization. "That was your mother screaming at me down here. I could feel her anger. She tried to bring me into death with her, with those needles and scalpels." Something else pierced the tunnel's dank mustiness at my words. "I smell it, Kevin," I managed to rasp. "I smell the blood. But you were already gone. How did the blood come back with you like all the rest of the smells?"

"I'm just a kid, Dr. Lindmark. My mom died. I died. That's what I know." Kevin's presence melted into the gloom. The fragile row of naked bulbs wobbled and swayed. Frigid wisps of empty coldness curled about me, like invisible exploring tentacles snaking ahead of something from deeper down in the tunnel. Something else that was coming.

His voice echoed at me from everywhere and nowhere. "She's here waiting, Dr. Lindmark. With all the rest." The pungent thick smell of old-fashioned glue blanketed the thick coppery smell, lingering even after Kevin's voice resumed. "But Dr. Morrow doesn't care about anything else besides his own escape. I feel the anger. Of Dr. Morrow towards the living, and of the dead towards Dr. Morrow."

A shrieking storm of ice swept down around me, erasing Kevin's voice and sweeping away the comforting aromas. Several of the overhead bulbs exploded and showered me with glass. I cowered against the wall and stared in utter terror as Morrow's deathly visage raged towards me. The tunnel beyond had filled with a damp, writhing mist.

Morrow floated closer, bottomless eye pits searing into me. A frosty vise clamped down around my arms. Something like a claw poked through my shirt in back and hurled me towards the fog that pulsed like a living thing. I held my breath so the acrid fumes wouldn't choke me. The gray-white wisps neither burned nor choked as I was dragged into their midst, but instead parted to either side. It wasn't smoke or fog or mist. Up close, I could see the bone-gray features of so many disembodied souls.

A low muttering rustled all around me. The faces and bodies of young people scarred by gaping bloodless incisions, old hunchbacked patients with breathing tubes obscenely protruding from their mouths, bandaged trauma victims. . . all loomed up at me, surrounded me. There was no smell or stench, nothing slimy smeared against me despite the gaping wounds and punctures that each had taken along into death.

"I will give you what you want," Morrow hissed in my ear. I dared not turn to see that face again. "One more chance to provide me a body, by *being* the body." The voice deepened to an invisible vibration that shivered through me. "The rest can be here forever. *I will get out.*"

An icy force pushed and dragged me further into the tunnel. Pain ripped down my arm as it caught on a rusted pipe. Lights swung wildly overhead. The muttering horde of souls parted to let us pass. I heard my shirt tear and felt more pain as my back scraped against rough concrete.

I opened my mouth to scream, but fear paralyzed my throat. I wanted to stop moving down the tunnel. I wanted the muttering to stop. I wanted the dead to leave me alone. *I wanted so much not to die.* All my plans, everything I'd set in motion, abandoned me as terror closed in from all sides. Too late. My head swam in time to the swinging lights above.

I fell heavily onto the floor as the cold released me. The murmuring quieted. Dim hazy light settled on two figures standing in the middle of the tunnel. Human figures. Familiar living people. Bethany stood with hands on his hips, looking more like a general reviewing his troops than a fellow human at the mercy of yearning souls. Beside him Leland Travis looked as grim and gray as a ghost himself.

"Lindmark." It was a declaration. Bethany's voice was oddly impassive. "We're here. Right where you told us to be."

I tottered closer to them on legs that would barely hold me. My back throbbed. I could feel a sticky wetness dripping down my arm. As I approached, I could see a steel table behind them, a cold metallic bed meant to be upholstered with body bags. A bulging IV fluid bag hung from an attached pole, next to a red crash cart brought in for my purpose. My death wouldn't work as Morrow needed, unless I could be resuscitated. I suffered a brief fleeting smile as I knew that crash cart would instead play into *my* plans, not Morrow's–if everyone did what they were supposed to do. Living and dead alike.

So far the living, Bethany and Travis, had done their part. Everything looked as I'd commanded.

"The crash cart. It's from years ago," Travis answered my unspoken thoughts in a distant tone. "Never was used, you know. At least as far as I can tell. Because the only patients who are wheeled down here are on their way to the morgue. Except my wife. That crash cart wasn't here then." His voice faded to a weak mumble. A shrill, ululating screech echoed up from somewhere in the blackness. No one else turned their heads or seemed to hear that eerie wail that filled my head.

Bethany pushed Travis aside and walked up to me. He gripped my arm and leaned close. I could feel the bristles of his beard. He stank of sweat, even more than usual. "You still good with this, Harry? This is murder you want us to do."

"*Good* with this? Hell no, I'm not fucking *good* with this." I could barely keep my voice from shaking. Images of Audrey and Connie surfaced in my thoughts and stoked my resolve. "But it won't end if I don't go through with it. He wants *me*, Martin. And he wants his freedom from this place. I can't have any more people die, especially after he'd led me into helping with some of those deaths." I put my mouth up to his ear and hissed, "But we'll get him, Martin. Just do what I told you to do. You have the drugs, right?" He nodded. I pulled back and looked into Bethany's eyes. "It's not that bad, you know. Because now I know there's something. . . *after*, for all of us. Maybe I'll see my baby. Just please," I locked my gaze on his. "Just make it worth it. Like I told you."

A blade of ice sliced between us and drove us apart. Morrow's voice rumbled from within the cold, shapeless glow and echoed off the tunnel walls. "You will do this. Or you'll die anyway, in pain." Terror squeezed down around me and sucked the strength from my legs. I wobbled, then sank to my knees.

"Shut up," Travis snapped. "Leave us alone and we'll get it done." I saw him dart a glance at Bethany. "You don't scare me, Morrow. Not anymore. Only life scares me."

"You ready, Lindmark?" Bethany asked. Something about his voice. It wasn't fearful or shaking. It was Bethany's normal voice. Was he brave, or still somehow disbelieving even at this late date? Maybe because Morrow hadn't threatened *him* along with Travis and me?

His grip tightened on my arm as he pulled me to my feet. "You need to get on the table now, Harry. Can you do it?" I shook my head. "Let me help." He hoisted me onto the stark metal table. Travis appeared at my side and rolled up one of my sleeves. His touch was gentle.

"Just. . . " Bethany swallowed loudly, then continued as he bent over my arm. "Just a little stick." I barely felt the jab of the IV catheter compared to the painful throbbing that wracked my body. Warm fluid ran down my arm a second later.

Each heart beat seemed to lift me off the table, as if that organ of life were pounding out its protest at the imminent trauma. "It's okay, Martin," I croaked. "It's okay."

I watched as Travis opened up the crash cart and nodded his head at several filled syringes lying in one of the drawers. He nodded one more time, then slid the drawer closed on the syringes I'd told him to get. He turned his back on me and started playing with certain dials on the defibrillator. The machine that would shock my body back from death. But Morrow didn't know everything. I was not going to let Morrow escape.

"Leland. Come here for a second." He squeezed past Bethany and leaned over me. "Leland, you brought all the medications like I told you, right?" I whispered to him. "The Pavulon, the morphine? *Especially* the morphine?" I didn't want to be aware. I did *not* want to be paralyzed awake. I wanted only to go to sleep peacefully and let it end. The morphine would do that.

"I got 'em, Harry. Just like you said," he whispered. "Just lie back. Martin and I can take it from here." He squeezed my hand. I remembered the first time he'd clutched me, so long ago. A repulsive claw then, his touch was now gentle, reassuring, needed. He stepped back wordlessly, walked back over to the crash cart, and continued to fiddle with dials on the defibrillator.

Bethany, meanwhile, was adjusting the rate of fluid dripping in my arm. He then unbuttoned my shirt and attached small pads across my chest. Pads to register my heart beat, but also to deliver deadly shocks of electricity at the right time. When he clipped wires onto the pads, a loud rhythmic beep from the defibrillator broke through the silence of the tunnel. My heart tones. The last sound I would hear. Would I hear those beeps slow to a crawl as the drugs took effect? Would I lose consciousness before hearing that one constant flat-line drone seconds before my brain succumbed and my soul left?

Bethany's voice interrupted my thoughts. "We need to know when you, um, when you pass, Harry. So we know when to resuscitate you. That's why we have to hook the monitor up. So we'll know when it's finished. When. . . *you've* left."

Straps secured my wrists to the table. I raised my eyebrows at Bethany, the beeping of the heart monitor sounding louder and faster. "Just making sure no unexpected involuntary jerk or twitches at the time of your passing dislodges IVs or pads, Harry," Bethany said, his voice coated with emotion. "I've seen it happen during other resuscitation efforts." He offered up as close to a smile of encouragement as his plethoric features would permit.

The monitor's beeping slowed, reflecting my trust in his answer. He and Travis had thought of everything that might make this as painless as possible for me. I stared up at the flaking ceiling, blood rushing and pounding in my ears in perfect time with the metronomic beeping of my heart. The monitor's steadfast proof of life barely penetrated the sudden quiet in the tunnel, so thick it felt almost tangible. I suddenly wanted to tear through the silence and the cold before they could smother me.

A deep rumble filled the surrounding frosty air. Coated with ice, filled with so much hate and hunger, I could *feel* the menace. "Do it now," Morrow intoned. "DO IT."

A voice from the grave, from that disgusting lusting soul. I was about to die. I looked up at Bethany. "You heard him, Martin. Go ahead. I'm ready." Tears ran down my face. "Just please make sure I go to sleep. Please Martin. I don't want to feel." A sudden awareness broke through the dread that had consumed all thought as I saw Bethany look up and nod. Bethany had heard Morrow? Bethany could hear the dead? He hadn't before, with Richman. Bethany was human, like Travis, and like all the others had been denied the connection with the other side that I was cursed with.

He turned back to me, holding a syringe in one outstretched hand. "Just before you die, Lindmark, I want you to know. You told me all your plans. Thanks for that. Might have worked, too. Giving yourself up for Morrow, then having one of us inject your body with the paralyzing drug and imprisoning him." He leaned in until his beard scratched my face. His words breathed against me. "He helped *me*. I owe *him*. You piece of shit."

My eyes widened. Martin Bethany's tone had deepened into an icy monotone, contempt dripping off each word. The monitor filled the tunnel with a rapid staccato of beeps as my heart rate quickened.

"You told us to keep your body paralyzed to keep *Sylvester Morrow* in the prison of your body on life support for as long as your body would last. Genius, Lindmark. But you told *me*. You trusted *me* to help do it." He lifted up the fiery red beard that had taken on a blood-red tint in the tunnel's gloom, revealing a small scar over his throat.

A tracheostomy scar. Similar to mine.

"I told you I had an accident in my internship year. I said I almost died, that I felt I deserved to die. Remember? I *did* die, Lindmark. Emergency tracheostomy, CPR, the whole thing. I passed through the in-between on my way to peace, eternity, whatever. Morrow was there, Lindmark. But I was brought back, thanks to all those trauma doctors. Before Morrow could steal what had been mine, my body. I felt his hunger then, and I took his message with me back to life after my resuscitation."

He pushed his neck with that vivid tracheostomy scar closer. His breath turned rancid, his voice graveled as if he were speaking through something that had decayed far back in his throat. "He told me he would kill every single patient I treated, unless I helped him escape. He would ruin my life, my new life that those trauma doctors had given me back. I'd never be the doctor I could have been, I'd lose my life's meaning, I'd be blamed for all those patient deaths, unless I helped him, Lindmark. Helped him come back from the dead. The weeks on a ventilator, the rehab, were all worth it. I regained my life, and I became the great doctor I once was. Again." His eyes stared with bloodshot intensity as they bore into mine. "I'm the best doctor here, almost as good as Dr. Morrow himself was. I've been trying to pay up ever since. You've kept fucking that up. Until now. Now you'll seal the deal, for *me*."

"DO…IT."

I became dizzy with terror at Morrow's hollow, throaty command.

Bethany kept up his stream of consciousness as he popped the cap off the syringe and tapped any air out of it. "Of course I didn't show up for Shirkey because he was supposed to die, not be resuscitated. Morrow wanted him dead, and so he was going to die. I never called any surgical resident. Why would you believe that, Lindmark? No one runs my codes. You believed that, and you believed that sob story about the old man and the fluid I drained. You're pathetic."

I struggled against the restraints as he plunged the needle on the syringe into the IV and emptied the morphine into me.

"I'll do everything you told us to do, Lindmark, except the last part. No paralyzing drug to lock Morrow in. Morphine, electric shock to ventricular fibrillation and death. Then electrical shock back to life and resuscitation. Just your body giving Morrow years of new life, the way it was meant to be. How does it feel, volunteering to give life back to Morrow? We're the same, Lindmark–both of us paying our debt to the dead. You, for the lives of others. Me, for my own life and reputation."

I struggled to sit up, to roll off, to escape, but I felt suddenly confused, wobbly. The morphine. . . Bethany pushed me back down onto the cold metal with one beefy hand. All my plans, ruined. I was watching Bethany prepare to electrocute my heart, but couldn't even raise my arms to stop what I'd set in motion. The reason for the straps became obvious. Everything turned heavy, as if someone had thrown a weighted blanket over me. Terror of imminent death battled with narcotic-fueled bliss for supremacy. Terror won out but couldn't overcome the dizziness that imprisoned me.

I turned at a sound and saw Travis limping over. His mouth was open but I couldn't hear what he was saying. He raised the red hazardous waste container over his head, then tried to overturn it onto Bethany. I felt Bethany's hand leave my chest and watched helplessly as he swiped a heavy paw at the old man. Travis reeled backwards back and sprawled onto the floor, spilling the container's contents harmlessly.

Bethany stepped over him and reached for the defibrillator. "I'll do this myself, Lindmark," he said with his back to me. I heard the machine release a beep that spiraled up into a loud whine, signaling it had been turned on and it was charging up to lethal potency. "After you're gone and resuscitated I'll finally put Travis out of his misery." I felt the straps around my wrist loosened then removed. "Don't want any restraint marks when I explain what happened," Bethany growled.

My head grew too heavy to look over at Travis. The ancient stained ceiling would be the last thing I saw. Somewhere up there Connie was sitting, probably explaining to Audrey what happened to her mother. Would she ever know what happened to me? My plans, all failed, because I'd trusted Bethany. No longer my life to protect theirs. Now my life to bring Morrow back, not imprison him.

The tunnel swam around me as the morphine bathed my brain. I couldn't stop it. It was too late to fight back. My thoughts jumbled pleasantly. Bethany's voice slowed into a slow-motion jumble. I wanted to scream because I was going to die for NO REASON, but my lips wouldn't work.

A strange muffled "Oof!" broke through the haze. My head was a leaden block of heaviness. It took a huge effort to turn it towards that sound. Someone else was moving down here with us. An old wizened black man, one twisted leg scraping against the concrete. I watched a strange scene weave back and forth in my vision. The old man held up a bat and swung at Bethany, who grunted again as the bat thudded into his upper back. I shook my head back and forth, but the vision didn't go away. Charlie Washington was standing over Bethany, hammering repeatedly at his back and sides with a bat stained crimson. But Charlie couldn't be here. He was in a nursing home, brain-damaged in a coma from Morrow. I'd seen him, right? The morphine was good. First the sleepiness, now visions of old friends. Was this a version of my life flashing before my eyes? The next step–nothing, forever.

I watched as the Charlie-vision stood in front of the defibrillator, punching buttons, turning dials. The machine's electronic whine turned louder. Charlie? It was supposed to have been Leland at the controls. Leland... where was Leland? I was able to turn enough to look down at the floor. The old man was lying on the ground, his open shirt exposing the same pads on his chest as Bethany had pressed on me. The world was spinning and turning black, but could still make out Travis attaching wires that Charlie, or a drugged hallucination of Charlie, had disconnected from my pads and tossed on the floor next to him. The shock of the unreal scene before me cut through the morphine's fog.

"He dies NOW. NOW." A frigid blast blew over me. Morrow's gravelly croak rose to a shriek. "NOW. NOW. NOW."

Bethany's bulk rose up from the floor and loomed over me, still holding a syringe. A long needle glinted in the light of the overhead bulb before disappearing into the IV tubing. I screamed at him but didn't hear any sound. He leaned closer to me, leering at me through eyes riven with bloodshot vessels. I struggled against an irresistible oblivion that seemed so welcoming, cracking my eyelids open enough to see Bethany straighten up and turn towards the cardioversion defibrillator. A baseball bat appeared over his head, then slammed down against his skull with a sickening crack. Bethany's face sank from view, then my world plunged down a hole. Blackness won out against whirling lights. I kept spinning, rolling, felt myself floating off the cart into the air. The concrete floor rushed up at me moments before pain exploded as I crashed face-first.

Travis and Charlie swam into view. Travis was still lying on the floor with arms outstretched, curling tufts of gray chest hair sprouting around the large pads. Charlie stood at the defibrillator. The smell of suntan lotion and popcorn wafted around me. Movie theater popcorn, drenched in butter.

"Dr. Lindmark," Kevin's voice pushed its way through the warm blanket of nothingness engulfing me. "We're going soon. My dad is taking me with him. He told me he would, because this time it's right. We're going to be together."

I reached out a leaden arm at the voice, felt Travis's arm. The constant electronic hum shrieked into a whistle, then a scorching shock ripped up my arm and lifted me off the floor. Colors, shapes, images of people and things from deep in my past exploded in my head. My precious baby rushed by me.

I landed heavily against a wall. A low unearthly growl of satisfaction vibrated around me, through me, into me. The revolting smell of charred flesh and burnt hair mixed with erupting colors and flashes. Something else penetrated through the swirling haze. There was no more beeping. My heartbeat on the monitor was gone. Blackness dimmed the colors then swept over me, closing in, drowning me. Silent blackness, no beeping. I was falling, finally dying. Morrow had won.

CHAPTER 27

Beeping. The monitor *was* still beeping. *I* was still beeping. My heart was *thank God, thank God* still beeping. Words started condensing from the darkness into full thoughts. Did dead people stay attached to their monitors in heaven? I finally opened my eyes but closed them immediately against bright heavenly light. I *was* dead. I had gone towards the light, just like everyone always said. I was in—

"Oh my God!" The voice was familiar. "You're awake! Hey, he's awake!"

A door opened and closed somewhere. My arm throbbed and burned. I closed my eyes and sank back to the dark.

"Harry? Harry?" That same familiar voice. My eyelids were heavy shutters I couldn't pry open. "I saw him open his eyes. I did, Dr. Northrup. That's why I called you."

Connie's voice. That's who it was. Connie must have died, too. She was here with me. I wanted to return to the warm comfortable peace when a grinding pain on one of my fingers jerked me into alertness. I pulled my hand away from whatever was biting down on it and let out a hoarse yelp. The pain immediately eased as I forced open my eyes and looked into a familiar smiling face. "You *are* responsive, Doc," Charlie Washington said almost reverently, squinting down at my face.

I saw the forceps in his hand and realized what had caused the pain. "That really hurt, dammit," I grumbled.

"Sorry. I had to know if you were in there." His toothy smile vanished as he leaned in closer and spoke with an oddly different emphasis. "If *you* are in there." He shone a penlight into my eyes. "That you, Doc? Is that *you* in there?"

Northrup's voice interrupted. "Thank you, Mr. Washington. I know you care. But I'm his doctor. Kindly stop handling my patient, if you would. Please let me by." The light clicked off.

I was *alive.* I wanted to scream it. There couldn't be forceps and hospitals and prim unsmiling doctors in heaven. The fog clouding my mind lifted and my thoughts raced. Morrow. The realization hit me like an almost physical jolt. If I had somehow come out of that tunnel alive, I hadn't lived up to my promise. Morrow must still be here. Connie, and Audrey, and Jesus. . . any of us were now going to die. I struggled to sit up in bed, but my arms wouldn't move.

"Harry, relax. You're okay, really, you're okay. Thank God." Connie's voice was soothing. I felt her hand clasp mine.

"Are *you* in there? Tell me now." Charlie had pushed his way past Connie. Sweat dripped from his forehead. I looked down at feeling something cold replace Connie's grip on my arm and saw a syringe clutched in Charlie's bony hand.

"Charles Washington! Please step back this instant." Northrup's command matched the stiffness of her expression.

The syringe didn't move, and neither did Charlie. "I'm his damn friend, Dr. Northrup. And I need to know that he's okay. That he's really Harry."

Connie broke in. "Of course he's 'Harry.' He's right there. And he's coming out of it. Are *you* okay? What happened to you all in that tunnel? Please, just—"

He was going to inject me if I didn't say something. I knew what he was thinking. "Charlie, it's me, okay? We went to the nursing home together. All the nurses there love you. I saw it, when we went to talk to Leland. It's me, Charlie."

He exhaled loudly. I saw him slip the syringe into his pocket. "Yep, he's okay," he said. His smile returned in its gleaming white glory.

"Those nurses do love me." He chuckled, that same noise of rocks rolling around in a hollow tube.

"What happened?" I asked. "What happened to me? It didn't work, did it?" A more desperate concern stabbed into the fog. "Morrow's still here."

Connie and Northrup looked at each other as they hovered over me. "Not surprising that there's still some residual confusion after that episode, Mrs. Lindmark," I heard Northrup say. "We need to keep an eye on him. But the fact he's as lucid as he is after what happened is a good sign." She looked down at me. "You need to rest, Harry." She glared in Charlie's direction. "Visiting's over. We're going to let you rest now." I heard her heels click a military retreat as she walked away. Connie leaned over and kissed me, then followed Northrup.

"I ain't gonna kiss you, Doc, but I sure as hell am glad you're back," Charlie said.

I closed my eyes again and sank back into the lumpy mattress, exhausted. The mist rolled back in. I didn't know if the fog was spinning around inside my head, or if my head was spinning around inside the fog. I didn't know, and I didn't care.

I was alive.

CHAPTER 28

Something cold traced an icy path down my chest, then pressed down on my stomach. I fluttered my eyes, but they wouldn't stay open. The large icy finger dug in over my heart.

Morrow's cold, lifeless touch. He was still here. Voices surrounded me.

". . . still not responding appropriately, Dr. Tanner. Should I just go on and present him to everyone?"

"You've already examined him, right?"

"Just did, Dr. Tanner. He's been unresponsive since Dr. Northrup claimed he woke up and said something."

"Just start from the beginning, okay?" the deep voice said, Lincoln Tanner's voice. "Stay organized."

A medical student? That's who was talking? And Dr. Tanner? Not so deadly.

The hesitant female voice again. "This is a twenty-nine-year-old male who—"

"We all know who it is, Deanna," Tanner interrupted.

I heard her clear her throat. "This is Harry Lindmark. He's, he, um, suffered an accidental electrocution during an attempted cardioversion. He suffered severe burns on his arm. . . "

My arm started to throb more insistently.

". . . a deep scalp laceration and concussion when he lost consciousness and fell to the ground…"

The ache in my head swelled and pulsed against my skull.

". . . and, um, finally, he's been only minimally responsive to his environment over the past week since it happened, probably from all the above."

A *week*? I looked up, panicked, into three sets of eyes staring down at me.

Lincoln Tanner leaned his large unkempt bulk over and peered closely into my eyes. "Welcome back, Dr. van Winkle," he greeted me without a trace of mirth. He shone a penlight into both of my eyes, back and forth. The sudden brightness pounded even more pressure into the swollen balloon my head had become.

"What happened? How—"

"Don't talk, Harry," he interrupted as he untangled his stethoscope from around his neck. I felt the same cold finger as before as he laid the stethoscope on my chest. "Deep breaths."

"But you said a week. How am I—"

"Please, just take deep breaths," he commanded.

I obediently breathed in and out several times until I could no longer contain my anxiety. "Linc. Dr. Tanner. It's me! Not some *patient*," I exploded, then winced at what I'd just said. "Look, sorry, but you said I've been here for a week? I've been like this for a week? What happened? What happened to my wife?"

"Relax, Harry, relax," Tanner replied.

"My wife," I repeated impatiently. "She was in the pediatric ICU. And Morrow is still here." I saw Tanner and his intern exchange a knowing look.

"Damage to higher cortical functions," Tanner explained quietly. He dropped his voice lower, but I was still able to hear his muttered words. "We'll need the neurologist to come back, maybe even consult psych, but it may be reversible. We'll hold off for now." He turned back to me. "You still need to rest, Harry," he said. "And as far as your wife, I think that's who I've seen come in to visit. So don't worry."

Don't worry? "You *think*? Was she or wasn't she my wife?" My plan. . . everything had been ruined.

"I don't know, Harry," he responded irritably. "I can't keep track of patients and families. I'm sure she's okay."

Tanner turned and walked away, then stopped and looked back at me after waving the others on. He leaned down, an odd little smile pushing at the corners of his mouth. "It's weird, isn't it Lindmark?" he said in a quiet tone. "First that Charlie Washington guy got electrocuted, and now *you* almost get electrocuted to death. You could probably publish this, you know? I wonder if anyone's ever written about himself in a medical journal. Weird, huh?" He offered one more reassuring glance and tromped out of my room.

Tanner's comments were as comforting as a fist. Something very bad had happened in that tunnel. Something very bad and very unplanned had happened to Bethany, and to Travis, and to me. Memories teased me with their impossible scenarios, but remained just out of reach of clarity behind the fog that wouldn't clear. Had Charlie really been there? *How* had Charlie been there? I'd last seen him comatose, probably forever. My friend, but never part of my plans. Because I'd confided my plan to Travis and Bethany. I'd given up my life, had relied on those two believers to trap Morrow in my body with the paralyzing drug. Fragments of people, of actions, sharpened out of the fog. Charlie had not only been there, he'd attacked Bethany. It was coming back. Bethany with a tracheostomy scar. He'd needed emergency resuscitation, from the looks of that scar. I shook my head to jar loose more memory. He'd turned on me in that tunnel, hadn't he?

But I was alive and I was *me*. Morrow had to be loose, and even more enraged, which meant he would keep killing. That realization sent my mind racing. He would kill all those I cared about. Where was Connie? And Audrey? Had Morrow and all those horrible dead things clutching and moaning in that tunnel already been at her?

I reached over, picked up the phone, and tried to remember Connie's phone number. Then I yanked the IV out of my arm.

CHAPTER 29

I bolted up in bed, sure that Morrow had arrived at my hospital room for his final revenge. Connie turned at the sound that had awakened me, oblivious to my sudden panic. Another knock sounded at the door, prompting me to smile and relax back onto the pillow. The dead didn't knock first. "Come on in," I called. My smile blossomed into a chuckle as a familiar stooped man shuffled into the room.

"Hello there, Doc Lindmark," he said in a voice still rusty with disuse. He shone his familiar toothy smile at me.

"Hi, Charlie," I smiled back at him. "Connie, meet Charlie Washington, a true institution in these parts."

"I know what you're thinking, Doc," he said. "And you're wrong. They're all my own teeth. Not a denture among 'em."

"Actually, Charlie, I was thinking that I've missed you. From the day you were electrocuted, I've thought about you. I didn't keep visiting you in the hospital, because we all thought you were in an irreversible coma."

"That's all right, Doc."

"I could have found the time, but I just didn't try hard enough. I'm sorry, Charlie."

"I knew you were busy, Doc. You, of all people, had a lot on your mind."

Connie rose from her chair beside the bed. "Sounds like you two have some catching up to do. I'll grab us something from the cafeteria,

Harry. Why don't you let Mr. Washington take you for a spin to see all the sights?"

"If there's a sight in this place that's worth seeing, Mrs. Lindmark, then it's escaped me over the last eighty or so years," Charlie said. "But I'm happy to take the doc around, anyway. Catch up, like you said."

Connie threw a threadbare hospital robe around my flimsy gown, stuck ridiculous no-slide foam slippers onto my feet, then she and Charlie helped me into a wheelchair. Charlie pushed me out the door into a hospital that had returned close to normal, without the lingering chlorine odor or disarray littering the hallways that I last remembered. Men in dark suits still mixed like unwanted weeds among the throngs of nurses, doctors, and patient families, but far fewer than I'd remembered.

"Why'd you do it, Charlie? *How* did you do it? Why did you lie there in the ICU, day after day, not responding to anyone? I knew your brain wave test was substituted for someone else's, probably so they'd just stop treating you and let you die. It was Morrow, right? For God's sake, you let them put a damn feeding tube in you. Even those high and mighty neurologists diagnosed you as irreversibly comatose. How the hell did you know what to do, or what not to do, with those neurologists? More important, *why* Charlie?"

"I was afraid, Doc. I've known about Morrow for years. Hell, I worked here when he was alive. Over the years I came to believe. . . " He stopped talking and pushed through the jostling crowd filling the hallway. Lunchtime had triggered the usual civilian and white-coated stampede towards the cafeteria. Even those men in their ominous dark suits joined the herd towards the cafeteria. His deep voice barely reached me over the din. "I came to believe that he'd never left, even after he died. Leland was never crazy. I've seen things happen over the years that no one could explain. Lots of people have died in this place. Natural deaths, but so many unnatural deaths too, Doc. I couldn't leave people at the mercy of those dead things that lingered, but I sure as hell wanted them to leave *me* alone. That's why I became a poor black uneducated transporter. And they did leave me alone–until Morrow tried to kill me at that code. Now I know why he tried to kill me. When I woke up, I figured I'd be better off *not* waking up."

Wait, what did he say? He knew why Morrow had killed him, or had tried to?

Charlie kept talking, oblivious to my turmoil. "My belief that Morrow was real. . . I think that's what he feared, especially the closer he got to escaping his eternity. After that last code, when I awakened from that electric shock, I knew my time was finally up because Morrow would finish what he started. I knew too much. I *believed* too much. All I had to do was keep watching what was poured or dripped into me until they transferred me out."

I couldn't believe what I was hearing. What this old man had put himself through. . .

"So that's what happened, Doc. They disconnected life support, thought I was hopeless. But I didn't die." He stopped pushing me and walked around to the front of the wheelchair. His features drooped in sadness. "There was no close relative to stop all treatment, so they kept taking care of me and finally transferred this bag of bones to a nursing home."

"But you were down in that tunnel, Charlie. How'd you know about all that? And why did you go after Bethany? He was, well, I thought he was on our side. He was gonna help put Morrow away."

"Leland, Doc. Leland came to see me in the nursing home. He was in here for a heart attack, you know."

"Yeah, I know. Believe me, I know." The image of Travis stumbling around on his bed begging for his son flashed through my mind. "It wasn't a heart attack. He—"

"Leland asked the nurses where I'd been transferred to. He talked his doctors into releasing him back to the same nursing home, which made the mistake of accepting him in transfer." A throaty chuckle lightened his story's grimness. "I bet his doctors were only too happy to boot his ass out of here, knowing Leland. Anyway, he told me everything that had happened and what you wanted him to do. He told me something else, Doc." He leaned down and stared at me. Brownish debris floated around the whites of his eyes. "He never trusted Dr. Bethany. So he followed him to where those drugs are kept, the ones that you told Bethany to bring. Bethany had left the paralyzing drug behind. Leland knew right then that something wasn't right, because without that drug there'd be no way to lock Morrow in your body. That son of a bitch ghoul would finally escape. Leland took it upon himself to steal that paralyzing drug. After letting me in on your plan he told me something else, Doc. He wanted to be with Kevin, giving up *his* body and releasing *his* soul instead of yours. I got ready to take over for Bethany, just in case. So that's what I did. But I just wasn't ready for what I saw that son of a bitch do to you."

I ignored the looks everyone was throwing at us as Charlie and I whispered in the middle of a crowded hallway. An ancient transporter and a recovering medical intern, looking for all the world that we were as close emotionally as we were physically. He shuffled behind me and pushed the wheelchair into the teeth of the throngs moving past. We eventually turned down a deserted hallway ending in a metal door. "Storage room, Doc. As the oldest transporter on earth, I know where all the quiet places are in this place. We need some privacy." He squinted at me. "I'm damn tired, Doc." He lifted my arm, then kept lifting until I rose up out of the wheelchair. "Don't mind if I do, Doc. Thanks." He settled heavily into the sagging seat of my wheelchair. I could almost hear his joints creak. He sighed, then stared up at me. "Leland ain't the only relic around here. I liked old Leland. I trusted him. I was his intern."

"You were his. . . you were a doctor?"

"First black doctor in training here," Charlie answered. I thought I heard bones crack as he straightened up. His gleaming smile faded. "I attached myself to Leland, 'cause he was one of the best doctors we had back then. And because he didn't mind working with a black doctor, if you know what I mean. Then Morrow died, and Leland started telling everyone about ghosts, and well, they asked me to leave along with him. Guilt by association."

I could only shrug, not really sure what to say.

"You better be sure a black man was allowed only one chance back then. I didn't bother trying to get into another training program. I needed to get back into this hospital because I believed what Leland was talking about. So I waited a year or so, then applied as a transporter. No one recognized me, probably because no one had ever bothered to really look at me when I was an intern. I was there when Morrow let Leland's son die. I was the only other one who knew the great all-knowing Dr. Morrow never left *here*, after he left life."

Charlie Washington had been a doctor. Jesus. So that's why he'd known what to do in the tunnel, with the defibrillator and the medications. Going from doctor to transporter with all indignities that demotion had exposed him to, then faking a coma with all the painful procedures and indignities *that* exposed him to. I couldn't help shaking my head.

"And you know what? Everyone ignores a transporter. Even the dead. So I stayed here and tried to help. They'd been here all along, the dead. Souls are meant for peace, Doc. But no one took their knowledge with them until Morrow. He knew the way back from death." He looked around uneasily. "Only Morrow could have known the way back was through the science that had failed him in the first place. You know?"

Yeah, I knew. "So what about Leland? What the hell happened, Charlie?"

I almost regretted ever asking when Charlie finally got around to the answer.

CHAPTER 30

Charlie waved his hand forward, like the head of a wagon train moving his people forward along the trail. I half expected to hear 'Wagons, ho!' come out of his mouth. I obediently started pushing the wheelchair back into the main hallway, until his next words froze me in place.

"Someone had to be offered up at that moment. Might as well have been someone without much else to lose. That meant Leland, not you. I didn't kill old Travis. I *freed* him." He twisted around in the wheelchair and raised his thin grey eyebrows up at me. "Get moving, Doc. You wanted to know what happened, well, take me to the ICU, Miss Daisy. And step on it." He turned back around and kept talking despite facing forward. "Leland told me a lot when he came to see me, Doc. Told me what to do in the tunnel, and told me what to do after." He patted his pocket.

The nurses and therapists stared as we wheeled past them into the Intensive Care Unit. The sight of a hospital doctor dressed in patient garb, pushing an orderly who normally did the pushing, was a strange reversal probably never seen before in the ICU and likely never to be seen again. We stopped in front of Bed 14.

"You don't miss a day, do you, Charlie?" one of the nurses said.

"I promised my old friend I'd watch out for him, Debbie," he replied as he pushed himself painfully out of the wheelchair. "Anyone else come to visit Dr. Travis?"

Debbie shook her head. I could see her trying to hide a smile.

"Well, he deserves better," Charlie continued. "Can we get a little time alone with him?"

"Charlie, you can get the whole day with him, if you want." She walked away, still shaking her head.

I followed the old man as he approached the bed. "They don't love me the way those nursing home nurses do." His smile shrank into a grim slash among the wrinkles. "But they all think I'm harmless," he added. An elderly unshaven man lay under the sheet, connected to a ventilator by a large tracheostomy tube that stuck up from his neck. Familiar gnarled age-spotted hands poked out from under the covers. The same gnarled hands that had gripped me when I first started, so long ago.

I stared down in disbelief.

"Look closer, Dr. Lindmark," Charlie said. He shook Leland's shoulder roughly. The old man didn't respond. He shook him even more violently. "Open your eyes," he commanded, but still received no response or movement. One of Charlie's eyelids twitched, otherwise he showed no emotion as he picked up a plastic syringe. Leland twisted painfully on the bed and tried to pull his arm away as Charlie ground the hard plastic against one of Leland's cracked fingernails.

"Jesus, Charlie, stop it. He's awake," I pleaded.

Charlie did let up, then glared down at Leland with an expression made of stone. "Look at us," he said, his tone devoid of its usual warmth and humor.

Leland stopped struggling and opened his eyes. I peered into them, hoping to soften such vicious behavior with a sympathetic look. He glared back at me with such fury I could almost feel the hatred searing me. Leland's entire body lunged up; I stumbled backwards as the ventilator alarmed with a shrill buzz.

Charlie pushed the old man back onto the bed. He leaned over Leland's contorted face grimacing in anger and mouthing words that wouldn't come out because of the tracheostomy. "You're supposed to be irreversibly comatose, remember?" Charlie said, his usual buoyant features still locked in stony dispassion. His hand crept into his pocket, then came out with a filled syringe. He shot a quick glance towards the curtains, then popped off the cap and plunged the contents of the syringe into Travis's intravenous tubing. Within fifteen seconds, the old man once again lay motionless and peaceful.

Too motionless.

"What did you do?" I hissed, horrified, even though I knew what he'd done. Nothing calmed agitation that quickly. He hadn't calmed Leland into peaceful quiet; he'd *paralyzed* him.

"Open up his eyes, Dr. Lindmark," he replied.

Just then, a nurse came through the closed curtains. She looked at the ventilator, then to Travis, then to us. "What's going on? I heard the ventilator alarm. Did the patient wake up?"

Charlie shook his head. "No," he sighed. "But you have to be a little more careful. The ventilator came disconnected from his tracheostomy tube. Check on him a little closer, okay? He's a personal friend of ours."

The nurse blushed and backed out of the cubicle. Charlie closed the curtains tightly shut behind her, then turned back to me. "Now, open his eyes."

Cautiously, I lifted up one sweat-drenched eyelid. The eye that stared back at me didn't move. The eye muscles were as paralyzed as the rest of his body. But deep within it, something seemed to be swirling. As I stared back, the swirling circled and floated up from the depths within. It was a fire, a churning eddying redness that gleamed out at me. The orb itself remained bulging and immobile, but the white around the pupil darkened.

I drew back from that bulging eye engorged with blood. "Seen that before, Doc?" Charlie asked.

A shudder ran through me. I *had* seen that look before. I had *felt* that look before. But never. . . so close.

This wasn't Leland Travis glaring at me.

It was Sylvester Morrow. I wanted to say something to Charlie but my throat had closed down.

"I thought so," he answered my stare. "Now you know. Leland's gone. He told me that letting you stay with your family would let him finally stay with *his*."

"His son's dead, Charlie. Kevin's gone."

"That's right, Dr. Lindmark. And now Leland is too." He lowered his voice and moved closer to me. "Before we ever went into the tunnel, Leland told me to give you everything we'd planned on, except the paralyzing drug. He came into the tunnel wearing cardioversion pads under his shirt. Morrow, Morrow's soul, would be so greedy to escape from his in-between that *anyone's* sudden death, *anyone's* shell of a body, would reach out to him. Like falling over a cliff when you get too close to the edge. You can't stop it. Even an old dried-up turd of a body." Charlie offered a wan half-smile. "His words, not mine. So Leland told me to shock *him* to death just before giving you that drug. And then I was supposed to wait long enough before shocking him back to life. Just to be sure he was gone and Morrow had taken his body, not yours."

Charlie peeked out through the curtain, then turned back to me, apparently satisfied with our privacy. "Leland knew Morrow's greed, his nature, would survive death. That was his weakness. And if Morrow didn't take the bait. . . " he paused.

"What, Charlie?" I prompted.

"He never finished telling me. I think Leland was counting on something else. Something beyond us." He looked around the small cubicle almost fearfully, then he shrugged and faced me. "I've been thinking about what he said for the past week. What Leland never finished saying to me makes me think of that old question. Did Sylvester Morrow jump, or was he pushed?"

Kevin's last words to me rose in my thoughts. He'd known Morrow, before and after death. He'd known a lot, that kid.

Morrow had been pushed. I couldn't resist a grin. "Ghost-on-ghost violence, huh, Charlie?"

"What was that, Doc?"

I shrugged. "Nothing, Charlie." I couldn't lose the smile. Kevin was definitely beyond the reach of the law. "Leland gave me my life, Charlie, I know that," I said. "But Morrow wanted *me*. I was ready, Charlie. I'm thankful as hell, but it should have been me."

"It almost was you, Doc. That shock got you too, because you rolled onto Leland as I was shocking him. Almost had two people to bring back down there. Fortunately, Leland got the better part of that electricity. Didn't hurt that you're about two centuries younger than Leland was. It also didn't hurt that you wanted to live, no matter what you'd planned. Leland wanted to go, Doc. He had nothing here. He just wanted to be with his son again."

"I hope you're right," I replied. "Leland deserved peace, no matter how he found it. And he deserved to play with Kevin again."

"You were right about Morrow."

"I was?"

"Morrow got his wish–he's back in the flesh. But not quite the way he'd wanted. He'll never get out until that body finally dies. Just like you'd planned. At that point it would be a natural *justified* death, finally allowing Morrow's soul to depart to an eternal deserving place." His weathered features wrinkled with a grin as he glanced downward in unspoken emphasis of the direction Morrow would take. "I'll make sure of it."

"How are you going to do that?" I whispered.

"How do you think? The way you'd planned. Everyone thinks Leland was irreversibly brain-damaged because of the code. From the 'heart attack' he suffered in the tunnel. As long as I keep injecting Pavulon, he'll stay paralyzed. Just like you'd instructed Bethany and Leland. Awake underneath, but brain-dead to everyone else."

"What about brain-wave tests, Charlie? They'll have to do that at some point, to clinch the diagnosis, right?"

"They already have," the old man answered. "Nothing that several hundred milligrams of barbiturates can't cover up. Guaranteed to get rid of brain activity until it wears off."

"But how—"

"You have no idea how little some crash carts are checked, Doc. You think over the years I wouldn't know which ones lay forgotten about? After that first brain-wave was done, I'd never have to 'borrow' any more of those phenobarbital syringes. Same for the Pavulon. After weeks and months of paralysis, his muscles and nerves will permanently turn to jelly. He'll stay imprisoned in that body, aware every second of every minute. Whether he's in here, or in a long-term care unit."

I marveled at how much this creaky, wrinkled transporter knew.

Charlie's grin widened, an expression born from years of suffering erased by moments of vindication. "I know what you're thinking, Doc. Don't forget, I was a doctor in here. Taught by the best–Doctor Leland Travis. I know all about these medications. We had paralyzing drugs, and phenobarbital, and death back then. It's been like medical school every day since then, listening to you know-it-all interns and residents talk about all your patients and great cases like I wasn't there. But I listened to every word."

"Charlie, I—"

"Not you, Doc." He clapped me on the back. "I mean all them other know-it-alls."

I looked over at Leland's body. The heart rate on the monitor had suddenly accelerated. Sweat had broken out on his mottled forehead. Morrow was in there, screaming in fury at Charlie's words. I'd be doing the same thing.

"But if he's declared brain-dead, they'll take him off the ventilator to finally pass away in peace. He'll just be released again." My own heart rate quickened at the panic that thought aroused.

Charlie reached into his pants pocket and pulled out a sheet of paper as wrinkled as he was. "Dr. Travis filled this out before going into the tunnel," he said.

I reached for the paper, but he smoothed it out then folded it and put it back in his pocket. "It's Leland's advance directive," he said. "All notarized and legalized right after you called him with your plans. It states that no matter what happens, he wants to be kept alive. No one's taking Leland Travis' body off life support for a very long time."

He leaned close to the body lying still on the bed except for its chest moving up and down in obedience to the ventilator. "For a very long time, Dr. Morrow. Because your old friend Dr. Travis made sure of it. Think of the money and manpower wasted. . . keeping you alive. Sound familiar? It does to me. Because Leland told me those were *your* words when you stopped his son's life support. But no one's stopping yours."

He pried open one of the old man's eyes, triggering rapid beeping on the monitor tracking Leland's heart rate. "So you'll just lie there, because that's what your advance directive says. Maybe, to break the monotony, there will be the occasional random painful neuro exam that some new doctor will feel obligated to do. Otherwise, awake and aware the whole time, maybe years."

He released the eyelid but kept his gaze focused on the paralyzed man on the bed. "I'll put it in words that so many of my people hear. Death penalty's off the table for Dr. Morrow. You can't kill something already dead. Instead, a sentence of life in prison."

"What if someone does a tox screen on him? What if someone screens for drugs?"

"What's with all the questions, Doc? Leland Travis has been ignored for years. Would anyone in their right mind waste time and money trying to prove someone would actually try to kill an old broken-down wretch like that?"

I peered down at the petrified body on the bed. "No," I had to admit. "I'd try to stay as far away as possible, and hope nature would finally take its course." Memories of that tunnel and its horrors pushed their way into my thoughts. "What about the rest of them, Charlie? All the souls denied their peace over the years? I saw them down there. I felt their hunger, their rage."

Charlie shrugged. "Even if they learn how to affect the physical world like Morrow did, they don't have his knowledge. I expect those trapped souls will stay trapped, angry, agonized, but as helpless now as they were before Morrow joined them."

I looked around me and shivered, half-expecting to see ghostly wisps of mournful souls floating about me. "So the dead never leave?

That's creepy as hell, Charlie." He just shrugged, but I couldn't help noticing his eyes also darted about.

I was still having trouble swallowing everything Charlie was thrusting at me. "What about other hospitals, Charlie? People aren't just dying unexpectedly or brutally here."

Charlie sighed. "Hell, I don't have a clue. I ain't a priest or ghosthunter, Doc. Morrow may have been a special case, filled with so much ego in life, then dying so horribly himself. No wonder death had so much trouble holding him. Hopefully, no other hospital has seen such stuff. All the same, Doc, I'd watch my IV very carefully no matter what hospital I'm in. And maybe pay attention when the air turns cold and the AC isn't on."

"But the computers, Charlie. The trust doctors *everywhere* put in them. It's that way all over, and getting worse."

"You're the one with the stethoscope, Doc. You and all them other white coat wonders. Maybe you'll just have to use it more." Charlie went back to just staring down at the body that once housed Leland Travis, saying nothing for an interminable several minutes while I stood by respectfully.

I finally didn't want to be close to the thing on the bed. "You hungry, Charlie? It'd be great if you would join Connie and me for some food."

"Damn, Doc, what an offer. Being treated to another round of the same hospital food I been eating for the last century. Sure I'll join you, but if that's the best you can offer, you're still gonna push me. I didn't save your life just to be rewarded with hospital food. And I sure as hell ain't gonna be a transporter anymore."

"Sounds fair to me, Mr. Washington. I mean, *Doctor* Washington." This time I matched his grin. Death and revenge hadn't taken everything. It was beyond the ability of simple words to express. I'd prepared to die, and I hadn't.

I was alive.

CHAPTER 31

The Sylvester Morrow Convalescent Center rose against the morning sun's glare as ancient and as decrepit as ever. It had been six long painful months since I'd stepped foot in the place, yet some unseen threat stirred my heart rate the minute I walked in the main entrance. I looked uneasily from side to side, but of course all I saw were the familiar sights of a dilapidated warehouse for the old, the demented, the forgotten. I no longer feared them, because I knew their kind would never be created again. At least not around here. Now I just felt loathing, except for one certain resident.

I'd awakened that morning as I had every morning since I'd been discharged six months earlier–headache, neck pain, muddled confusion that refused to clear. All the ugly reminders of that day in the tunnel. But as that fog finally cleared, I had been gripped by a resolve to finally confront the loose ends I'd been avoiding.

"Well hey there, Dr. Lindmark," one of the nurses greeted me. At least some people refused to pretend they no longer knew me. "Long time, honey, but it's good to see you back. Did that handsome friend of yours come too?"

"Um, it's *Mister* Lindmark now, I'm afraid," I answered. "And no, Charlie couldn't make it today. You only have me."

"We see enough of Washington anyway," another nurse said. "I think he visits so much because. . . " she paused and winked an eye. "Because I think he's attracted to me." She giggled.

I looked at these guardians of the nursing station, each one more portly than the next. White uniforms strained to contain bulges. "Maybe, maybe," I answered. Her nametag was dwarfed by the breast over which it was pinned. "Gladys, can you point me in Dr. Bethany's direction?"

The hall stayed gloomy and thankfully empty as I walked over scratched linoleum under ancient chandeliers. I found Martin Bethany sitting at the only piece of furniture in the room besides the bed, a worn desk backed by a large mirror.

"Dr. Bethany? Martin?" I couldn't contain the disbelief in my voice. Were it not for the name taped to door I'd have been concerned I was in the wrong room. The face reflected in the mirror was gaunt. The fiery red beard was gone, replaced by bronze stubble pockmarked with scars previously hidden. One corner of his mouth drooped and dripped saliva. The eyelid on the same side was wide open and almost never blinked. It was a crooked maniacal expression born of the severe blow to the head Charlie had landed. "Martin?" I repeated.

The man in the chair turned away from the mirror and looked in my direction. His bulk had shrunk to only mildly overweight. One arm hung limply and ended in a hand that was curled and contracted in on itself. The other hand clenched as he glared out at me with palpable hatred.

I advanced on the half-paralyzed wretch in the chair. "With your medical skills, Martin, you could have done so much more." I easily avoided the spittle he blew out at me. "Leland Travis was not quite the pathetic old loon you dismissed him as, was he? Old Leland was on to you. He told Charlie to be prepared. Charlie would never have done what he did had he not realized who you really were and what you were doing, because Charlie is an honorable man. So is Leland. *Was* Leland, I mean." Bethany's hand scrabbled against the wooden chair.

"You two must be sharing some good stories, as long as you've been in here," Gladys said from behind me. "So you got to let me in on—" She stopped talking then hurried past me. "What have you done to yourself, hon?" she said as she saw his scratching fingers. "We're going to have to put some mittens on you if you're going to hurt yourself like that." She clucked in disapproval. "That homeless monster really did in one of the best doctors there was," Gladys said as she straightened up. "Poor guy just trying to run that code in a place no one else had made it to, and he gets hit over the head for his troubles. Poor thing never had a chance. Never did find that guy, did they?"

I smiled at the story Charlie and I had created. A drug-seeking, drug-addled homeless person camped out in that subterranean passageway had attacked a heroic Martin Bethany with a bat while desperate for drugs. Such a believable scapegoat, especially as innocent homeless addicts had indeed been found by hospital security before. "No idea, Gladys," I replied, unable to tear my gaze away from the broken replica of a hothead physician. The tracheostomy scar stood out like a scarlet hyphen without the camouflage of fleshy folds and beard.

"You going to stay for mealtime, hon?" Gladys asked.

I looked at the battered remnant of Dr. Martin Bethany. The trail of dead and broken bodies he'd left behind in the name of Morrow's madness slithered through my memories, and I wanted nothing to do with mealtime, or bath time, or any other time with this ghoul of a human. "I'm good, Gladys," I said, then turned my back on Martin Bethany for the last time.

I was hoping my next stop would be as vindicating. I drove past the hospital's employees' lot, trying to ignore the sharp pang of sadness, and eventually found my way into a distant space meant for patients and families. All the privileges of being a doctor had been closed off to me and would likely stay that way. Even crossing the threshold of the main entrance felt a violation of the conditions that had been forced on me.

Nurses and therapists who I'd known and worked with threw me a sideways glance or pretended to look straight ahead as I passed. Rumors about what had happened in the tunnel had started even while I was recovering and had grown with each passing week. Nothing had ever been proven because the truth would never be believed, never mind proven. The only witnesses besides Charlie and me were dead or incapacitated beyond speech. The rumors and suspicions remained just that, too impotent without evidence to ignite actual legal proceedings.

I sighed and walked on, comforting myself with the same thoughts I'd had since the tunnel. Losing my license was a small price for gaining my life and recovering my desire to *have* a life. No one stopped me as I entered the long-term care wing, breathing in antiseptic air that seemed to have scrubbed each cubicle clean of smells and human touch alike. I peered into one particular cubicle, then breathed deeply and walked towards the bed. My heart pounded as familiar tendrils of fear wrapped around me.

The face was as gaunt and drawn as a skull but was still recognizable as Leland Travis. The tracheostomy tube, deprived of any support by the emaciated tissues of his neck, tilted painfully to one side. I pulled the sheets away from his body. Ribs poked through the papery skin of his chest. His arms had curled and shriveled into feeble bony appendages, his skin blotched and bruised from countless intravenous catheters. Someone had finally ordered a permanent catheter placed into a deep vein in one elbow. Even that buried plastic catheter hung limply, without flesh or muscle to prop it up. I reached out and pushed open both eyelids. Sweat beaded up instantly on his forehead.

I looked into those eyes. It struck me that the overhead light must have been as blinding and painful as the midday sun to someone who'd laid in the dark for so long. I kept his lids open but moved slightly to try and shield them from the light. The whites of his eyes grew bloodshot with angry blood vessels the longer I stared into those orbs.

I released the lids and locked Morrow's soul back into the darkness. Feeling everything, hearing everything, suffering every second from an irresistible urge to move and relieve the maddening itch of perpetual immobility. The feeding tube and the ventilator ensured that existence would go on. Charlie's reliable injections had ensured an eternity far worse than the one from which Morrow had escaped.

As told by Charlie, the lawsuit he'd filed as Leland's designated power of attorney against the Sylvester Morrow Convalescence Center had been settled in Leland's favor. The nursing home had offered little defense against the charge of negligence by permitting one of its mentally impaired residents to wander out, somehow make his way to the hospital, then suffer a heart attack deep in the tunnel. Charlie had told me the award money would support Leland's existence, and Morrow's prison, with full support until nature finally took its course.

Charlie's grinning features rose in my thoughts. He'd flitted in and out of life at the hospital as invisibly as a ghost himself. Now he'd chosen to live out his life in eerie guardianship, one aged remnant of years past watching over another.

I glanced around the cubicle one last time, my last look at Morrow. The room was silent except for the incessant mechanical breathing of the ventilator as it hissed mockingly at the still form on the bed. I drew comfort knowing that when Travis's ancient body finally gave out, Morrow's release would be a deserved, expected, dignified death assuring his soul would pass by the in-between to whatever fate he deserved.

A strange sound reached me from somewhere near the bed. A high-pitched, fleeting squeal.

Or a faint agonized scream?

Nothing else moved in the room except the ventilator tubing inflating and deflating. The muffled screech escaped again, and again. It had to have been pressurized air escaping from some tiny leak in the ventilator tubing. It had to be. Right?

CHAPTER 32

The image of Leland's body and that distant endless shriek haunted me for weeks. The brightness of the park with all its squealing children and harried parents finally managed to loosen the grip of that memory.

"Hey Harry. Harry!" The voice jolted me out of my thoughts. "Over here."

I turned and saw Connie sitting on a swing by herself. "Where's Audrey? I thought she was with you."

"She's playing baseball with your patient." Connie pointed toward a distant ball field. "You know, with Ma and Pa Kettle."

"Norm? Norm Strickland? He actually came?"

"He and the missus," she affirmed. "Must've come over fresh from gathering in the harvest. He even brought his own baseball bat."

"Maybe I should go over there and help him out. Norm was in a rehab hospital for months. Audrey may be a little too much to handle."

"If you ask me," Connie said, "I think you'd be doing him a favor by letting him spend a little time playing ball." She smiled and shook her head. "That sounds so strange. '. . . playing ball with Audrey. . .' That little girl has come a long way since, well, you know." She looked at me. "Anyway, I also think you'd be doing his wife a favor by letting her watch them play together. Norm has been smiling more than Audrey has."

I couldn't help smiling myself. Norm Strickland considered himself master of the infield as well as the cornfield. My smile faded. Maybe he imagined Timmy holding the bat again. I breathed in the grass and trees and sunshine. "This park is just the right place for all of us. Even the ones who aren't here, like Leland," I said. "All those outings with his son, some of them must have smelled just like today."

A sudden breeze fluffed against me. Did someone laugh? I looked around, glanced over my shoulder, but saw no one else nearby.

"Harry? You okay?"

I turned back to face Connie. "Yeah, I guess." I couldn't hold back any longer. "Well no, Connie, I'm not so okay. I'd been reading all my journals and reviews to prepare for returning after my appeal, catching up on syndromes, medication doses, and diagnoses. Then I got a call from the state Board of Healing Arts." I averted my eyes. "A while back. I should have told you, Connie. But I was too ashamed. And with all of Audrey's adoption stuff finally happening. . . "

Connie rested her hand on my arm.

"They said the investigation just left open too many questions about what happened, about what I had done. That tunnel left one person in a permanent coma, another disabled from an attack by someone who was never found, and me barely surviving electrocution. They're like everyone else, Connie. Something happened to Leland, never mind the missing drugs and the morphine found in my system. Too many rumors about me, but maybe I'd brought them on myself. They denied the appeal for reinstatement of my medical license, Connie. So no completion of internship, no completion of anything." The words soured in my mouth, but the expected anger didn't erupt. I felt somehow calm and unaffected. "They did say that if I get psychiatric treatment and clearance after these next six months, they will reconsider."

Connie's grip was reassuring. I squeezed back in appreciation.

"Ever since that phone call, I realized I've been catching up on all the wrong things, instead of what really matters." I exhaled a deep breath. "It's really all okay because. . ." I caught myself before I could say it. But I thought it. The wonder of it had finally dawned. I'd been allowed to see what was beyond. I'd been granted the gift of knowing that there *was* a beyond. I couldn't even think about good or bad, justice or reward or punishment. It didn't matter. We all went somewhere after. And that was good enough for me. Good or bad, we don't just. . . end.

"Harry?"

I looked up, startled. Connie was looking at me with a concerned expression. "You okay?"

The breeze felt good. The sun felt good. "Yeah, I *am* okay."

Neither of us said anything for several seconds. Then Connie tightened her arms around me. "I love you, Harry Lindmark. Doctor or no doctor."

The sudden throb of my side and back under her embrace brought me back to other things I'd witnessed, other horrors that dampened the awe of what had been revealed to me. I suddenly didn't want to talk about it anymore. What happened in that tunnel needed to stay in that tunnel, but haunted me relentlessly.

I disengaged myself from her hug. "Maybe I should go over and rescue Norm. I'm not sure he should be playing baseball after everything he went through." I tried to spot them through the playgrounds and trees. "The Stricklands may want to just sit down and have something to eat."

"Or, maybe you're getting hungry?"

She was probably right. As I approached it wasn't hard to spot the field they were playing on. Fields one, three, and four were crowded with scurrying, yelling midgets and crowded bleachers. Field two, however, stood out. A small wheelchair drove repeatedly between home plate and first base. A tall man stood close to home plate, holding a wooden bat. A solitary woman sat on the front row of the bleachers. From a distance she looked to be wearing a floral curtain.

Norma Strickland waved at me as she noticed my approach. I walked over and took out the gift I'd stuffed in my pocket. "Quite a team you're cheering on out there, Norma," I greeted her.

The smile that broke out on her features matched mine. She started to respond but I couldn't hold back any longer, reaching out the stuffed animal and placing it in her lap. "I'd put it in a pocket of white coat so long ago, Norma," I said. "I've been waiting to see you and Norm for so long, because Timmy's bear needs to be back home. With his parents."

She clutched the ragged stuffed bear up to her chest and hugged it. Tears ran down her cheeks as she gazed up at me. I felt my own eyes burn as emotion overcame both of us. Her lips trembled but words caught in her throat. I nodded and offered a reassuring smile before turning away, knowing all that passed between us was best left unspoken.

My walk towards the field broke into an eager jog when I saw the small electric wheelchair veer out of the base path and bump over the hillocks of the outfield towards me. Halfway to Audrey, a soft gust of cool air brushed against me. An odd little current of air, carrying with it something else. A sudden aroma hit me.

Popcorn, fragrant buttery popcorn.

My heart thudded against my chest. The pleasant aromas grew even more tantalizing as I hurried towards Audrey. It had to be *them*. I looked in all directions, trying desperately to find where Kevin-from-heaven and his father had to be, and swerved at the last minute to avoid running into a boy and his father.

The boy was holding a box of popcorn. I looked in the direction from which they'd walked and saw the refreshment stand where dozens of sizzling hot dogs and mounds of popcorn released similar aromas. I smiled ruefully at my imagination still playing tricks with me, shrugged, and turned to catch up with Audrey when something banged into my shins. The grass had muffled the approach of Audrey's wheelchair, which had stopped only inches from my legs.

"Evil child." I frowned, but couldn't maintain the façade as she glared in unspoken disdain. "I suppose you thought that was funny."

Her smile twisted crookedly. She opened her mouth and released a strangled gurgle. Her speech sounded as twisted and distorted as her body had become. The low oxygen levels she'd suffered had stiffened her diseased muscles even more. The breathing tube in her throat had scraped her vocal cords raw, paralyzing one of them. Her voice had become a strangled rasping, each syllable more work than it should have been.

Morrow had gotten his revenge. He'd taken the one thing that had kept the world laughing *with* Audrey instead of *at* her. A little girl who'd conquered the world with her voice had been robbed of that gift. I followed her as she spun around in her wheelchair and set off across the grass. My anger melted as she released loud, twisting squeals of careless abandon. Only Audrey could get locked away bit by bit and not know any better than to keep having a good time.

I was out of breath by the time I reached the infield.

"You come to watch, or to play?" Norm Strickland greeted me. His tattered overalls hung loosely on his gaunt frame. Thinning strands of hair couldn't quite hide the odd sunken dent marring one side of his forehead. He braced his lower back with a knobby hand as he bent over and picked something up from the dust.

I recognized it immediately. The scratched wood still bore a faded crimson blood stain that had sunk permanently into the grain. The mystery of that bat turned out to be not so mysterious after all. Leland had seen a nurse toss the bat aside in the midst of the chaos and chlorine fumes the day of the pool disaster. He'd picked it up and had kept it for reasons known only to Leland Travis. Charlie relayed to me that Leland had presented him the bat when he'd visited him in the nursing home as if it were a housewarming gift. After Leland had told him about my plans, Charlie had decided it might come in handy when hearing of Leland's suspicions about Bethany. It did.

I looked at the bat still stained with the blood of too many people on it, innocent and evil alike. It had become a talisman, first an instrument for evil then a weapon against evil. As I watched Norm lay the bat almost reverently in Audrey's arms, I knew its journey had finally ended in the best possible way, put to its best possible use.

I picked up a baseball glove lying on the infield dirt. Connie had remembered to bring it to the park, just as she'd remembered to save it for years because she'd believed for years. I pounded a fist into the glove, stirring up a cloud of dust.

"Hey Audrey, why not show off what you learned to your dad?" Norm said. He wrapped Audrey's small hands around the grip of the bat as best as he could.

"I'm not sure she's used to that 'Dad' thing, Norm," I said. "I can't even get her to call me Harry, much less 'Dad' yet." I was relieved to see her crooked smile answer me. I lowered my voice and murmured to Norm, "Her own father, when we finally tracked him down, was more than happy to have us adopt her. I wasn't sure which surprised him more–that she was still alive, or that someone wanted her." A sudden cold breeze wafted against my arm, but the infield was as still and quiet as it had been when I'd first approached. I peered in at Audrey. "Just keep your eye on it, okay?"

Audrey rolled her eyes one more time, but squeezed her hands together more tightly. Timmy's bat looked as though it weighed half as much as she did. I shrugged again, unwilling to spoil Strickland's fun. I walked several feet away, pretended to wind up into my best Big Leaguer's pose and released the ball in a slow, arcing curve. It floated past Audrey and landed squarely in Strickland's glove.

"Stee-rike one!" he proclaimed.

Audrey's smile persisted undeterred. "Good try, Audrey," I said. "Don't swing too early on this one." I tossed an even higher and slower pitch and held my breath until it again floated untouched over home plate into Strickland's waiting glove.

"Stee-rike two!" This time, Strickland patted Audrey's shoulder reassuringly. "That was a good try, anyway," he said. It sounded as if he was talking to someone else, maybe a son cherished but gone. I heard a childish giggle from somewhere, a sound way beyond what Audrey's damaged voice box could generate. I looked more closely towards home plate as I heard another chuckle. Norm peered into the sunny, clear air around him. That happy chuckle prompted me to do the same thing, a little uneasily. Nothing but the bright afternoon surrounded me.

"I think she wants that next pitch, Doc," Strickland called. "It's a whole new season. Let's start it out right."

I heard another soft chuckle that seemed to come from everywhere.

"Whatever, Norm," I responded, the words catching in my throat. Nothing else would sound right. "All right, Audrey, you heard the man. One more chance." I backed up several steps as Audrey whirred and clicked the wheelchair into position. She spun around several times, stirring up a cloud of infield dust.

I peered in at my daughter. "Hold it tight," I called out, then assumed what I hoped was an intimidating squint. Strickland settled down into a catcher's squat. I wound up slowly, stopping dramatically at the top of my wind-up, then let the ball fly towards home plate. It arched lazily, almost in slow motion. As I watched it, the cheers ringing from the other fields faded. The sun became brighter, almost blinding. The ball slowly curved down towards home plate. Audrey looked at me for the briefest of moments. She cocked her arms back then whirled forward, extending Timmy's bat out in a mighty swing. It connected squarely with a loud, satisfying crack.

Cheers rose up again in my ears as the ball exploded up and out over my head, over second base, out into center field. It rose unbelievably high until it cleared the center field fence in a powerful home run blast. I turned around to see Audrey holding her hands over her head in jubilant exultation. A home run! A walk-off win. The cheers became deafening.

"Doc? Hey Doc! You okay?" I blinked several times as Norm called out to me. The cheering faded into the distant shouts from across the park, the blinding light faded to the warm haze of the afternoon sun. I returned to reality as the image of that mighty swing dissolved. Audrey was still strapped in her wheelchair, slumped in the only position that her twisted body permitted. The baseball rested several inches away from where it had plunked onto the bat cradled in her arms. I unstrapped the restraints as gently as possible, tossed the bat onto the ground, and lifted her from the wheelchair high into the air.

"Did it, Da, did it!" she warbled. Her glasses were crooked; her smile had reappeared in all its misshapen glory.

"You sure did," I whispered. "We finally did it." Her head was framed in the bright rays of the sun as I thrust her higher into the air. "Major hit, Audrey. Knocked 'em all in." It suddenly became harder to talk. I lifted her slight form even higher up into the sky. "What say we celebrate with some popcorn?"

THE END

AUTHOR ACKNOWLEDGEMENTS

Dreams are meant to be pursued, and hopefully but not necessarily achieved. As the saying goes, it's as much the journey as it is the destination. I have pursued dreams of finding the right partner for life and marrying her, raising a family, being proud of that family, becoming a doctor, and publishing my writing. I'm fortunate enough to have enjoyed each journey, and to have reached each destination. Strangely, I held all those dreams as possible except the last one, which I regarded more as a pipe dream that belonged to so many other luckier or more talented writers. Black Rose Writing, and in particular Reagan Rothe, have allowed me to realize even that last impossible dream, and I will be always grateful for such trust, encouragement, and investment.

From those other dreams have sprung those to whom I owe so much. My wife and my children have showered me with love and unwavering support while offering objective and honest critique. Words cannot adequately express how much I owe them, and how much I revere them. Finally, I also owe much to my youngest son Andrew, who passed away much too early but still set an example of excellence in all endeavors and an unquenchable love of life for me to live up to.

ABOUT THE AUTHOR

Scott Eveloff, MD, is a pulmonary physician with thirty years of experience treating seriously ill patients. He has appeared on *The Dr. Oz Show*, ABC's *20/20*, and *Inside Edition*. His insider's knowledge of the many ways to harm patients in today's hospitals as there are to heal them prompted his debut novel.

Dr. Eveloff is an exercise fanatic, alternating between weightlifting and aerobics. He loves to travel but hates cruises and can often be found attending concerts of his favorite (aging) musicians. He is enjoying retirement with his supportive physician wife. Spending time resuscitating plot lines instead of patients, he remains motivated by the comforting recollections of growing up and by his late son Andrew, whose boundless enthusiasm lives forever like the characters he inspired.

NOTE FROM SCOTT EVELOFF, MD

Word-of-mouth is crucial for any author to succeed. If you enjoyed *Do Not Resuscitate*, please leave a review online—anywhere you are able. Even if it's just a sentence or two. It would make all the difference and would be very much appreciated.

Thanks!
Scott Eveloff, MD

We hope you enjoyed reading this title from:

BLACK ROSE writing™

www.blackrosewriting.com

Subscribe to our mailing list – *The Rosevine* – and receive **FREE** books, daily deals, and stay current with news about upcoming releases and our hottest authors.
Scan the QR code below to sign up.

Already a subscriber? Please accept a sincere thank you for being a fan of Black Rose Writing authors.

View other Black Rose Writing titles at www.blackrosewriting.com/books and use promo code **PRINT** to receive a **20% discount** when purchasing.